Stonecaller

Talisman Series, Volume 2

J P Wagner

Published by J P Wagner, 2021.

STONECALLER

First edition. September 10, 2021.

Copyright © 2021 J P Wagner.

ISBN: 978-1990862038

Written by J P Wagner.

Also by J P Wagner

Avantir
The Guardian of the Sword

Talisman Series
Stonecaller
Talisman of the Winds

Standalone
The Search for the Unicorns
Railroad Rising: The Black Powder Rebellion
Maid of the Westermoor

Watch for more at www.revjpwagner.com.

For Lila, Carol and Jimmy

Chapter 1

The sky was bright blue and cloudless, making his wide-brimmed hat critical. Not the kind of country to be crossing alone, Qedrim knew, but he'd worn out his welcome with the caravan a few days ago.

He snarled at that thought. They hadn't *proved* he'd been cheating at gambling, and what if they had? Everyone did, or would if they were able. What had finished it, of course, was when that Morrkerr-eaten young fool pulled a knife. So when Qedrim had used his own knife to finish the matter, that old bugger of a caravan-master had driven him out, as though Qedrim were the one at fault.

Qedrim stabbed his stick viciously into the grassy ground. Well, he could be thankful his Talisman Against Lameness was holding up. When the talisman ceased to work, he'd be leaning on the stick like an old man, and that rankled him.

Medium-tall, smooth-muscled, usually nimble, Qedrim seldom had to lack female company. When his leg went Chaos Away, though, he turned into a pinch-faced cripple, old before his time.

He paused, listening. Yes, he'd heard a sound, someone over the next rise. It had been a shout. To be taken as trouble until proven otherwise.

Qedrim toiled up the rise. The caravan trail took the easy way around, marked by ox-dung and ruts of oxcarts. The ox dung varied from being a few days old all the way to rich grassy lumps.

Even with the Talisman, his leg didn't like this. Qedrim was not about to wander around a corner into something which might be trouble. He was not going to skyline himself coming over the hill, either. He crawled the last several feet on his stomach.

Better be alive and feeling foolish than be genuinely foolish and suddenly taken dead for it.

When he got to the top of the hill, he saw a situation which was abundant with possibilities.

There was a tumble of rocks down there, next to a spring. Near the spring was a pack-mule, his packs on the ground nearby. In cover, behind scrawny bushes and rocks and the like, were about a half-dozen ragged bandits.

The merchant, the owner of the mule and packs? There he was, in the tumble of rocks, near the water. He wasn't truly visible himself. Just a slight movement, and a bandit behind a bush pitched over with a small arrow in him.

The other bandits weren't discouraged. Yet. It was still five to one, no, six to one, he'd missed the one moving cautiously on his belly. From the looks of it, the merchant wouldn't be around for long.

There was another movement, higher in the rocks, and another bandit crumpled. No movement from the first place, though. He must be biding his time. It was impossible for the merchant to have gotten from one place to another so fast.

This also meant Qedrim had to do something soon. No altruism, here. Once they finished off the merchant, they might well find Qedrim's tracks. Then they'd be on his ass in a shake of the Old Woman's Apron.

He reached into his pouch and pulled out his sling. It was a long while since he'd come happily trotting down from the Arndal Hills, sling in hand, ready to make a living with someone's army. He grimaced at the memories, and again at his leg's sympathetic twinge.

Qedrim was going to have to skyline himself, after all. He could do all right on one knee, but for certain he'd do better standing.

He put one of his special white stones in the sling; at these odds, he'd need every advantage.

Standing, he whirled the sling three times round his head and let go. The stone flew. A black speck spinning through the air. Unerringly striking the shaggy head of bandit behind a bush. The man yelled, and sprawled out from his cover.

The bowman looked up, spotted Qedrim, and drew his bow. Qedrim dropped another stone in his sling and whirled it. The arrow dropped in the grass several feet downhill. The bandit wasn't used to shooting at these distances.

He was just putting another arrow to his bow when Qedrim's stone got him.

There was another man below the hill, on his feet, whirling a sling. This brought back the memory of Qedrim's first battle. It was under a bright, hot sky, a field of green grass and daisies and bluebells. He and the others doing the usual slinger job. A scattered screen across the light infantry's front, harassing the enemy advance. Across the field were another screen of slingers, doing the same job for their side.

Your normal target was the people the slingers were screening, if they were close enough. But otherwise you whittled away at the slingers.

Of course, he never knew which one of the enemy got him. He felt a glancing blow on his left knee, and the leg refused to hold him up. A friend had helped him get back behind the lines, and later that same day that same friend had taken an arrow and died.

All this went through his mind as he moved to make himself a poorer target, and dropped a stone into his own sling.

Then the slinger's stone went wild, and he fell with an arrow in the back.

"Thank you, merchant," he muttered, then sent his own stone at another target.

He'd better use his next stones well. He wanted the merchant to feel at least a bit indebted to him.

What remained of the bandits were running. Best not let any get away, in case they developed some courage and came sneaking back later that night. His stones flew as fast as he could make them.

He came down carefully off the hill. The merchant would be wary. It would be interesting to find out what was in the mulepacks.

There was no sign of the merchant until Qedrim got close enough to the spring to smell the fresh water, and the scent of the bushes growing nearby.

His first thought was this was a child. But children, especially children only a little taller than his waist, did not grow thick beards. Nor did they have lined and weatherbeaten faces.

The man wore a leather tunic and trousers, and a forward-flopping pointed leather cap. All were decorated with patterns of stars and flowers and winding stems. He also carried a crossbow. Qedrim heard of them, but had never seen one. They had decent range, but were slow to load, giving a poor rate of fire.

The little man was smiling broadly, though, and that bode well. "A good day to you, O lame slinger, and my thanks. I shall have to reward you."

Qedrim laughed, at least partly in response to having survived a fight. Memories of stories leaped to his mind, stories Old Baksha used to tell, away off back in the hills. You rescued a strange-looking person, and he offered you a reward...

"I'd like the power to move mountains, I'd like to marry a beautiful Princess, and I'd like to live happily ever after."

'And I'd like you to turn your back for just a moment.' Qedrim added as a silent afterthought.

The little man's eyes opened in what was clearly feigned surprise. "Ah, the Old Tales! How lovely! But let me introduce myself; I am Shapak-ailesh, a merchant in various gewgaws and trinkets. And you?"

"Qedrim, of no particular place."

"Ah, Qedrim the Lame Slinger! Very pleased to make your acquaintance! If you'll accompany me, I'll see to your reward. I shall have to do a bit of hasty travelling to make up for what this ambush has cost me."

He turned and began to step toward his mule. Qedrim took a quick step forward, reaching for his dagger.

Shapak-ailesh turned, as if recalling something he'd forgotten to say. Qedrim's leg gave way, and he collapsed with a grunt of pain.

"Oh my goodness! Has your Talisman failed you, then?"

"Yes," Qedrim replied, through gritted teeth, "And it shouldn't have!"

Among the jobs he had taken, after his leg had healed enough to walk on, was as apprentice, pupil, and general servant for a magician. A crabby old man who barely rated the term 'hedge-wizard.' Qedrim had swept the shop, handled some simpler herbals, and learned some of the less complex talismans.

It had started with him bartering his assistance for the Talisman Against Lameness. Then worked its way into a near-apprenticeship, though no specific agreement was ever made.

He knew this Talisman Against Lameness. The talisman lasted longer. Much longer than this. And the talisman failed bit by bit, not suddenly.

Of course the apprenticeship hadn't lasted. Old Freyollach was scant with his pay, and had the nerve to take exception to Qedrim's selling a few handfuls of poppy and the like, to make up for it.

He looked up at the little man. "How did you know I was wearing a Talisman?"

The little man shrugged. "I have several ways and means of knowing certain things, O young and pain-filled slinger. But I think

I have something which will help. It will not be counted against your reward, of course."

He went rummaging through his mule pack, and came back with a small strip of grey ribbon. The ribbon was about a thumb-breadth wide and two forearms long. "Here, wrap this around your leg, either inside or outside the trousers. It will have an immediate effect, though it will take a while for you to be able to move with comfort."

He glanced around. "We will have to camp here tonight."

Qedrim wondered about the little man's sanity. He seemed too trusting of someone he'd just met. Despite the fact that person had helped him against the bandits. Then he began to wonder. The Talisman had failed at just the right moment, at least from the little man's viewpoint.

Had this strange little fellow had something to do with it?

Now he, Qedrim, had put on a Talisman the merchant had provided, put it on without thought for what this strange talisman might be. A Talisman of Obedience was possible in theory, though it was beyond Qedrim's competence. Qedrim had heard of these talismans, but it was never a matter of first-hand knowledge. It always involved some third cousin's best friend, who either had a near escape, or was taken with one, escaping only by some clever trick.

He had discussed, with old Freyollach, some possibilities of various talismans. Some, such as the Talisman of Instant Travelling, were possible in Theory. But no one had ever been known to have made one which worked.

He reached a hand down, furtively, toward the knot. He had no trouble touching it, which was a good sign. One thing which went into a Talisman of Obedience was a charm against taking the talisman off.

Well, whatever this grey ribbon was, he'd better be careful for a while. Learn what he could, and not make any moves until the right time.

Shapak-ailesh busied himself with setting up a meal, dried meat, bread, and watered wine. During all the activity, Shapak-ailesh kept up a constant chatter. Going on some long discourse about some general and hypothetical notion. Only now and then asking his guest for a response. Then carry on as if Qedrim had said "yes," or "no," whichever had been expected.

"Here we are, O Hungering Slinger of the Deadly Aim! It isn't much, but it will do for travelling."

The portion he gave to Qedrim was a fair-sized one, which made Qedrim suspicious straight off. People always had a motive for their generosity; what did the little fellow want?

Well, he wasn't going to ask. Let the little fellow bring it up first, and see if it were something he'd want to try. If it were, he'd make the little merchant pay more than a meal's worth.

He had to keep in mind there was more to Shapak-ailesh than volubility. He'd been doing a fair job holding off the bandits, though there was no doubt Qedrim's arrival had helped. Nor was he willing to believe that his talisman had up and failed on its own like that, just as he was making a move. Caution was a wise notion, at least for a while.

It was still hard to equate the chatty little fellow with some serious danger.

The wine Shapak-ailesh shared was nowhere near the sour stuff commonly taken on journeys. Somehow or other the wine didn't taste as if it had been brought any distance on the back of a plodding mule, stirring up all the sediment on the bottom.

This, added to all the other things he had witnessed and experienced about the little man, kept Qedrim alert for the trap.

When the meal was over, and everything packed up, Shapak-ailesh spoke, in the manner of one getting down to a subject which had been put off for too long. "Now, about your reward for assisting me. You have asked something which may take a little time to arrange. No, no, there's no need to speak; I ought to be ready to wave a hand and have your three wishes come true.

"I, however, am not so gifted as that. We can make a start, though. Reach into your pouch and bring out one of your special stones."

Qedrim was reaching into his pouch when he stopped. "How do you come to know about my special stones?"

There were certain stones, he'd learned as a child. Smooth white oval stones. And not even every smooth white oval stone, with which he could hit small targets at amazing distances. He could recognize them by the feel. After he found they didn't work for others, and only got him teased, he stopped talking about them. He never stopped using them, though.

Shapak-ailesh merely smiled. "I know a number of bits of lore and story, O Suspicious Slinger, this and that, here and there. Suffice it for the moment that I am aware of your stones.

"Now take one out, and let the stone lie on your palm. Examine the stone carefully. Hold the stone in your mind. Every crack and discolouration. Every slight difference to its shape. Imagine, even, that you are seeing inside it. Everything about the stone is in your mind, its particular weight, the shape specific to this stone alone. Now, tell the stone to jump. Go on, tell it."

It wasn't as if the little man had given him an order he had to obey. More that the quiet voice had put his mind in such a state that doing what he was told seemed the only right and natural thing to do.

"Jump, stone!" he told the stone, almost quietly. The stone leaped perhaps a finger-breadth, and Qedrim swore. "Old Woman's Apron! How did you do that?"

"I did nothing, O unbelieving young slinger, only convinced you that you could. Consider, if you would, why you consider these stones special; you can do things with them which no other can. So it stands to reason you can do other things with them.

"And ask yourself, 'What is a mountain made of?'"

"Stone of course, but—-"

"You will argue and argue in face of the evidence of your eyes. Yet I assure you. If you start with the ability to move certain stones, you will, with practice, be able to move other stones. And at some point you will indeed find yourself capable of moving mountains." He shook his head as if confused.

"Why one would wish to move a mountain is a thing which escapes me at the moment. No doubt you have your reasons, and they are good ones."

"Nonsense! I'm no magician, all I can manage are a few simple Talismans. You did this!"

Shapak-ailesh sighed and shook his head. "O Lame and Doubting slinger, make this test. Hold the stone again in your hand, and when you are ready, make the stone move. I will turn my back, you do everything as you did before, and when you are ready, call on the stone to jump. If it does so when I'm not looking, you can hardly blame it on me."

Qedrim glowered. There was something going on here, something he didn't understand. He took up the stone again, and stared at Shapak-ailesh who smiled and turned his back as promised.

"Jump, stone!" He thought the stone wiggled, though his hand was shaking.

"Not so easily, O hasty young Qedrim, you must meditate on the stone first. Look at it carefully, make yourself fully aware of it."

"Old Woman's Apron!" he muttered, but went through what he could remember of the process. He began focussing on what the stone looked like in the flickering light of the fire.

"Jump, stone!" The stone leaped in his hand, perhaps not so far as the first time, but it had definitely moved.

This time he didn't drop the stone, just stared at it. There was something to what the little man had told him. He could hit difficult targets at incredible distances with these sorts of stone. Could he command them to do more? What else might he do with them?

"May I look now," asked Shapak-ailesh.

"Yes, you might as well."

"So it moved?"

"It did. Did you put some sort of spell on it?"

"Tsk, tsk. Such a doubtful and distrustful nature! It will do no good, of course, for me to assure you I have done nothing to the stone, only give you a lesson. The work is all yours. The ability all yours. One with which you were born, but might never have used for more than hitting impossible targets. Try it again, from time to time, with that stone and with others.

"Perhaps no more tonight; it is a thing like the using of new muscles, it will take time to develop.

"But the more you practise, the better you will get. Eventually you will not need to speak, merely think what you want the stone to do."

Qedrim, still not quite accepting the notion he could move stones with a word, returned the stone to his pouch. Yes, he was going to have to keep an eye on this little fellow.

Shapak-ailesh smiled at him. "It grows late, and we ought to be sleeping soon. But do me a favour, tell me one of the tales they tell in your homeland."

"'Tales?' What was this now? What was he up to?' Qedrim struggled to do what he could to hide his suspicion, for all the good it would do him.

"Yes, tales. I collect stories, epics, romances, even philosophical discourses. What sort of tales do they tell in the winter nights in your homeland?"

"Tales of my homeland?"

"Why, yes, for certain. Don't worry, even if you tell the tale badly, I will still be interested."

Qedrim clenched his teeth. People might say all kinds of nasty things about him, but no one had ever said he couldn't tell a story.

"I'll tell you about North Wind Woman. You ever heard any of her stories?"

Shapak-ailesh considered. "I think not. Go ahead."

"So. Here it is. North Wind Woman went out one day, walking to town to buy a fat pig. She had her hair all bound up on her head, and fastened with two long pins.

"And as she walked along, up came Rock-Monster. Rock-Monster said, 'I'm going to eat you, North Wind Woman!'

"'Pressing me is not good,' said North Wind Woman. She shook down her hair and a little fire came dancing along and burned Rock-Monster's butt, so Rock-Monster ran away yelling.

"And North Wind Woman continued on her way.

"But Rock-Monster went and talked to his friend Swamp-Monster. 'I found North Wind Woman alone, but she drove me away with fire.'

"'Hah! You don't know what you're doing! Come along with me, the two of us will be too much for her.'

"So Rock-Monster and Swamp-Monster went and found North Wind Woman. 'We're going to eat you, North Wind Woman,' said Swamp-Monster.

'Pressing me twice is bad,' said North Wind Woman, and she shock down her hair. So two fires came dancing along and burned Rock- Monster and Swamp-Monster on the butts, so they ran away yelling.

"And North Wind Woman continued on her way to town.

"But Rock-Monster and Swamp-Monster found Deep-Earth-Monster and talked to him. 'We found North Wind Woman alone, but she drove us away with fire.'

'Hah! You two don't know what you're doing! Come along with me; the three of us will be too much for her.'

"So they found North Wind Woman as she was walking along. And Deep-Earth-Monster said, 'We're going to eat you, North Wind Woman!'

But North Wind Woman said 'Pressing me three times is too many!'

"And she shook down her hair, and a fire came raging and burned up Rock-Monster, Swamp-Monster, and Deep-Earth-Monster.

"And North Wind Woman went on her way to town to buy a pig. So they tell the tale."

Qedrim looked at Shapak-ailesh. He'd even finished the tale with the traditional phrase, 'So they tell the tale.' He wondered if the little man knew that tradition, or recognized it at all.

Shapak-ailesh considered for a time. "No, I hadn't heard that one. Very interesting. A very forbearing and formidable woman."

"Well, that's the story they tell. I think it's a bit stupid, myself."

The merchant's eyebrows rose. "Indeed? And why would you say that?"

"Because she ought not to have allowed them so many chances. If she'd burned up Rock-Monster the first time around, she wouldn't have been bothered again."

Shapak-ailesh chuckled. "But then there'd have been no story, would there?"

"Chaos Away with the story! That's the way the world works! People who have power use it, and don't worry too much about anybody else!"

"Tsk tsk, so bitter indeed, O young slinger! Suppose I tell a tale to make you smile?"

"Oh? Yes, I need a smile. Go ahead, tell your story."

"Indeed I will.

"You see, it happened that there was a man in a far-off kingdom. He was not an extremely bad man, but it chanced that he offended the king three times. After the third time, he was brought before the presence of the King, who sentenced him to death.

"The man at once cast himself to the ground before the King. And said, 'O King, Most Mighty and Powerful King, if you will allow me to live for a year, I will teach your favourite horse to sing hymns to the gods!"

"This intrigued the king so much that he set the sentence aside, and said, 'You will be given a year. In that time, if you have not taught my horse to sing, you will die.'

"'Agreed, O Most Mighty and Merciful King.'

"And as he was walking out of the presence of the King, one of his friends approached him and said, 'This madness! In a year, you will be executed!'

"But the man smiled. 'In a year, many things may happen. The king may die. The horse may die. I may die. Or perhaps the horse will learn how to sing!'"

Qedrim could hardly avoid a smile. "That's the way of it; another day is another day! And that's the way of power, too. Kings, nobles, caravan masters, they use their power as they see fit. And the rest of us must go along with it, and stay out of their notice."

"O dear, O dear, O most cynical slinger! If someone does you good, you will be looking forever around and about to see just what might be the trick!"

"Of course! Don't go telling me that anyone does anything for anyone without expecting something in return! I watch out for myself, Because no one else will."

DAWN WOKE HIM. HE COULDN'T recall anything after the argument over the little man's tale. Had something put him to sleep?

A blanket covered him, a thin one, but warm enough for all that. He moved his hands and feet, but the little merchant had not bound him during the night when he was so sound asleep.

That didn't really allay Qedrim's doubts. Shapak-ailesh might be being paid to deliver him, and easier to convince him to walk somewhere. Walking on his leg wasn't going to be easy, just yet.

"Aha!" The cheery voice rang out. "He is awake! Good, good! We will eat a bite, then we will travel!"

"We? I don't think my leg will allow me to go anywhere much today."

"Oh, I think you will not find matters so terrible as all that. Here, have some bread. You slept well?"

"Very well," he said, his suspicions coming back.

The little man held up a small but strong-looking hand, waving as if warding something off. "No, nothing I did. Or at the least, my part in it was minor, teaching you that trick with the stone. I said it would tire you, and it did. And you may or may not know that pain itself can be wearying, and you were in some pain.

"Oh, of course, after you fell asleep I put a blanket over you to keep the cold from waking you.

"Now, eat."

So they ate. Qedrim discovered that, other than a few twinges now and then, his leg was in fact much better.

While Qedrim was still eating, Shapak-ailesh went over to the mule, and began talking to the animal. "Now," he said, "we come to this part of the day. Yes, indeed, it is time to put your pack on for travelling. Come, now, what will our guest think of us, if you so refuse to take your part? Of course, he looks rough and rustic. But has there never been such a man which hid underneath such an exterior the soul of a philosopher?

"And indeed, he knows, as well as you and I know, that the nature of beasts is to be servants of men. Will you thus go against nature, against all the philosophies of the wise? For surely they are wiser than you or I, and thus they do declare. Some will even declare that for a recalcitrant beast such as yourself, it may be necessary to take up a philosophical stick and whack you on the backside.

"Yes, now, that is better."

Had he not known better, Qedrim would have said he was a harmless, fussy, little man.

With the mule finally resigned to his lot, Shapak-ailesh was back beside Qedrim. "Well, young Qedrim, do you need a hand getting to your feet?"

The thought of someone who stood barely waist-high on him giving him a hand to his feet brought an expression of scorn to Qedrim's face.

"I think I should be able to manage."

His leg, however, seemed determined to tweak him at strange times. Movements which usually had no effect were suddenly sending stabbing pain through his knee. Getting up was not a simple process. By the time he was on his feet, he was aware of the pinched feeling in his face as he gritted his teeth.

"Morning is always the worst," said Shapak-ailesh cheerfully. Why shouldn't he be cheerful? It wasn't him who was having iron spikes driven through his knee.

"I hope you're not expecting me to travel at any speed. I think I'll be doing well to make it from here to the main track."

"Oh, you'll do quite well. After a bit, your knee will stop hurting altogether. And besides, I do not use the main track anyway."

"So what do you do? Fly?"

"Oh, no, I use the Hidden Ways. Now, take a step."

He took hold of Qedrim's arm as though to help him along, and took a step.

They stood in a deep wood, tall evergreens on every side. If the wood was an illusion, it was a very good one, for the scent was not only of evergreens but of other woodland growth as well. Startled, Qedrim put a foot wrong, and gasped as his knee let him down.

"Careful!" warned Shapak-ailesh.

"Oh, yes, I'm very careful. What is this?"

"A stop on the Hidden Ways, as I said. Now we have to take another step. Are you ready?"

"Not that it would have mattered at all if he weren't ready. The little man took his sleeve again and took another step. Qedrim, without having taken a step of his own, was standing beside him on the edge of a huge lake. Out on the lake giant serpent-like things were swimming. They were apparently playing, for they lept out of the water and dived, going over and under each other.

"Best not stand here too long. Come along."

Now they were on a cold and snowy plain, whiteness stretching out on all sides as far as they could see. Shapak-ailesh stepped again, and now they were on a green plain, and only a score of yards away was a large skeleton. The skeleton had huge wings, and the bones of the wings lay extended on each side of the body.

The skeleton was easily as long as twenty men, and the skull itself was as tall as a tall man. All around the skeleton, nothing grew, no blade of grass, no smallest weed. A patch of dead soil, vaguely the shape of the skeleton itself, wings and all, held the bones. Beyond that border, the field was green.

Qedrim looked down at Shapak-ailesh, who looked back up at him. "There are strange things, even dangerous things, in the Hidden Ways. But I only stop to investigate on occasion, when I have no important schedule to keep."

"And you have a schedule to keep now?"

"Yes. One more step, please."

They were now in a grassy meadow in a mountain pass, running water next to them, and small bushes growing here and there. "We will camp here for the evening."

"Where are we?"

"On the border of Higfrod."

"Higfrod? But that's—-"

"A fair distance from where we started. An advantage of traveling the Hidden Ways. The folk in this land, for the most part, speak the Common Language. You may find you like the place."

Qedrim frowned at Shapak-ailesh, his eyes carefully surveying the merchant, "But if you could just step into the Hidden Trails or whatever you call them; what was that business of standing off the bandits back then?"

"I had to wait for you."

Qedrim's hand went for his knife. "For me? Why? I don't even know you!"

Shapak-ailesh waved a calming hand. "No, no, I have no nefarious purpose in mind. I promise, by the Lady of Praises, I mean no harm to you."

Which might have calmed Qedrim's mind, had he not had experience with people and promises.

"Consider the facts," said the little man. "Had I wanted you dead, I could have killed you while you slept last night. Does that not suggest I mean no harm to you?"

"Or that you plan to deliver me somewhere, alive, for someone else," answered Qedrim.

"O suspicious young slinger! Have you made some enemy who would go to so much trouble over you?"

"A man like me makes enemies, and sometimes I haven't been able to make sure they were safely dead when I left."

"And which of these alive and unsafe foes might be up to such a complicated scheme as you suggest?"

Qedrim had to admit, though he wouldn't do so aloud, no enemy he could think of could afford the cost of such a scheme. A man of his standing rarely numbered rich merchants among those who actively wished him unwell.

One heard other things, though. While not necessarily connected with any enmity, there were said to be magicians wanting live people to test spells on, or to supply certain organs or bodily parts for special spells or talismans.

"Come now, O slinger of magnificent suspicions! I have already sworn that I mean you no harm. Ease the grip on your knife."

"All right, then." Qedrim eased his grip on his knife. He was not, however, easing his grip on his suspicions. Qedrim continued watching, without seeming to, for any untoward motion. He hadn't altogether given up the thought of killing the little man for his mule and goods. That, however, was a thing he would have to give much more thought to, since this fellow was more than he appeared.

"But aside from all great assurances that you mean me no harm, why were you waiting for me, then?"

"O, it was a simple matter of seeing if you were the person I sought, and making sure of that. Giving you a few hints, and letting you go on your way."

"And you do this without asking me for pay?"

"Why of course. There are some things to be done, and you are most likely the man to do them. And no, I will not tell you what these things are, for that will make you more determined not to do them.

"Now, would you mind looking around for firewood? I suggest you use care. This would seem to be a safe neighbourhood, though one never knows."

"No, one doesn't, does one?" Qedrim tested his knee. It hurt a bit, though not so badly as to be disabling. "Yes, I think I can handle firewood."

One suspicious part of Qedrim's mind suggested to him taking part in the camp-chores was meant to make him feel one of the party. Inasmuch as two could make up a party, that is. He would have to take care just how much he allowed himself to accept that.

When he had gotten out of the little man's sight, a notion took him. Reaching into his pouch, he took out one of his special stones. As he had done the previous night in the firelight, he concentrated on it, on every aspect of it. Then he said, "Jump, stone."

The stone leaped in his hand. He stood there looking at the stone for a moment. So. Either the little man had some means of keeping track of just what he, Qedrim, was doing, or he had put a spell on all of Qedrim's stones. Or else he, Qedrim, was doing this all by himself.

The simplest answer was that he was doing it himself, which was a bit too much strangeness for him.

He shrugged and went back to collecting wood.

THAT EVENING, AFTER supper, Shapak-ailesh said, "I fear I may have taken you somewhat off your intended route. You had pressing business back there, had you?"

"If I said yes, would you retrace our steps tomorrow?"

Shapak-ailesh smiled broadly. "If you said so, young Qedrim, I would have to inform you that you were fibbing most wickedly."

"So you have a Talisman of Truth-telling, do you?"

'What things might I have told him that weren't true?'

The little man raised bushy eyebrows. "Ah, and are you familiar with such, O young slinger of the grim mood?"

"Not really. I know they exist. Old Freyollach did mention them, but only slightingly. He claimed no one could talk about himself without adjusting the facts a bit. So if a person had a Talisman of Truth-telling, all you'd find out was that everyone were liars."

"Myself, I think he said that because that kind of Talisman was beyond his ability, and he knew it."

"Oho! So you are greatly learned in the art of making of Talismans?"

Qedrim felt himself blush. "No, not greatly learned. I served as an apprentice to a magician, a bare hedge-wizard. Whose chief living was love-talismans, and those an uneven quality. I learned how to do some simple things, before he and I came to the parting of ways."

He was concerned the little man might pick up on that 'parting of ways' and ask awkward questions, but he did not.

"Oho! So you're a man of many skills, then?"

"I can do a lot of things, some of them better than others." He noticed the defensive tone in his voice, and hated it. He liked to make the most of his achievements, but Shapak-ailesh had already hinted he could tell truth from lies. Bragging to acquaintances was one thing. Bragging to a stranger who recognized it for what it was. That was another.

It was almost as if Shapak-ailesh had read his mind. He held up a hand in a warding gesture. "No, no, I was not trying to bait you, merely making an observation that you have several talents, the better to make your way in a harsh world."

Which only annoyed Qedrim the more. "And you know all about this harsh world, don't you? A merchant such as yourself, with your ability to slip about from here to there unnoticed!"

The bushy eyebrows rose again. "Oh, I have my little advantages, it's true. But everything is not for free. And it was certainly a harsh lesson in life for those bandits. And consider this; if I could always slip away from trouble, what need have I of my skill with a crossbow?"

Which was a matter worthy of thought.

Shapak-ailesh went on, with the slightest of pauses. "We are, however, straying somewhat further from my original question, and the direction my thought was taking. I plan to go to the city of Higfrod. Of course, Higfrod is not so much a city as a very large town. I think, though, that I can sell a bit of this and that there. If you'd like to accompany me, you're welcome."

"I'm not a merchant."

"Of course not. Nor had I thought of you as an apprentice or workman. I merely thought you might be willing to accompany me to the town. Once there, I can go about my business, and you can go to yours. Of course, if you wish to hire yourself out as my assistant—-"

"No, I don't think that will be necessary."

Shapak-ailesh smiled, as if he'd just brought a business deal to an very satisfactory close. "Just remember, I have to see to the remaining portions of your reward. But don't forget to practice with your stones. In fact, I think you ought to do a little practice before you go to bed."

Qedrim shot him a suspicious glance. *'You do, do you?'*

He dug one of the stones out of his pouch. After staring at the stone for a bit, he said, "Jump onto my knee, stone!"

The stone obediently hopped off his hand and landed, not quite on his knee, but close. Qedrim looked up at Shapak-ailesh.

"No, I know you don't believe me, but it really is you that are doing it."

Qedrim continued to eye him with mistrust.

"Oh dear, oh dear! How young and suspicious we are! Look, I will turn my back, put my fingers in my ears, and you can give the stone another command and see what happens." He turned and put his fingers in his ears.

Qedrim, curious now, looked at the stone and aid, "Roll to my thigh, stone!"

The stone obediently moved toward his thigh, though it stopped after a palm-width. He was still sitting looking at it when Shapak-ailesh spoke. "May I look again?"

"What? Oh, yes, of course."

"And did it work?"

"Not completely, but it did seem to try."

"Ah, yes. Be sure though, that after sufficient practice, the stone will do just as you say. After all, you do use those special stones to great effect in your sling, do you not?"

Qedrim didn't answer. This little man seemed to know altogether too much about him for comfort. He had now set aside any notion of trying to kill this little man for his mule and goods. He would settle now for getting away from Shapak-ailesh safely.

Shapak-ailesh smiled his vexing smile. "I assure you, if you continue to practice, there will come a time when you will be able to make any stone of any size obey you. And I refer to any stone whatever, not merely the ones you call 'special.'"

Qedrim considered the thought of hurling boulders as though they were pebbles. What might he be able to do with such power? He might, at the very least, win bets on his ability to lift heavy stones? How much might he win by being able to lift a stone without touching it?

"I see by your face that you are attracted to the notion." Shapak-ailesh appeared a little sad. "However, I suspect that I would not care to hear some of your speculations. If I thought it would do the least good, I would lecture you on careful consideration of the use to which you put this power."

"Or you'll take it away?"

Shapak-ailesh shook his head. "No, I doubt I could, whatever I might desire. But think of this: A lion can be fierce and powerful, easily a match for one man. But if the lion becomes too troublesome, several men band together to kill him."

"Is that some sort of threat?"

"Not at all. Merely a prediction of what may happen, if certain circumstances arise.

"But there is still time. You can move a pebble, but it will require more practice to move the pebble exactly as you wish. And it will require still more for you to do serious harm with a stone. Other than using it in your sling, of course."

Qedrim was set to thinking. He'd known of wizards who'd been suspected of selling curses. They were usually hedge-wizards, with little ability to begin with. Mobs had gathered, though, and in many cases, torn them to shreds.

He knew too much ability in gambling, not necessarily cheating—though everyone did it—could result in some poor loser going after you with a dagger. If that loser felt himself outclassed, he might gather several friends. Yes, you'd have to think things through carefully before you started taking people's money.

But-—"This business with my special stones. Are you hinting I already had power over stones?"

"'Power over stones' would be putting it a bit strongly. You had some power over certain stones, though scarcely developed to any degree. After all, your range and accuracy with these stones in your sling was something which you hardly took thought over. You would have gone on with that capacity unchanged forever."

"And you used some spell on me?"

"O, ever suspicious one! No, I merely called your attention to your ability, suggested to you how to train it. Which means the first part of your reward was dreadfully easy to supply."

"I see." Qedrim had thought his knee didn't hurt so much any more. It was possible that tonight he might be able to put a knife in the little man, and relieve him of his goods. He put that thought away from him. At times, Shapak-ailesh seemed eerily close to being able to read Qedrim's mind. Much better to wait and find some other easier prey.

Best not to think of Shapak-ailesh at all, and rather think what sort of game one might make out of the ability to move and place stones.

HE WOKE UP NEXT MORNING with the same thin but warm blanket over him. In the background Shapak-ailesh's voice cajoling and threatening the mule to allow himself to be loaded with packs.

"Some beasts, you understand, do not have such accommodating masters. Some would not put up with such fractious and dilatory attitudes. Some would, indeed, have already taken to the practice of carrying around a big stick with which to chastise animals who seem not to know their places in the world. Yes, that's better. And yes, indeed, I shall want to be sure the cinch is tight, so don't be swelling your belly with air like that."

Qedrim was annoyed, to say the least. He'd slept the night through, missing any opportunity he might have had to rob the little merchant. The worst of it was he'd slept so soundly that Shapak-ailesh might well have put a knife in <u>him</u>. He was suspicious, and more than suspicious, magic had been involved. A sleep-spell on the blanket, for instance, which the little man had tossed over him while he slept.

He got up and pulled off the blanket; he considered leaving the blanket in a wadded lump, but decided not to. Let the little fellow think he didn't suspect anything. Let him begin thinking of Qedrim as harmless. He folded the blanket neatly.

"I thought we might just eat a bit as we went," Shapak-ailesh said. We could be in Higfrod by noon."

"Wouldn't it be faster to use your Hidden Ways?"

"Why certainly, but it would be a waste. Consider: We appear out of thin air in the Market Square, and cause such great suspicion among the people that we can hardly do anything. How can one trust a merchant who is able to appear and, it is assumed, disappear at will?

"So we need to pick a place which is definitely uninhabited. Meaning outside the walls, at any rate. And walk from there. So, using the Hidden Ways to move such a short distance would be on the order of lifting a boulder the size of a house in order to crack a walnut."

Qedrim nodded. Not that he agreed completely. His knee was still not easy, and he disliked the thought of walking. It was Shapak-ailesh's choice whether or not to use the Hidden Ways, and there was no way Qedrim could compel the merchant.

Chapter 2

The trip was an easy one. There was a well-travelled trail, the sky was fair, only an occasional cloud in sight, and the grass and wildflowers provided their illusion of peace and tranquility. Along the way Qedrim took a couple of rabbits with his sling, not even bothering with the special stones. Each time, Shapak-ailesh accompanied him off the trail to pick the rabbits up.

"For our supper?" he asked the first time.

"If we wish. If not, I'm sure I could sell it for a couple of coppers in the town."

After the second rabbit, Shapak-ailesh's comment was, "Very accurate with that sling of yours."

"Yes. Back in the Arndal Hills where I came from, we start with the sling as soon as we start walking. I'm one of the best."

The little man looked up at him. "You are, are you?"

Qedrim shrugged. "Think me a braggart if you wish. I am quite good with the sling"

'And you aren't giving me a chance to put a little distance between the two of us so I might crack you on the head with a stone, are you?'

The scent of town, wood smoke, charcoal smoke, and the aroma of a packed mass of humanity, reached them well before the sight of the city itself.

The town in main was well-made, and made of stone; there was plenty of such material hereabouts. As with all walled towns, buildings of various sorts had sprung up outside the walls to accommodate increased population.

As Qedrim came up the road, city guards were forcibly removing one shelter which had been set up on the road itself. The husband

26

was standing by, with a guard's spear at his throat to keep him quiet. The wife was screeching incoherently at the guards who went about their business, ignoring her.

The Captain of the party, gruff but not rude, said "Come, mother, you know the law. No building may block any street or road. We asked you once to move four feet over, we come back and you've made no attempt to move. So we do what we have to do."

Qedrim frowned. "Why did they put their house there in the first place?" he muttered to Shapak-ailesh. "Did they think the town would let them be. You don't pick a fight you can't win!"

"Impossible to say why. Sometimes when you have so little to lose, simply picking a smooth spot for your tent, even for the time being, knowing you'll be evicted, seems worthwhile. Or perhaps there was no thought at all, just setting up the tent, no consideration for either permissions or disallowances.

The city proper was more solidly built, most of the buildings were made of stone and mortar. One could tell which were the houses of the more affluent; the stones were squared and fitted regularly. At last they came to the market place.

Shapak-ailesh turned to Qedrim. "You're certain you don't wish to stay with me?"

"No, I think not."

'And don't pretend you're not glad to see the last of me!'

"We may part ways for the moment, but we haven't seen the last of each other," Shapak-ailesh carried on. "We still have some unfinished business."

'Have we indeed, little merchant?'

QEDRIM WENT LOOKING for a buyer for the two rabbits. He sold both of them to a woman of middle years, a woman of the town, and got two coppers better than he might have, on the grounds that the skins were whole and unmarked.

He put these coppers together with a bit of his own money, then bought a few items. He then sat in the marketplace and put together two Talismans of Fire-starting. He concentrated on speed, not quality, and the two talismans he produced would work well, though not for an extended length of time.

He chose his first customer with care, a caravan master wearing dark leather vest and trousers, with a turban round his head to keep off the sun. "Sir, do you wish to buy a Fire-starting Talisman? Very useful for those times when you need a fire, and quickly."

The fellow spoke the Common language, but with an accent Qedrim couldn't quite place. "This has some advantage over flint and steel?"

"Yes, indeed. with this, there is no concern about having tinder kept safely dry at all times. You simply take a twig, like so, and hold it in your hand, while holding the Talisman in the other. You then say "Fire! And behold, the twig burns!"

"I see. And what do you ask for this thing?"

Qedrim stubbed out the burning stick on the dirt of the marketplace. "Two silver coins."

"Two silvers? Ridiculous! Two coppers."

"For two coppers I will tear the thing to shreds first. I must at least recoup the cost of the material. One silver and five coppers."

They finally made the bargain at one silver and two coppers, a little better than Qedrim had actually expected.

The next customer was a mercenary soldier, a light spearman, wearing a leather cuirass and carrying a much-used shield. He bargained harder, and brought the price down to one silver.

Qedrim considered this fine; the firestarters he made would work, and work well, but only for a time, after which they would cease to work altogether. That would not be for a month or two, though, at which time he hoped both customers would be too far away to bring back any complaint.

With a little more money in hand, Qedrim went off to find a wineshop.

HE WANTED A WINESHOP of a certain quality, not the best, but certainly not a dive. His main requirements were that there be people, and people who might be separated from their money. A certain establishment named The Copper Bowl seemed a likely bet. It appeared to pay off when he stepped inside.

At one table sat four men, strongly built, probably small farmers, squat and solid, with hair varying from a bushy black mop to a balding crown to a hairless head that gleamed faintly with sweat.

He bought a cup of wine and carried it to the table. "May I join you gentlemen?"

Politeness and courtesy were not necessarily the signs of weakness some considered them to be. In certain situations, they were essential tools.

The four glared at him with unwelcoming faces. Qedrim maintained a smile, not the sort of broad smile which made people wonder what was behind it, just a general good humoured expression. "My name's Qedrim. I've only arrived in town today, and I'd like to hear the latest news. Don't want to run afoul of the wrong people. Do you mind if I join you?"

One of them finally shrugged, and hitched his stool over. Taking this for as effusive a welcome as he could expect at this table, Qedrim reached back with a foot and hooked a stool over from another table, then sat down.

"What d'you want to know?" said the bald man brusquely.

"Just about anything and everything, I guess. Until a while ago, I'd scarcely heard of your city, now here I am. Is this a good or bad time to be here? No pestilence or war breaking out, I hope?"

The bald man frowned. "Might not be the best time to be here. War's coming on."

"That's not good. Who's troubling who?"

"The Kharmista of this province, she's being pressed. The Kharmost of Daura, he's determined to take over Higfrod. Up until last hear he couldn't do much, because our Kharmista, the Lady Annavristi, she's related to the Kings of Dai'vlash. Last year the old King died, and there was some fuss over who should take the throne.

"That meant B'tlas of Daura had a chance; first he suggested marriage, agreeing to give up his present wife, but Lady Annavristi, she'd have none of it. So now he's putting it out to the people that he's mortally insulted, demands surrender or war."

Qedrim nodded. "They go to war, and we underneath, we try to keep our heads down."

From the expressions, that was not quite the thing to say. Had he fallen in with a band of patriots? He was trying to come up with something to ameliorate the effect of his latest statement when the bushy-haired one said, "You might find yourself recruited for her army. Or are you any good with that sling at your belt?"

'Well, Old Woman give you grace for that! Saves me the trouble of having to work round to it casually!'

"Best you're likely to see!" A brag was the best way to handle this lot.

"That good? But of course, you wouldn't claim to be second-best, would you?" The others merely nodded, grinning, letting young bushy-hair carry the conversation.

It was no difficulty at all to play insulted. "I'll bet you three silvers I can hit a target the size of a man's head at fifty paces, three times in five!"

'Aha! Got you now!' Qedrim thought as he maintained a stoic face.

"Oh, sure! Everybody's heard of Kedrim the Deadly, from here to Suragos!"

'And you've never been more than a day's trip from your farm, have you?'

"It's not Kedrim, it's Qedrim. And if you haven't got the money to put up to watch me, then stop gabbling. Here's mine!"

He slapped a silver coin on the table glancing at the profile of the woman shown on it.

'She's got a big nose, hasn't she?'

Ignoring his friends' protests, the young man put a coin on the table himself, "There you are! Now show us!"

Qedrim leaned back. "This isn't my town. You find a target, and a place to set it up, then find me. I'll be here." He looked at the bald man. "When he's got things set up, you'll hold the bets?"

The bald man eyed at him closely. "All right."

No one spoke any further word of warning, but Qedrim knew he was in a tricky situation. These fellows might not take kindly to him taking advantage of their younger friend. Well, there would be nothing they could prove about it, one way or another. He'd simply have to keep his eyes open in case someone decided on their own that this stranger had been cheating somehow.

THE YOUNG FARMER, THALDO by name, had picked a spot on a hillside. Qedrim wasn't sure if he'd picked that spot to make things a bit more difficult for Qedrim, or perhaps because there was little flat land hereabouts.

The target, on the other hand, was perhaps a a little larger than an average man's head, though not likely large enough to make a significant difference. Qedrim was happy to see a small group, no great crowd, but sufficient for the moment, had gathered to watch.

He checked over the field the young farmer had picked, studying the ground, as though that mattered. One could, of course, whip three stones in a row into the target, but it might suggest to Thaldo's friends that the young man had been set up for a fall.

He made a show of carefully picking a stone from his pouch; all that mattered was he pick one of his special stones. He tested his footing; this mattered, a little. A rolling pebble or the like underfoot at the wrong moment might just put this shot off.

He swung the sling three times round his head and let go. The stone leaped out so fast as to be lost from sight, then smacked into the target and bounced away. Ignoring the crowd's murmurs, he picked another stone, and sent it, too, whipping down the range. Another hit, of course.

They murmured louder now, and he chose another stone and slung it down the range, missing by a hand's breadth.

More murmuring. Now, another choice; finish it fast, and have Thaldo's friends thinking he had taken advantage of the young man, or another miss, then a final hit, and risk seeming to be having some fun at Thaldo's expense.

He thought he had read the crowd's reactions right. His next shot hit home.

The only problem might be if they thought he was using some kind of magic; of course, doing this trick too often gave a fellow a bad name, and he'd had magicians called in before, a time or two, at the other fellow's expense, and they could never find a trace of magic involved.

Indeed, they might decide to mob him on the grounds he'd used magic, proven or no. He was ready for that. The fact was, he could make about any shot he wanted with his special stones, occasionally at ranges bordering on the fantastic, and who could fault him for using that fact to make money on?

He turned to Thaldo, staying aware all the time in case people were moving in behind him. "You satisfied?"

One had to watch one's expression, too, especially in a strange town. Say something which sounded like you were rubbing it in, that might bring payback from Thaldo's friends, and Thaldo himself, if it came to that.

Thaldo handed over the money, frowning. "You are good. Good enough to find yourself recruited, willing or no, for the Lady's Army."

"Not me! I was in an army once, got my leg bashed up. No more armies for me! I can use a sling, but I'm not much good on long marches."

"Huh!" That statement appeared to have lowered him in Thaldo's judgment.

'Old Woman's apron! Why should I involve myself in someone else's war? And if it becomes needful, I put aside my Talisman Against Lameness. No army's going to buy a Talisman just to keep one slinger on his feet.'

He spoke aloud. "Would you like to get some of your money back?"

The young fellow sneered. "Bet against you again? What kind of fool do I look like?"

"Old Woman's Apron, no! I meant, you set up another match, this time you lay bets with people in the crowd, betting on me to win. You maybe lose your original bet, but you make money anyhow. Then we split fifty-fifty, and I won't even insist you pay back my silver." He watched Thaldo as the young man considered.

"Come on! You didn't lose all your money today. I saw you laying side-bets on my third and fourth shots."

Thaldo smiled and it did not surprise Qedrim to see a shamefaced look. "All right. Suppose I set up another match. You want me to do it right now?"

"No, work on getting bets in overnight. Meet me at the same place tomorrow, the wineshop we met in."

"All right. Just don't go getting yourself so drunk you can't see the target, let alone hit it."

The youngster just had to get a little dig in, make himself feel better.

"You just see to your part, I'll see to mine."

IN FACT, QEDRIM DIDN'T do much drinking at all. He did a little cautious gambling, but luck wasn't with him and he knew better than to keep playing, hoping his luck would change.

"One sure bet," he thought wryly, "is that it won't."

He did find a quiet corner to practice having his special stone unwatched. He already had some notions as to just what sort of game he might use them in.

Next day he put some more money into material, and put together another talisman, a water-finder, and he sold it to a farmer. "You'll never regret this," he told the man. No more digging wells in the hope there's something at the bottom. Now you'll know where there's water."

This talisman was of better quality than the one's he'd made the previous day. The fellow would get at least a year's use out of it. How often would a farmer use it? Get out to his farm, find a new spot for a well, maybe rent it out to a neighbour or two, then the thing would probably sit on a shelf for a few years.

It might be only the farmer's son or grandson who noticed the talisman wasn't working any longer.

Though the farmer had been a sharp bargainer, in the end, Qedrim had increased his stock of coin a bit.

He knew well enough the sling-hustle would only work until the word got round, and in a small place like this, which wouldn't be more than a few days. He knew he'd have to find something else to do. Gambling was no sure thing, unless you had some means to bend the odds your way a bit. Even then, people noticed you were too lucky, and avoided playing with you. Or they caught you doing something that went against the rules, and which made bigger problems. As if any one of them wouldn't do the same, or worse, if they thought they could get away with it!

Higfrod wasn't a large city; he should be able to last for a year doing this or that game, then he'd probably have to move on. Which brought to mind another fact. Thanks to Shapak-ailesh and his Hidden Ways, Qedrim didn't know exactly where the nearest city was. He'd have to work that out, though there was plenty of time.

It would be nice if he could make a big score now, take some rich fool for a lot.

He shook his head. Mess around with rich people, they could make bad trouble for you. Often as not, they had contacts in other cities, people who owed them a favour or two. The likes of Qedrim didn't have any allies at all.

It was him against the world, the world against him, and he had to watch just who he skinned, and how badly.

THALDO WAS ALREADY at the wineshop when Qedrim showed up. The young farmer grinned at him.

'Old Woman's apron, man, why don't you just hire someone to go round announcing we're in this together?'

None of Thaldo's friends from the previous day were with him, Maybe he hadn't told them, or maybe they hadn't wanted to find themselves involved in something which might be shady.

"So, Qedrim, you're ready?"

He shrugged. "Ready."

Thaldo had set the target up in the same place, and this time the crowd was a bit bigger. Among the crowd were other farmers, and other folk beside who looked like the sort to bet on anything. There was even a robed Kondellini among them. Very far from home, that one.

Qedrim varied his techniques this time, hit the first one, missed the second, then hit the third and fourth.

From the sound of the crowd, a lot of people had bet against him.

That fool Thaldo, grinning broadly, came up to him with a handful of silver. "Not here!" Qedrim whispered sharply. "Back at the wineshop!"

The boy's face fell. Well, so his feelings were hurt. Better some hurt feelings than a beating, or worse, from a crowd who'd lost their money.

Back at the wineshop, Thaldo pushed the money across the table with a sulky look on his face. Qedrim didn't so much take pity on him as decide to teach him some facts. After all, the two of them might work together a bit more.

"Look, boy, you don't wave fistfuls of silver in front of a bunch of people you've just skinned. In this case, handing me a bunch of money merely tells them they've been had, they've been talked into a sucker bet, and the two of us had worked this out between us."

"But we had!"

"Yes. And some people, having it rubbed in their faces, can get downright nasty. You collect your winnings with a smile, not a large mile-wide grin, and you share out the loot later on, quietly."

"You sound as though we're going to do this again."

Qedrim shrugged. "We can. Depends on a lot of things. I think it'd be best to lay off the sling-game for a few days; we do the same thing too many days in a row, word gets around faster, nobody'll bet against us. Not only that, we'll get the name for running a game, and have the Watch on our heads, or whatever they have in these parts to keep order."

"Besides, don't you have to be back at the farm?"

Thaldo looked up. "No, not me! My brother Goldat is going to take on the farm. As for me, I'm going to join the Lady's Army.!"

Qedrim barely managed to keep himself from saying something like "Old Woman's apron, what for?" but he remembered in time the young fellow's expression when he, Qedrim, had made his pronouncement on armies the day before. He restrained himself to merely saying "Oh?"

Thaldo kept the conversation going. "I'd say it's only polite I offer to buy you a cup of wine."

So they sat for a while, Qedrim trading stories of far-away and exotic lands for chitchat on the ins and outs of life hereabouts. Qedrim had spent the odd moment hoping Shapak-ailesh would be eaten by Morrkerr Deathlord for bringing him here. He would have to find out, and quickly, what direction he ought to go. He disliked being in a city on what was the losing side of a prospective war. That meant the possibility of a siege, and worse yet, sacking, neither of them things to be desired.

Which was most likely why he decided to start on his new game. "Listen," he told Thaldo, "you start off betting against me. Then when we get some people over here looking on, you start making some side bets on me. And don't worry; no matter how mad it sounds, I'll win."

Thaldo was still taking in this sudden change of subject when Qedrim reached into his pouch and took out one of his special stones. "See this? I set it on the table here, like so. Now, without touching the stone or the table by any means, I can make that stone leap from here to the table's edge."

"Nonsense!" Thaldo didn't have to work at all to sound skeptical; all the better. As long as he remembered his part, to lay off some side bets.

"Nonsense, is it? Look, here's five coppers. Cover that!" It was a small bet, but it was a start.

Thaldo was staring at him. "Come on, boy! You're quick to say 'nonsense' but slow to put your money out!"

Of course, that pushed the boy just far enough. "All right, here's five. Show me."

Which was fine, as far as it went. If the boy had a bit of sense, He'd have started getting people in already. Well, Qedrim could do that himself, though it put everything on him, made him the sole target if things turned nasty.

He looked around. "Anybody else want to get in?" Eyes were turning in their direction, eyes which showed varying states of intoxication.

"I'm betting, without touching the stone or the table, I can make that stone jump to the far edge of the table. I got five coppers out now; anyone else want to get in?"

A husky blond fellow *What country does that pale hair come from I wonder?* walked over in the careful way common to drunks and slapped down a silver coin. "No strings?"

"No strings." Qedrim pulled out a coin to match, noticing idly the blond man's coin showed the picture of some strange ruler, along with a foreign inscription.

"Anybody else? Come on, come on, this's hardly worth the money!"

After a little more coaxing, he had a nearly reasonable sum of money out in front of him.

Qedrim stood and moved back from the table so they could see he wasn't touching it. "Anybody want to check for strings?"

Someone was actually sober enough to take that measure. He moved his hands all around and over the table, and certified it free from strings or wires.

Qedrim looked at the stone, fastened it in his mind, and said, "Stone, jump to the edge of the table!"

The stone jumped, and landed just short of the table's edge. There was some muttering, a bit of it bad-tempered.

"Some kind of trick!" someone shouted.

"Well of course it's some kind of trick. But it's a trick I know how to do. Want me to show you again? Put up some money."

The blond man said, "Right. I'll put up some money, but this time I get to hold onto your hands."

"Hold my hands, hold my feet, anything you want. I just have to be able to see the stone and talk to it."

This brought some new bets, and at last they were ready. The blond man took hold of Qedrim's hands in his own pair of strong calloused hands. "Go ahead."

The stone had been placed, not exactly where it had started, but near to a quarter way around the table. "Jump to the edge of the table, stone!"

The stone jumped. Once more some in the crowd shouted. The blond man let go Qedrim's hands, spun him round by a shoulder. Qedrim's leg, talisman or no, betrayed him momentarily in the twisting motion, and he stumbled. The yellowhair's rough hand caught him by the front of his tunic.

"You'll tell me now you did that!"

"I tell you how I did it, you'll be winning bets instead of me." This was a bad part. How drunk, how angry, was yellowhair? Was he ready to be influenced by argument or sense?

No, he was bringing up a fist. Qedrim had not had so much to drink, though, and as a boy he had learned a lot of wrestling tricks in the Arndal Hills. He slapped a hand on the fist holding his tunic, lifted and twisted, forcing yellowhair to turn away from the pain. Slapping his other hand on the man's elbow, Qedrim sent him flying at the wall.

Qedrim immediately began scooping up money from the table into his wide-brimmed hat. A few coppers and silvers slipped away, tumbling to the floor. He didn't bother with those; the fight was beginning, and mostly it was a case of anybody hitting everyone else; he wanted no part of that.

He saw Thaldo hanging onto a handful of money in his shirtfront with one hand, while warding off a couple of semi-drunk attackers with the other. Qedrim hit one of them behind the ear with his cane, stuck a foot behind the other's knee and pushed him down.

"Come on, boy, let's get out of here! And watch out!"

At its start the fight had been over the bet, but in a flash it turned into a wild any-against-all affray. He shouldn't have made the second bet, pleaded tiredness or something. Not his fault the people were so edgy here.

Qedrim knew very well that his best position, when the Watch came to deal with the matter, would be seated comfortably in a wineshop some distance from the centre of the trouble.

It required some skillful use of his stick, as well as his knees and feet, to get to the door. Luckily, Thaldo appeared to have the sense to follow him. Once out the door and and a few steps away, he slowed down.

"Hold up, Thaldo. Running away will merely get people's attention. You know a place they won't cheat us for a night's lodgings?"

"Yes. Follow me. And thanks for getting me out of that business."

"Huh! You're hanging on to money I have a share in. Otherwise, I'd've let you get your head bashed in."

"Right." The boy didn't believe him. Well, if he lived long enough he'd see that everybody was out for themselves. Most likely he'd die first.

HE SPENT MOST OF THE next morning buying material and putting together talismans in the markets. He thought that, considering last night's excitement, he'd be best to stick to talismans. Talismans cost more in time and money to make, but most times you could manage it so the fellow who bought the talisman didn't come back with a band of friends, a bunch of clubs, and a bad mood.

This time he intended to make some fire-starters, a couple of water-finders, and a Talisman Against Lameness.

While he was sitting there in the market there was a sudden stir as a column of mounted soldiers rode through. From the chatter he gathered this was the Kharmista. He glanced up. It was always good to know the faces of the powerful, if only to avoid coming into their sight.

His first thought was that there was a die-cutter somewhere who deserved to be whipped. She didn't have a big nose. Strong, yes, high, yes, but not that great honker pictured on the coins.

Other things struck him. She wore armour and a sword, and the sword was not one of those decorated, bejewelled monsters, useless in a fight. It was a warrior's tool, made for her size and weight, and meant for use.

"Poor girl" he thought. "Even here, in the midst of the people who say they love her, she knows she's not safe."

For some reason, it didn't feel as good as usual to have his view of the world confirmed. Everyone was looking after themselves; some decent people got squashed while it was happening.

The column stopped. This wasn't some ordinary procession, but they were here for a purpose.

A part of the column moved around the Kharmista and her immediate guard, and people drew back to allow them room. In the midst of this group was a tall and powerfully-built fellow, whose clothing declared him to be one of the upper class. He looked and carried himself like a Lord, though he wasn't wearing any armour or weapons, and his hands were bound behind him.

Some of the escort got down, and pulled him from the saddle, though they didn't let him sprawl on the cobbles of the Marketplace.

That was the only consideration they gave him, for they roughly pushed him to a kneeling position. A herald spoke, trained voice carrying to all corners of the square.

"People of Higfrod! This man, Hol'kas son of Vodithar, has betrayed the Lady Annavristi of Higfrod. Not being content with spreading malicious lies against her, he has even gone so far as to attempt the formation of a cabal to overthrow her.

"Though the Lady's generosity and mercy are great, certain things cannot be forgiven For this cause, it is decreed that he should be executed here, and his head displayed for a sign of the Kharmista's justice!"

A soldier, an ordinary cavalry trooper, though somewhat stronger in the arms than most, stepped forward, drew his sword, and in one strong, clean blow, cut the head from the guilty Lord.

They left the body to lay there in the street, though Qedrim supposed that eventually a crew would come along to dispose of it, likely tossing it on a dung-heap. They took the head with them, in a basket brought for the purpose.

It seemed to Qedrim the Lady was not going to go down easily, but he wondered how much use this execution would be. It was good she had the strength of will to order such things. But how many other Lords were going to be looking at the comparative sizes of the Lady's forces and the forces of B'tlas? And how many of those other Lords would at least consider a separate bargain with him?

Everyone looked out for themselves, after all.

The column moved on out of his sight, and he went on with his work. Qedrim took it as a good sign one of the people who paused to watch him work leaned on a cane and limped, in the manner of one who had the joint-pain. "Hah, uncle, I have just the thing for you!"

Old eyes stared at him, hostile at being hailed by a foreigner, a hostility further fuelled by continual pain. "And what is it you imagine I need?"

"Look at this!" he rolled back his trouser-leg to show the wreck which was his left knee. "I went to the wars, as a young man. I took a sling-stone in the left knee that ended my career.

"And you can believe I was lame and in pain, too. Then I discovered the making of this."

He held up the Talisman Against Lameness, "You see, I wear one as well."

He still wore his own, as well as the thing Shapak-ailesh had given him. Sometime, he'd have to remake his talisman, if it were possible, though for now the little man's talisman was doing well.

The old man frowned. "Oh, yes? And its cost is equally astounding, I suppose?"

"Now, uncle, you wrong me! If you go shopping for a ham, the best ham always costs a bit. All I ask is three silver coins, and you'll be free of pain for half a year!"

"Three? Ridiculous! Did I accidentally come out of the house today with 'Fool' written on my forehead? Suppose I pay you a copper for that thing, and find that it doesn't work. I'd be willing to bet you'd be nowhere around, would you?

"With such an attitude, do you ever buy anything? Look!" Qedrim demonstrated one of his firestarter Talismans. "See? These work, just as advertised. And I guarantee the Talisman Against Lameness will work as well."

"Oh? And how? I'd be willing to bet you'll tell me I have to wait a day or more for the full effect. By that time, where would you be? Halfway to Ta'chol I suppose?'

Qedrim shrugged. "You're right. Something like this takes a bit of time to work. And nothing I could do or say will convince you it does work. So off you go, save your money, and rejoice as you limp about the next year that you have your money, and having that money in your fist is worth all the pain!"

The oldster's face became even more forbidding. "I would surely not pay three silvers for it. One, perhaps."

'Got you, did I?'

"One does not begin to pay for what I put into it. Two silver and five coppers."

The price ended up at two silver and one. With a Lameness Talisman, Qedrim always gave a warning. "It should last for at least four, possibly as long as eight months. If it does not, come back to me."

The truth was, they seldom lasted longer than three months, but by that time Qedrim should be somewhere else. And if by chance a dissatisfied customer should find him, he'd be all apologetic about magic's adventitious nature, and offer a cut rate on a replacement.

Strangely, he found his mind drifting back to the Kharmista from time to time during the day.

At these times, he considered this the way of the world. Everyone was out for themselves. From all he'd heard about the situation, she was about to fall, hard.

Those eyes would be staring out over that proud nose from the top of a pike, and wasn't that a shame?

He shook his head. And wasn't it a shame Qedrim had to keep his mind on his work, or he'd starve?

HE DIDN'T DO ANYTHING big for the next few days. He'd developed another game involving his stones, in which he,d take two special stones, balance one on the other muttering "Stay there." He would then bet a few coppers no one else could do it.

He kept the stakes low; a few coppers was not a really big win, but they added up. This one seemed more like a matter of steady hands than something halfway to magic.

Mostly, he'd been too smart to press his luck too far; the last few days were an exception. He'd pushed his luck much too far and too fast, getting into the big stakes where the chances were high someone was going to be upset about the amount they'd lost.

Despite all efforts to lie low, on his third night working this new game, he suddenly saw a blond head pushing its way across the room. A second glance told Qedrim yes, it was that bad-tempered yellowhair, and he was a little more sober this evening. He plainly recognized Qedrim, for he was surging this way determinedly.

Qedrim didn't want another riot tonight. He scooped a handful of coppers from the table, tossed them in a scatter in the blond's path. "Have a good time on me, lads!"

He scooped the rest, as much as he could, into his hat and his shirt-front, and made his way out the side door to the alley. The alley, of course, had been used as a latrine for generations by the wineshop's patrons, and it stank, badly, but Qedrim wasn't paying particular heed to that. His concern was more whether yellowhair was drunk enough to be determined to follow him, or sober enough to realize that if he went back out the front and circled to the alley he might meet Qedrim at the alley's mouth.

In this case, yellowhair apparently hadn't thought that clearly and Qedrim headed off, unfettered, through the darkened streets. By now he knew several places where he could stay and, even without the coppers he'd scattered or hadn't been able to grab from the table, he was adequately in funds to be able to pay for his lodging. He even had several talismans he hadn't yet sold.

His mood was still bad. Why did yellowhair and his old grudges have to come along tonight? When you were gaming for coppers, you couldn't afford to let any get away, and he'd let what—twenty?—get away.

Worse waited him next day.

HE WAS LEANING AGAINST a wall in the marketplace, with his talismans on display, idly juggling one of his special stones, causing it to leap from palm to fingertips and back again. It was a fine afternoon, and he was enjoying the heat on his chest, though his hat kept his face shaded.

Once more the Kharmista and her party rode through. Nearly everyone stopped what they were doing to watch, and to call greetings to her. Again, it occurred to Qedrim to feel sorry for the woman. She rode so bravely through the Marketplace, fully armed and armoured against whoever or whatever might attack. Yet she acted as though there were little to worry about; did she actually think she could survive?

She must have her doubts, for there was an archer up there on a rooftop, keeping watch on the crowd.

A moment later several things occurred to him. Only the one archer was in sight, and the man was not exactly standing where he could watch the crowd. He seemed to be skulking up there, trying to remain hidden.

Then he realized this was no guard, this was an assassin, looking for the best shot.

Without hardly thinking about it, Qedrim whipped his sling from his belt, dropped the stone into it, and began whirling it around his head. The assassin was standing, drawing his bow; Qedrim let loose his stone. It was a far shot, but not that far, especially not for one of his special stones.

The man went back and down, but he had already loosed his arrow and was reaching for another when he fell.

The marketplace crowd broke into shouting and screaming. There was confusion in the Lady's party. Was she down? Suddenly someone was pointing to Qedrim, standing there like a fool with the sling dangling from his hand.

The had surged forward to get close to the Kharmista, now they were beginning to surge his way.

It took only an instant for him to realize what was happening, then he whirled and ran. The crowd came after him. He rushed through streets, up alleys, but the noise of the crowd told him they were still behind him.

Then without warning he was in a blind alley, with nowhere further to flee. Old Woman's apron! He hadn't been in this city long enough to get to know all its ins and outs, and here he was, trapped!

The crowd continued to press toward him, and behind the crowd he saw horsemen. Not only were the citizens after him, but the Kharmista's bodyguard as well. Why hadn't he let well enough alone? Saving the Kharmista's life like some stupid hero! This is what it got him, torn to pieces by a mob.

The crowd swarmed toward him, screaming their fury, and the horsemen in back continued to push their way forward. Ah, wonderful! He would be pummelled to death under authority's watchful and approving eyes.

He tried one door in desperation. Locked, of course, and much too solid to break in. He rushed to the next door, but before he reached it heavy hands grasped him, and fists pounded on his back. He fell, and the kicking began. Something hit his head, and the battering of further blows drifted away into darkness.

Chapter 3

Consciousness returned, and with it pain. He was lying on something soft, not like the pallets they laid wounded slingers on. Something was wrong with that thought. No, the wounded knee was some time ago, this had been...what?

"You're awake? We were afraid we'd lost you."

A face was leaning over him, a weathered face, with a neat grey-tinged beard and short hair. No one he knew. What was happening?

Qedrim managed to produce some sounds, then forced out a word. "What?"

The face smiled. "Don't remember? No surprise. You took some knocks on the head. What happened was that an archer took a shot at the Kharmista, and hit her. Not straight on, but close enough to be scary. You used your sling and picked off the archer, who was just readying another arrow. Good shot, by the way.

"There were some in the back of the crowd who saw the sling in your hand, and took you for the assassin. Wardesh guard and guide, the real attacker was on the roof in plain view, but you had a weapon in your hand, so you must be the attacker!" The head shook in disbelief. "People can do the stupidest things, especially people in crowds. Anyhow, the lot of them took off after you.

"But I came along too, and between me and two of my lads, we managed to get through to you and beat them off. You took a bit of damage, though."

"Remember. Some," Qedrim mumbled.

"Yes. The Healers will be happy. They said in cases like this, a person often didn't remember anything. You do remember saving the Kharmista?"

Talking was getting a bit easier. "Remember that." He managed. He wasn't going to go into any stupidity about it not being any of his affair. Not to this fellow.

"And you were rewarded for it with a beating, almost death. I apologize for the people. They love the Lady, they worry for her, they know the political situation we're in. So in the same place where someone shot at the Kharmista someone sees a weapon in a foreigner's hands, the results are predictable. Though perhaps not forgivable."

"Accept—-apology."

'And stop nattering about it before I say something like "I knew it was a bad notion at the time!"'

This reminded him that, as things stood, he wasn't likely to be able to put many words together. He felt the corners of his mouth twitch.

The man leaning over him paused, and took a deep breath. He looked over his shoulder. "I promised the Healer not to overtax you, and I promised to tell the Kharmista when you were awake. She wants to talk to you."

"Right." Words would come, but making sentences was still difficult.

"She'll be here to see you in a while." The man looked back over his shoulder again. "Yes, yes, I'm going! I had to at least give him her thanks, didn't I? Yes, I know, nothing counts but what you can grind up into a powder and make into a medicine."

Qedrim, to the extent it was possible, followed the broad back out the door. His neck was stiff as a board, and his head ached foully. So they were grateful, were they? A man might make something out of that. Be careful not to ask for too much or you might...

WHEN HE WOKE AGAIN, a woman was bent over him. Yes, that engraver deserved a whipping; the nose was a little large, but not that bad. She smiled at him. "They say I shouldn't trouble you too much, and Gwothernan has already passed on my thanks, but I wished to do so in person. They say you're young enough you shouldn't have any trouble healing. You'll be my guest until then, and at that time I'll give you a more tangible expression of my thanks."

He was still having trouble getting words out. For true and sure he knew the kind of thing he ought to say. "No reward is necessary," or that sort of nonsense. He also knew that "How much?" would give a poor impression, possibly even decrease the reward. Being a Friend of the Kharmista could have its benefits, if a man used it right.

"Did what I could," he finally managed. Words were still a little troublesome.

"Yes, and a fine reward you had for it! I hope we can make it up to you, in these troubled times."

This brought to mind the fact that being a Friend of the Kharmista might be an unpleasantly short career.

She leaned down and kissed his forehead. "Get well soon, friend. Wardesh knows I need all my friends at this time."

She was gone.

QEDRIM BEGAN TO IMPROVE, then began to improve rapidly. The Healer, a wiry little man with great strength of both will and body, got him out of bed by force, if need be. "Don't want to be coming down with the lung-fever, do you? Sooner you're up and around, the less the risk."

No, Qedrim didn't want to come down with lung-fever. Nor did he want to lie around. He wanted to see what might come of this "Friend of the Kharmista" business. A bag of silver at the least, he reckoned. Maybe even some sort of official recognition, which he might build up into something more.

"I can talk to the Kharmista face-to-face. You have a problem, tell me, I'll take it right to the Kharmista." That was a bit bald, but he could dress it up to look right and fancy. Make a bit of silver before people found out he couldn't do as much for them as they could by going out on a hillside and shouting their trouble to the wind.

'That wasn't the right thing to do this time.'

Where had that thought come from? The right thing to do, any time, anywhere, was what profited you, yourself. You start getting sentimental, you end up starving.

One day a servant, wearing the better-quality clothing worn by the higher nobility's servants, appeared beside Qedrim. Along with a Healer.

"He's healthy enough to leave here?"

"Yes, and we can use his place. All he needs is to exercise a bit, not let his strength fall off."

It irked Qedrim to be discussed as though he were a horse at the market, but restrained himself. He would wait to see what kind of reward he was going to receive.

The servant was a cheery sort. He was well-fed, though not fat, but clearly on his way to becoming one of those chubby, bustling, fussy sorts. He had an oval-shaped face, the usual Gafrodi dark hair, and a nose which looked as though it had been the model for those coins. It dominated his face, and made him look slightly foolish. He seemed to act a bit foolish as well.

"So, Qedrim of Arndal," this was said as though Arndal were a city instead of a vague geographical area, "are you ready to go?"

Qedrim shrugged. "I didn't have much when I came in here, so I haven't got any gear to pack up. And some kind soul has seen to the washing of my clothing, so I'm reasonably presentable."

The servant looked him up and down. "'Presentable' in some quarters, but not, I think, for the Kharmista. But we will see to that. Please follow me."

He gestured down the hallway with long-fingered hands. You may call me Fallash."

That superior attitude tempted Qedrim to trip him as they walked the marble halls. But Friends of the Kharmista did not brawl with servants in the hallways.

The chamber Fallash led him to appeared small, in comparison to the common rooms of inns where Qedrim had been used to sleep. It contained only one bed, so he suspected he had the whole chamber to himself.

A set of clothing, Gafrodi cut, was lying across the bed. "If you please, sir, the clothing is a gift from the Kharmista. When you are dressed, I will take you to her."

'Which is as close to "hustle your butt" as a servant wants to come when addressing a Friend of the Kharmista.'

Qedrim was becoming very pleased with this new status.

Fallash hovered while Qedrim dressed, seeming always on the point of reaching out and squaring something away. The trousers were loose, dark brown, and tied at the waist. The tunic was dark blue, lacing up the front. The boots were dark leather, and gentle on the feet. Fallash grimaced when Qedrim insisted on fastening on his old Talisman Against Lameness and the ribbon Shapak-ailesh had given him. Albeit both were under his clothing and out of sight.

The servant looked him up and down. Twitched Qedrim's tunic into an invisibly better line. Then, brushed off a speck Qedrim couldn't see, and nodded. "Yes, that's fine. Please come along, then."

The servant led Qedrim along another set of hallways until they came upon another servant who stood waiting at a doorway. Fallash turned Qedrim over to this servant. While no words of introduction were spoken, the second servant clearly knew who he was expecting.

He bowed slightly to Qedrim. "Please accompany me."

The servant opened the door and they entered. The Kharmista was seated at the far end of the room, on a chair placed on a raised stone dais.

"When I present you to the Lady, you will bow."

Qedrim nodded. Already he was being irked. But he held himself in check with the knowledge a little restraint now would allow him to make more sure of the situation later.

He noted style and fashion at the Kharmista's court favoured plain clothing, cut plainly. To that, however, each person added their own little touches, bright sashes, jewellery, and so on.

A Kharmista requires certain courtesies. Though not at all like the Great Kings people told tales of. Those whom Thogor Peacemaker had swept away. Those rulers who had required the highest nobles to come into their presence kneeling, and bowing their heads to the floor until the Great King might summon them to look up.

Here, it was enough to bow deeply from the waist, and to not stare at the Kharmista's face.

Just to be getting away with something, Qedrim bowed a quarter-bow, winced, and stood again. "I regret, Highness, that I cannot yet bow quite properly."

'And if it reminds you of what I deserve, so much the better.'

She gave a little laugh. "Thank you. A Kharmista does not rate the title 'Highness.' 'Lady' will do very well, here."

For an instant he had the urge to say something, anything, just to hear that laugh once more. But he managed to suppress that silliness. He also knew better than to speak again unless she asked him directly to speak.

"You have saved my life, Qedrim. For that reason I feel it necessary to reward you fittingly. First, is this." She held out a small leather bag, the size of one of Qedrim's fists. "Come, take this directly from my hand."

He did so, and from its feel and weight, it was over a hundred silver coins.

"This is an immediate reward. I also desire to give you something which is perhaps more valuable. Take this, and read it."

It was a small rolled scroll. Opening it, Qedrim found it was written in the Common Language, though with a few little changes in verb-forms and wordings. He'd learned his letters, more or less, from the hedge-wizard Freyollach, but this was hard going for him.

The Kharmista, likely assuming he couldn't read at all, said, "It is a deed of gift to you, for a piece of land one plough-day in size. For your use, inalienable and indivisible."

"What does 'inalienable' and whatever mean?" It came out sounding more brusque than he had intended,

She laughed again. "'Inalienable and indivisible.' It means the property cannot be sold, given away, nor divided up in order to sell or give away part of it. That is to protect you from swindlers and cheats. It is land enough to start you as a small-farmer."

"Thank you very much, Lady." A piece of land he couldn't sell was no great gift, in his mind, but at least there was the money. Proper courtesy in this instance was still the best notion; you didn't complain in front of the Kharmista. Besides, she'd start laughing again.

'Shut up, Qedrim you fool! Are you turning all sentimental, now?'

She was speaking again. "Further, you are invited to accept my hospitality for the next while. When you are well enough, we will ride out to view your new land."

He bowed again, and his wince was not altogether affected. "Thank you, Lady."

"Nonsense! I am the grateful one here. Now, my servant shall find a seat for you over by the wall. After all, you've just gotten out of a hospital bed."

With a touch to his arm, the servant led him away. By some magic, or more likely by some clever anticipation on the servants' part, a stool appeared.

So Qedrim sat listening to the court's business. This Lord's complaint meeting that Lord's defence, and so on, and so on, had little meaning to him. So, he spent most of his time making schemes to use his bag of silver as seed to build up even more.

The main trouble was making a fortune from the sort he commonly hung out with would be a long process. A copper here and a silver there, was all he could count on. What he needed as some young Lord with a lot of silver and a fair deal of gullibility. Of course, that would have to be someone with enough respect for Qedrim the Hero to overcome the notion of speaking with Qedrim the street-scum. So. He had a little time yet, as the Lady's guest, to—-.

"Qedrim?" Gwothernan was standing over him, almost looming. There was a touch of menace to the noble.

"Sir?" Qedrim looked up, pretending bafflement. *'Morrkerr eat me if I jump to my feet for you!'*

"It's my duty to look out for the Kharmista. As such, I go digging around to look into the character and motivations of those who, for one reason or another, find themselves close to her." He held up a hand to signal Qedrim to silence. "I agree, it is scarcely likely anyone would go to the trouble you have merely to get close to her. The deed, the fact you saved her life, is not lessened, no matter who you might be. Still, I have my duty to do. I find Qedrim from Arndal has been in this town for only a short while. During which time he appears to have been strangely fortunate at betting. That he makes strange claims, bets on them, and wins.

"This does not show an intent or even a bent toward treason. But that sort of person might well stir up trouble in her court now, at a time when we most need unity. I do not intend to let that happen."

"Sir?" Qedrim put on his best bewildered look. Doing that was going to annoy Gwothernan, but better that than defy him, or outright deny any bad intent.

Gwothernan, however, nodded, as if hearing what he expected. "I didn't expect any more of you. And I can't toss you out while you're still her hero. But I can keep an eye on you, and if you put a foot too far wrong, I'll get rid of you one way or another, and trust my credit with the Lady is high enough to keep me above suspicion.

"So you might play a game here or play a game there, but make sure you don't stir things up too much." Gwothernan turned and walked away.

Qedrim's immediate reaction was to go seeking, as soon as possible, some careless young Lord to cheat. What saved him from doing anything rash was partly his own good sense. And partly the fact he couldn't go roaming around until the Lady had dismissed the court. Long before that, he had quieted himself and determined he'd arrange things so he was rich and gone before Gwothernan was aware of it.

When the court was dismissed Fallash, the servant who had seen to his dressing, met Qedrim outside the doors. "It was thought you might appreciate a guide back to your chamber, sir. It was also thought you might prefer a rest before dinner."

"I'm to dine with the Kharmista?" That startled him.

"Well, yes sir. Not at the highest table, if course, but she would have you share meals with her, while you are her guest."

Well then! If he were to be sharing meals with her and the whole court, he'd be able to look for a likely prospect among the Lords.

Carefully, though; Wardesh knew who Gwothernan's spies and sources of information might be. It would be a shame to be tossed out without having the chance to get a little more ahead in funds. With this lovely bag for seed and all...

He was glad for Fallash's presence. He didn't think he'd be able to find the chamber on his own. The chamber was way back in the corner, near to, but separate from, the Palace servants' quarters. He might be a hero, saviour of the Kharmista. But he could imagine the fuss and fury which would come of trying to put Qedrim, a man of no family, up among the Lords and fancy folk!

Back in his chamber, he found all his old garments, including his sling and pouch of stones, were gone.

"My things! What's happened to my things?"

"Your—ah—garments, sir?" The short pause made it sound more like 'Your pox-ridden rags.' "They were disposed of, sir."

"I see." It occurred to him he didn't need the clothing, not with what he was wearing. He wasn't going to let the servant have it all his own way though.

"But I need the sling and stones. They're important to me."

There was no change in Fallash's expression. "I will see to it, sir."

Indeed, when he came to lead Qedrim to dinner, he presented the battered pouch and sling.

"Thank you." he said on a sudden whim.

There was a flicker of expression on the man's face. "My duty, sir."

AS THE SERVANT HAD indicated, Qedrim was not at the highest table. He could, though, catch a glimpse of the Kharmista if he leaned his head just so, and looked. He didn't do that very often; he didn't want to seem like a yokel. He did hear her laugh from time to time, though.

He knew, from rumours, the nobility had special manners to be used at the table. He watched his neighbours, doing as they did, and thought he managed things not too badly. He found himself wishing he were seated nearer to the Kharmista, and when he found himself wishing that, he scowled and took hold of himself.

'Old Woman's apron! You're like a boy with his first crush on a neighbour's daughter! You you don't belong here and you know it! Just find an opportunity, make some money, and be gone!'

He glanced around the table, assessing his table-mates as possible quarry. He warned himself to be careful; no sense messing things up by being in too big a rush.

At one point he saw Gwothernan's eyes on him from further up the table. It almost seemed to him Gwothernan was reading his thoughts. Hearing his unspoken plans.

He shivered, and started talking inconsequentialities with his neighbours. He'd learned, over the years, to take an interest in what people around him thought. Though it taxed him to act as if a particular fashion of embroidering for men's sleeves was a matter of great importance.

THE SERVANT FALLASH was outside to guide him back, though he was quite sure he would have managed it this time. He hadn't even had that much to drink.

Somewhere in the middle of the night a sound wakened him. A strong hand gripped his, and he was on a sandy plain with a bright moon shining overhead.

Shapak-ailesh stood over him, with his mule standing in the background.

"I apologize, O heroic slinger. I wished to speak to you, and it seemed better not to do so in the Palace where someone might well be listening."

"So instead, you drop me out here in the cold. What do you want?"

"I see you have already met the Kharmista. She is not precisely a princess, but close enough."

"Princess? What does that have to do—-? Oh, my so-called reward."

"Yes. I had been trying to work out a way to bring the two of you together, but you managed it on your own."

"Suppose," said Qedrim sarcastically, "suppose I take the least bit of this nonsense in earnest. Surely even you know there's a war coming on, a war the Kharmista is not likely to win, or even survive?"

"O most pessimistic slinger! You will simply have to make sure that she does win, and survive."

"Morrkerr-eaten nonsense! I'm one man, wit a few tricks, a sling, and a bad leg! What d'you think I can do?"

"The best you can, of course! If I had all answers to give you, why then you'd do nothing for yourself, and never learn a thing. But I think it is time we went back. It's not likely, but you might be missed if you stayed away too long."

THERE WAS A CERTAIN tension around the Palace the next day. Fallash professed to know nothing about it. For himself, Qedrim felt the servant considered Qedrim to be slightly beneath him. For Fallash did as little as he could for him without risking trouble. And whatever he did do, he did with flourishes which seemed to say 'See how superior I am to you, who came off the streets only a day or so ago.'

Qedrim understood his own status as hero had its limits. He might demand a servant be whipped. But if no words were spoken, and he could only point to a certain manner, it would only appear that Qedrim himself were putting on airs. So he had to put up with the petty slights a crafty servant could get away with, in certain situations.

Let the servants be. More money was likely to be found among the Lords. In particular, the younger ones, who had not yet learned to be careful of what bets they laid, and with whom.

Some Lords were willing to grant him at least a little acceptance on the grounds that he had saved the Kharmista. Others felt he had only done his duty to the Kharmista. But that mere fact did not warrant his being allowed in to rub shoulders with his betters.

One of the younger Lords, more appreciative of Qedrim's deed, was willing to talk to him. "The day has come. For the past months, we've all been madly collecting troops. But today the last of the diplomatic maneuvering has been come to an end. Tomorrow, or the next day at the latest, we'll be going to war."

He said it with all the cheery insouciance of one who has never seen war. Qedrim was tempted to pull up his trouser-leg and show what war had done for him. That, of course, would make the young fellow think the less of him, and Qedrim needed to be accepted, at least for now.

"Sir," he said, opting for a polite but minor honorific, "I'm a foreigner, and newly arrived. I know little of the local situation. Would you mind telling me what's happening?"

"Of course. It's B'tlas of Daura, of course. Everyone knows his reputation. How he fancies himself something of a magician. Even to the point of using his own folk to test his spells. So when he wants to join our land with his, we Gafrodi must resist.

"And now, with the rule of the Kingdom of Dai'vlash up in the air, our Lady is more vulnerable. Our army is about the equal of

Daura's, in size and in ability, but they say B'tlas has some kind of magic troops at his disposal. And so we of Higfrod find ourselves pressed."

"He uses magic?" A safe comment, and one which would likely elicit further information.

So it proved. "Indeed. He uses magic. But the word is that not all his spells are always fully effective. And that sometimes they have effects other than those intended.

"One thing he has had some success at, he's used his magic to sink deeper and more extensive mineshafts. That has made him rich.

"On the other hand, there was the endeavour with the sheep. He produced sheep which were bigger than normal, near the size of a small cow. That gave him more fleece and more meat for each animal. On the other hand, those sheep required more grazing, and in some places grazed the hills down to the grass roots. In the spring, many of those hills, without the grass to hold them, were eroded away. His next move was to take over more land, much of which he ruined in the same way.

"He finds it hard to admit a mistake, B'tlas does. He wouldn't have the animals rounded up and killed. Instead, or so the story goes. He introduced a sickness among them by magical means. Killing them thus, and making it appear like something beyond his control. And not the end of a magical effort gone wrong. But the strange thing is, this disease seemed to cause only minor illness among the normal sheep. A very interesting coincidence?

"To give the man his due, he did use his magic to recover the hills he had ruined. But at the cost of five years where no cultivation or grazing was allowed. Five years when the hillsides produced nothing.

"They say the five years were up last spring, but only a few cultivated plots have been allowed, and no grazing.

"There is another story, that he's tried several times to conjure a dragon, but has never managed to do so. Rumour has it that all he has been able to produce several large, deformed, lizards, which did not survive.

"So given that. When we hear he's magicked up some fighters, we wonder just what sort of fighters these might be. And whether or not there might be some hidden problem with them."

"I see. So no one worries much about the war, then?"

"Oh, no, I don't say that at all! It's just we don't have too much concern over his magic."

"Oh, I see."

THE REAL SURPRISE CAME next morning, with a sharp and penetrating rap at his chamber door. Since he didn't rate a personal servant, only Fallash. When a servant's assistance was necessary, he opened his door.

Gwothernan was there, scale armour and all, a pair of soldiers with him. Gwothernan was looking grimly cheerful.

"Good morning, Qedrim. The army is marching, with the Kharmista at its head. At this time, her money is better spent supporting fighting men. Not a crippled adventurer out for any copper he can get.

"Yes, the money she has given you is yours. I wouldn't presume to take that, and you deserve it for what you did."

"Now please come with us."

It was quite clear the two soldiers, Gwothernan's men, would be only too happy to lay hands on him and march him along like a felon. Resistance would lead only to indignity. As he gathered his few possessions, he asked, "Why do you assume I can't be of any assistance?"

"Assistance? Hah! What would you do? Get B'tlas into one of your games and cheat him out of his land and title? Come along!"

So shortly, Qedrim found himself looking at a closed and barred palace door.

He scowled, then shrugged. "Who needs it? I have a tidy bit of money, and it means a lot of seed to make a nice game or two."

A walk through the market showed few people were about. And of those, even fewer were the sort to get into any sort of game with. Qedrim stopped and bought an apple from a fruitseller's stall. He commented to the woman, who was short and round and rosy like one of her own apples, "There don't seem to be many people about."

She laughed, a little bitterly. "It's the war! The young men with little sense have gone off to be soldiers. then the recruiters came through and hauled off most of what were left. Then a good few decided to go off following the army, to see what bits and leavings they might find in the trail of the soldiery." She spat on the ground. "The sort who rob corpses after a fight."

He raised his eyebrows. "Oh my, oh my!" he said. "They've all left? Without me? I'll have to hurry!"

The woman looked at him sourly. "Wars and battles are nothing to make fun over. I had a son, once, taken off by the recruiters to be a spearman in the army. I only heard, much later, from someone who'd served alongside of him, that he'd died. And now—-" She clamped her jaw tight.

It was plain to Qedrim she'd had another grandson, maybe more. Gone off in this latest army, and was merely waiting for the bad news again.

He decided, in short order, his own best interests lay in the army's wake too. There were few enough in town for games, and many of those were being very cagey with their money. If the war went badly, if there were a siege, they'd need all they had.

There were still a few who were willing to take a risk in the hope of winning a bit more. But it was plain it would be hard scraping just to stay even.

There was one other thing to say for being out with the Army; he wouldn't be cooped up in the city if it came to a siege. In fact, if things went that bad, he might just wander over to B'tlas. With the new silver mines that young fellow had talked about, there might well be a few pieces of it not being carefully looked after. Even the old sling-dodge might make him a fair bit of money.

He spent some money, with care, because he knew full-well the markets were full of people willing to take his money for shoddy goods. He bought a blanket, a packsack for a bit of food and the like, and a hooded raincape.

Thus equipped, he set out on the trail.

He planned to stay among the camp-followers. Old Gwothernan might not like seeing him there, if he happened to notice. But the likelihood was he'd merely shrug and figure he'd been right about Qedrim. Qedrim would make occasional affrays among the soldiers. He would do this often enough to find who might or might not be willing to bet on a little trial of deftness, stacking the stones, and the like.

Of course, that grade of soldiers had little money. Still, a copper or a silver here or there would be all to the good. There were always some who were sure they couldn't be outdone, certain they knew every trick going. Those were the ones he could make money off of. You simply had to make sure you didn't go to the well too often. Soldiers tended to be a tough lot. It was hardly likely any officer was going to care about a gambler bilking the troops who happened to get a couple of spears rammed through him.

HE DIDN'T BOTHER RUSHING out of town. The army had marched out this morning, moving at the usual army pace, the speed of the slowest man. Well, perhaps not the absolute slowest; anyone too badly lamed would be left behind to make their own way. Quite often squads of tough troopers would scour the path behind the army, picking up stragglers and keeping them moving. There was no likelihood of a battle being fought in the first day or so, and a lamed man might be in condition to fight in a day or so.

This meant the army didn't travel very fast. He might not catch them up today, but he would likely do so tomorrow.

For all that, the camp followers would be a shapeless mass following in the army's wake, with no one among them to keep any sort of order. Their only set goal would be to have themselves set up for trade by the time the troops had finished setting up camp for the night.

He'd come up with the first of that lot sooner or later, and with no urgent need on him—for once!—to get there and make money.

He set to fiddling with his stones as he went. He was still working out the kinds of things he could do with them. It appeared Shapak-ailesh was correct. The more he practiced, the easier it became to move them.

He had one bouncing on his hand as he walked, then just to see what would happen, he tossed it up and said, "Go ahead."

It continued to float along ahead, at about the same distance, no matter whether he hurried or slowed. He was watching it so carefully he missed an uneven spot in the trail, stumbled, and nearly fell. When he rose, the stone was still there, floating at about the same distance in front of him.

He brushed off his knee and muttered "Too much of a distraction. He looked at the stone. "Suppose you go along at an arm's length to my right."

The stone obeyed. Qedrim started walking again. "Old Woman's Apron! A man could go half-way honest with something like this. 'Come see Qedrim the Magnificent, watch him make the stones dance!'"

By late afternoon, he had five of his special stones drifting along in a flock beside him. He made them travel in various formations, a line, a V-shape like a flock of geese, two lines, a pair of columns, and whatever shape he could imagine.

He reached into his pouch again, and the stone he took out was not one of his special ones. Well, what about that? Hadn't the little fellow said after a bit he'd be able to handle any stone?

He took it up and ordered it into position. It went, although a little grudgingly, if such a term could be applied to an inanimate stone.

It was not possible to describe it exactly, but it required a little more effort to make that stone go and stay where he wanted it. He settled for having the six of them moving around, keeping up with him, dipping, swooping, changing directions, according to his command.

However, long before he came up with the first—or last?—stragglers of the camp followers, he had brought the stones all safe back into his pouch. He wasn't entirely sure what he might do with the stones, but there was no point in spoiling the surprise.

Qedrim wondered idly about how the Kharmista was dealing with this business. The picture came clear to his mind, the proud-nosed face, lined with cares, a laugh that—-.

'Stop that, Qedrim! The likes of you don't go chasing after the likes of her. Trying to pull that sort of thing, all you'll get for it is stomped like a bug. You're out to make some money, in just the place Gwothernan doesn't want you to be.'

EVEN BY QEDRIM'S BROAD standards, the crowd who followed the army were a bad lot. For most of them, the major reason for following the army was to rob the slain on the battlefield. As often as not they weren't too picky about who was considered slain. Quite often, they themselves made certain the body they were robbing was actually dead.

Some of them also sold things that a soldier on the march might use. Most of the women among them, perhaps all, were prostitutes. A soldier, for whom any day might be his last, might well be willing to pay for a night's companionship. And, a man who had survived a battle might well want to celebrate his survival.

WHATEVER HIS FEELINGS might be for the crowd in which he found himself, Qedrim kept those feelings to himself. No sense at all in riling people he was going to be making a living off.

He did little, to start with. His clothing, fine as it was, would have made him stand out. But on the way he'd done a little scuffing and staining with grease. Which left it looking more like something some upper servant might have discarded. The cloak he'd bought before leaving town helped. The best one could ever say for it was it was of uneven quality. When it was wrapped round him, it served to hide his clothing.

For all these safeguards, he got suspicious looks here and there. This sort of people distrusted anyone and everyone, particularly the unfamiliar. Some were merely less careful than others about letting it show.

For his own part, Qedrim kept to himself. People like these didn't ask personal questions any more than they welcomed questions about themselves.

Qedrim still had his own food. But, just to keep from being stigmatized as a total outsider, he paid two copper coins for a share in a astonishingly good stew. He sat with the others, took a small part in the conversation, even told a few jokes to prove he had a sense of humour.

There wasn't a lot of conversation, which was just fine with him. Qedrim could well afford to take his time. He'd wait until he was accepted, in the sense that the camp followers accepted anyone. He would use the time to smell out who had a bit of money here or there, and who might be parted from it.

He found a place to sleep, off from the rest, and slept warily, something he was used to from his travels with the caravan and back when he was in the army.

By the next evening he had become familiar, though still not familiar enough for personal questions or answers. That time might never come.

Though by no means a forced march, the trek had its own rigours. The trail was dry, and the camp followers forever breathed the dust the army cast up. As they wound along between and sometimes over hills, they could sometimes watch the army weaving along like a long millipede. Many feet stepping along, the wink of sun on weapons, armour, and accoutrements.

As much of the countryside as Qedrim ever saw, in the haze, was the grey dusty road winding, twisting, turning, crossing rivers.

He was careful not to do too much with his special stones, only balancing one or two of them on his hand. Something which looked like a nervous habit. On occasion, he would cause a pebble beside the road to roll over. Being careful to be at a sufficient distance so no one could suspect he was doing it.

As time went on, he came to be sufficiently accepted for some of the the camp followers to gamble with him. He played honestly, rolling the Dwarves' Bones, winning a bit, losing a bit. There still wasn't a lot of silver among the camp-followers, and no one was betting high enough to matter. As for Qedrim, he'd save his tricky stuff for a time when he could actually make something out of it.

He listened to all the rumours, granting little credence to any he couldn't somehow test for himself. Depending on who one believed, they were anywhere from four days to four weeks from meeting the enemy. People swore their cousin's best friend had spent a night with Gwothernan, and he told her it was so-and-so many days. These were the ones to put least stock in.

So it came as a bit of a shock one day when they heard the enemy were in sight. There was the rumour at first. Then, there was the sudden stir and flurry among the army which said this was more than mere rumour.

A force of Gafrodi cavalry herded the camp followers into one bunch, the most telling evidence. For, any of the camp followers might have been a spy, waiting for the proper opportunity to slip over to B'tlas to let him know just who and what composed the Kharmista's army.

This close watch would last until the battle was about to be joined. Then the cavalry, or most of them, would return to their places in line. No one on foot was likely to be able to rush over, bypassing the line of battle, and get to B'tlas in time to have any effect on the fight.

The thing to do, of course, was to wait until the bulk of the cavalry had gone. Then manage to slip out and get as close to the line as possible. One would thus be ready, when the battle was over, to get out and look among the dead for anything of value.

Of course, one didn't want to get too close. If it happened to be one's own troops which got driven off the field, one might be run over in the crush. Furthermore, enemy soldiers with their blood up would make little or no distinction between soldiers or civilians. In fact, any civilians they met would likely get skewered. This was because the soldiers would likely recognize what the civilians had been there for, and look upon them with even less respect than the crows and vultures who would gather afterward.

Qedrim managed to work his way near the edge of the herded camp-followers. He didn't do anything further at once. Even when all but ten of the troopers had been called back to the lines, he held his place.

Someone way off to the right made a sudden dash, and a trooper was after him in an instant. The sudden squeal told everyone the fool hadn't made it.

Someone had had to be first; Qedrim had only been determined it shouldn't be him. Nor was he the second. After the second the rush started, and there were too many for the troopers to stop. Not that it mattered; it was too late for any spy to change the outcome of the battle.

Qedrim went with the rush, avoiding places where the troopers already were, or were making for. "Might be good sense to see what the Gafrodi are up against," he thought. "And if necessary get myself well out of the way."

At last he found himself a place under some kind of berry-bush, on a hillside, where no one would notice him. He was on the army's extreme left flank.

Up the shoulder of that hill were a force of cavalry in careful lines. Probably the cavalry reserve, from what Qedrim recalled from earlier battles. At the top, just hidden from him, was probably where the Kharmista was, and most likely Gwothernan as well.

Would she really lead her cavalry into battle? Or would she leave that to Gwothernan?

In the front were the infantry. Mostly light infantry, in the places he saw, shield and spear, axe, sword, or dagger. The phalanx was probably to his right, hidden by the hill. Now the army were advancing. The slingers had taken their places, flinging stones at the enemy. His leg twinged suddenly, then settled down again.

He saw the enemy as well, out there in the distance. On this flank, what would be the right flank of the Dauri army, was a force of light infantry. They looked strange, and even stranger when they came near enough for him to make out any features. They had dark blue skin, lumpy-looking bodies, and wore only a breechcloth. For arms they carried only a sword, no shield.

Off to his left, slingers and archers, flank refused, protected these swordsmen from an enveloping attack.

Further over he could now see a part of the Dauri phalanx, coming at their steady pace. Their lines dressed as though with a rod, their pikes presented.

What was it about those blue-black swordsmen in front? Having only a sword and shield made them light troops. But they had more cohesion than light troops. They were more like heavy infantry, the phalanx, without pikes or shields.

They did not suffer at all from the slings and arrows of the covering troops. Even stranger, they advanced silently, no battle cries of any sort.

Now the battle was joined, with the ring of steel and the sounds of men shouting and screaming.

Those blue fellows seemed immune to weapons. A straight blow bounced off them. A grazing blow scratched their hide, leaving a greyish streak, but no wound.

Here and there one of them went down. Those who fell did not suffer wounds as a man might, but rather broke to fragments like a pottery jar. Why were some smashed, when others did not suffer at all?

The light infantry in front of Qedrim were not up to this sort of task. The blue warriors showed no great expertise with their weapons, but then they did not need to be. They were constantly hewing, shrugging off return blows and still chopping. No matter how poor their swordsmanship was, one of their blows was sure to strike home in the long run. Their blows struck home more often as the men in front of them began to panic and lose their own timing.

It was no surprise to Qedrim when the Gafrodi in front of him broke and fled, leaving the blue-black men, still near five hundred strong, advancing through the gap.

Then, wheeling in a maneuver which would have done credit to the phalanx, they attacked the Gafrodi flank.

Qedrim, though no expert in tactics, realized that if Gwothernan didn't act fast, this would be the beginning of the end of the battle.

The commander's reaction was quick enough. A large portion of the cavalry reserve went thundering down the hillside toward the enemy.

"Come on, come on!" Qedrim's oft stated notion of this war having nothing to do with him seemed to have gotten lost. Fists clenched, he saw the cavalry clash with the blue-black men. More of them shattered before the force of the cavalry charge. But whatever they had for minds, the ability to panic was apparently not included.

They turned and wielded their swords in a seemingly clumsy fashion, ignoring defence, going all out on the attack. They held the cavalry, who were bogged down in the melee. The clash with the unyielding infantry having cost them their impetus. They were left to stab and hack and try to force their way through.

Qedrim lost track for a moment of what was happening. He dropped and lay close to his bush, while the disordered Gafrodi light infantry went pouring by on each side.

When he looked again, the Dauri cavalry reserve, or a good part of it, were dashing across the rear of their own lines. Most likely to wheel around into the gap the Gafrodi light infantry had left.

When the remainder of the Gafrodi cavalry reserve went galloping down the hill, Qedrim saw the Kharmista was indeed in front. If the enemy cavalry were going to attempt to hit the infantry flank, the last of the Gafrodi cavalry were going to try to take the Dauri cavalry in their flank.

Qedrim saw in the front ranks of the enemy cavalry a man, distinguishable by better-quality armour—also highly decorated—who appeared to be their leader.

Hardly thinking, Qedrim pointed at a rock peeking out of the soil. "Up!" he said, pointing at it. Shedding bits of dirt and strands of grass, it lifted into the air. He pointed down at the enemy cavalry. "Go down and knock that fellow out of his saddle!"

The rock flew fast, almost as fast as if it had been thrown with a sling. If one could imagine such a thing as using a head-sized rock in a sling. Despite that speed, Qedrim saw it hit the man, catching him full in the chest. The Dauri officer flung up his hands, falling backward out of his saddle.

Qedrim felt a sudden weariness, as though he had carried the stone at a run down the hill and slammed it into the man's chest. His vision closed in, and he felt himself fall.

Chapter 4

He couldn't be sure how long he was unconscious, but when he became aware of things again, the battle was in its final stages. The Gafrodi, despite attempts to put troops into the gap left by the fleeing light infantry, were withdrawing up the hillside. They were not going easily; dead covered the ground behind the Dauri line, and by no means most of them were Gafrodi.

Even as he watched, groggily, the battle seemed to settled down into a solid heaving, screaming thing. The cavalry battle, in the midst of the line, had also sunk to a seething mass of struggling men and horses. The sound of men screaming was bad. The screaming of wounded and dying horses was horrible.

And then the enemy began to withdraw, slowly. However, Gafrodi lacked the strength or the will to advance. The battle, for all the struggle and slaughter, was no better than a draw. They would likely camp the night and next day—perhaps—go at it again.

Qedrim hauled himself to his feet and began moving slowly off the field. *'Now why did I go and do that? Near killed myself for the sake of knocking down a cavalry commander!'*

He knew why he'd done it, of course. It was all the help he was able to give the Kharmista riding into battle. He also knew he was going to get nothing out of it. What could he do? He felt his face twist sourly at the thought of saying, "Oh, by the way, Lady, I magically knocked the enemy cavalry commander out of his saddle with a big rock? D'you mind if I hang around a bit longer?"

He should be making his way over to the battlefield, though possibly he should wait until night. Trying to slip past the soldiers who'd seen their comrades die was not likely to be among the safer things to do when on your way to rob the battlefield.

A hand took his arm. As he whirled to strike out and free himself, he was somewhere else. He was on a different hillside, green grass, a stream winding down below, and no sign of a battlefield. Shapak-ailesh released his arm so that his struggle to free himself ended in him falling to the ground.

"Silly boy!" the small merchant admonished him. "One shouldn't get so close to battles. They can be tricky things. Even without overtaxing oneself to throw a big stone."

Qedrim dropped a hand to his dagger, then remembered some of Shapak-ailesh's skills. "I didn't really ask for your interference, you know."

"O, but I haven't finished working out your reward yet. I couldn't have you dying before that happens."

Qedrim stood glowering at him. "Now what? Where have you brought us, and how do I get back?"

Shapak-ailesh shook his head, a little sadly. "Such a rush, and for what? Well, getting back is simple enough, if you will let me take your hand a moment. What you'll do when you get there is another matter. I'd strongly suggest you stay off the battlefield; it won't be safe, not until you've had a bit of rest. And even then, it won't be the best place to be."

"Thank you for your warnings. Suppose I decide what's safe for me and what's not?"

"Ah, well," said Shapak-ailesh with a small sigh. "Some will refuse to be warned. Here, let me take your arm, O most recalcitrant slinger."

A moment later they were back. Not precisely on the battlefield. Nor even under the berry-bush where Qedrim had watched the fight. But, it seemed, some distance in the rear of the Gafrodi camp. Even behind the area where the camp-followers bivouacked.

"What's this?" Qedrim demanded. "We're a mile from the battlefield!"

"And the safer for it. Ask yourself if you'd prefer to do anything but rest, just this moment." Suddenly the little man was gone.

Qedrim growled to himself, turned toward the battlefield, then decided against it. He found a place where he could tuck himself out of sight and sleep for the night, and sleep he did.

RUMOURS ABOUNDED. THEY'D won. They'd lost. They were about to advance. Any moment now the order to retreat would come. The Dauri had some magical ten-foot-tall soldiers who couldn't be killed. Well, they could be killed, but only if a man happened to be a seventh son.

The enemy commander, or even B'tlas himself, had been killed by an arrow, a javelin, a lightning-bolt. No, he hadn't been killed, merely hurt, and now he was going to use his magic to get even.

NEXT DAY THE ARMY WITHDREW.

This caused dismay among the camp followers. An admission of defeat, leaving the enemy in possession of the field. On the other hand, even the camp followers were aware the enemy had been fought to a standstill. And, the enemy losses were surely no less horrific than the Gafrodi's.

Any political ramifications of victory or defeat had no consideration for the camp followers. What worried them was the possibility the enemy would pursue. And, in that pursuit, would overtake them. They were with their own army on sufferance. For the Dauri, they would be anathema. Any who couldn't keep up with the oxtrain and what protection the guards of the oxtrain were able to supply, were doomed.

Qedrim, kept up quite well with the plod of the oxen. Which made him wonder how long that Talisman of Shapak-ailesh's would last.

Qedrim took note of the paucity of the rearguard. Gwothernan must be very confident no enemy were going to follow them.

'And a man could get taken dead relying on that kind of thinking, Qedrim. Watch out for yourself!'

There was a contingent of slingers among the rearguard. That made sense. They had the ability to harry an enemy without having to move into any formation. A force of light horse backed them up. Troops who were also mobile, good enough in a stand-up fight. Yet they were able to avoid being entangled in a melee and overrun.

A horseman came dashing up along their backtrail. He was a dusty young fellow who had a rag around his upper right arm from yesterday's fight. Qedrim guessed from the speed, that he was carrying bad news to whoever was commanding the rearguard.

Sure enough, a messenger came shortly to the slingers' commander. Of course, Qedrim was not able to draw close enough to hear what the messenger said. But the commander of the slingers shouted orders and his men began to push backward to take a place at the rear of the last of the oxcarts.

Qedrim found himself drifting along with them. No, it wasn't his fight. But he could either help the slingers or wait until the enemy overwhelmed them. Then use his few stones before they cut him down. Being with the slingers might not be much more safe, but it felt just a little more so.

The slingers noticed his presence, and some pushed him away. "You stay away, grave-robber! Don't get in the way of real men!"

An angry response would serve no purpose. Of course, the slingers would feel that way towards anyone who appeared to be part of the group of hangers-on. He pulled out his sling. "You let me try, I'll show you how well I can use this."

The commander was a grizzled little man wearing a garment made of some sort of hide and a hatchet stuck in the leather strip that made his belt. He gave Qedrim a quick look. "No time for foolishness. We have a fight coming up."

"I'll throw one stone, longer range than you'd bother with. If I bring down my man, you let me stay with you. I won't slow you getting into action."

The commander snorted. "Up the stakes one. You miss, I chop you down there and then for wasting my time. Still want to try?" The old eyes said clear as words that he expected Qedrim to turn and go.

"All right."

"Huh. Your head. And if you don't do your shot in plenty of time for my boys to get into action, my hatchet's waiting."

Qedrim gave him stare for stare. "And it'll stay waiting until it rusts." He picked out one of his special stones. With the practicing he'd done he could likely use any stone at all, but he'd take no chances.

The enemy were coming into view now, despite the dust. Light horse, of course, Qedrim noticed; they'd be the best for harrying and wearing down a defence. Soon he was able to distinguish one person from another, though it was still impossible distance for a sling.

On they came. There was a constant winking on someone's head out on the battlefield; most likely a helmet. Qedrim shrugged. Good a target as any. "See that shining helmet there? Whoever it is, I'll bring him down."

"Destroyer's teeth! I'll believe that when I see it! That's impossible distance, even for the best!"

"Just a moment yet." Qedrim knew he could make the shot. But drawing attention for accuracy was one thing. Drawing attention for making an utterly impossible shot was a thing that might lead to trouble.

At a point beyond reasonable range, but about right for what he wanted, he said "Now!" He swung his sling three times round his head, then let go. The stone went faster than his eye could track it, and suddenly the man he'd aimed at fell from the saddle.

"Not bad," allowed the grizzled commander. "You know how to take orders?"

"I've done so before."

The man eyed Qedrim again. "Huh! Well, you follow my orders, move when I say move, stand when I say stand. Do the wrong thing and I'll chop your Morrkerr-eaten butt. Understand?"

"I Understand."

The battle Qedrim had been wounded in had been one of the stand-up kind. The slingers screening the main line of battle. This was something different, a fighting retreat. Which meant continuous withdrawal, endlessly flinging stones and pulling back.

Even Qedrim realized, as much from talking to old soldiers as anything else, that they were not likely to prevent the attacking light horse from coming into contact. The slingers at last dropped back through a phalanx, which opened gaps in its ranks for them to pass through.

They continued to throw stones over the heads of the phalanx. The light horse were shying away from the sharp points of the phalanx pikes. At the last moment, the Gafrodi light horse came up and took them in the flank.

And the Dauri fled.

The Gafrodi light horse pursued only long enough to be sure the enemy were gone, then came trotting back. Qedrim was a little shocked to see Gwothernan in charge of them.

Even worse, the commander pushed his helmet up and back on his head for better vision. Then he came trotting over to the commander of the slingers. Simply one of those things, to give them a little encouragement, Qedrim knew how it went.

Of course, there was Qedrim, in his once-fancy suit, showing up like a flame among the hide-clad slingers. It was too much to hope Gwothernan wouldn't notice him.

"You, there! What are you doing here?"

"Helping to guard your arse, Lord Gwothernan, sir." There was no sense at all in either trying to mollify the man or run from him.

"You are, are you?" He turned to the commander of the slingers. "Belsando, how did this man come to be with your people?"

Belsando was concerned with only one thing, not knowing anything of Qedrim's history. "Sir, he showed us a shot I'd've called impossible, so I let him join us. He's done well today; I'd need a fair solid reason to let him go."

He gave Gwothernan a steady look that said that Qedrim was one of his men now. He was due all the protection Belsando was able to give.

After a moment of trading looks, Gwothernan smiled. "Fine. Just be careful what sort of bets you make with him." He rode off.

Belsando looked at Qedrim. "He doesn't like you."

"No."

"Hm." The elderly eyes measured him anew. "Seems to me there was this story about some foreign slinger picking a bowman off a rooftop when he was shooting at the Lady. That'd be you?"

Qedrim resolved to be very careful in his dealings with Belsando. This was not just some old man. From bits and pieces of nowhere clear evidence, the old slinger had come on the truth.

"It would."

"So, what did you do next? Try to steal her silver dinner plates?"

"No, nothing like that. Gwothernan is suspicious. He asked around about me, found I was known for winning bets. When the army marched, he tossed me out."

"So you followed along, just to show him?"

"Yes." Close enough not to be an exact lie.

"Hm." Belsando cocked his head a bit. "And show him just what, I wonder? No, don't answer. I need a good slinger more than I need to work through a whole raft of words to find out just what's true and what's feathered goats. Just one thing; will you swear you mean no harm to Lord Gwothernan?"

"By the Old Woman's Apron, I swear." It was even the truth. If he ever saw Lord Gwothernan all alone, with no one around to say what had happened, maybe. But the likes of him didn't talk publicly of killing Lords.

Belsando looked at him a moment longer. "Right. You got enough ammunition?"

"Some. I'll see what else I can find."

This wasn't the territory to find proper smooth sling-stones. But there was always something. He thought about trying to call back his special stones. But that was quite a distance. All that way the army'd pulled back. It wasn't likely he could do something like that and not be noticed.

A man making long shots was one thing. A man calling his stones to come back to him was something else again. Most likely something scary enough to undo all the good he'd done for himself today.

That, along with Gwothernan's warning to Belsando, didn't make for easy living, nor much possibility of making money. Whatever money might be made in an army making a retreat.

Just get your ass out of the trouble you're in right now, Qedrim.

He messed with the slingers that evening. His abilities and his actions that day having shown him worthy of their company, he was welcomed. Perhaps not warmly welcomed, but at least accepted. The food was not good, nor plentiful, but he'd known worse from time to time.

The next day was a repetition of the last, in the sense of what sort of fighting they did. The enemy this time were more cautious; they didn't really try to close with the slingers.

The slinging was at extreme range. Qedrim tried to make every shot count, but also tried to avoid showing off. Most of his long shots were well within a slinger's normal range. He didn't do anything stupid like trying to miss. In a situation like this, the fellow you missed might well be the one to get close enough to put a spear in your guts.

Given the sort of fighting that was going on, everyone slinging stones in their own time, it was not likely anyone would notice that one person seldom missed.

He tried, covertly, to pick up stones without touching them. Still, good slinging stones were rare, save when the path of the army went over a stream-bed, or a place where there was plentiful gravel.

He did make one small test, muttering an order to one of his stones to hit the target and return to him quietly in the evening.

He spent much of that afternoon worrying about whether the stone might come back and land on his lap in the middle of supper. That would certainly require more explaining than he wanted to do.

As a matter of fact, it did exactly what he'd have told it if he'd been going along beside it whispering into the ears it didn't have. As he was wrapping himself in his blanket and preparing for sleep. He felt a single light tap on his shoulder, and his hand went for his dagger.

In the darkness, he could see nothing further than a few feet away. Something was on his knee, but there was no sign of any human anywhere. He reached out carefully, and touched the stone.

"Well done," he muttered to it, softly enough not to be heard at any distance.

'I suppose I ought to have commanded you to return quietly, but not to scare me out of my skin.'

He started off the next morning with his bad knee a little stiff. He wondered how long the little merchant's talisman would hold up. He'd never asked Qedrim to pay for it. And on the basis that you got what you paid for, and then only if you were careful about it, how good could a free Talisman be? He wished he'd made one of his own to have in reserve, one he was sure would work.

The stiffness worked its way out by midway through the morning, and there really wasn't time to fret over it. For one thing, the enemy tried to catch them by surprise, before they were on the move.

It didn't work out as well as the enemy had hoped. Though he might be irascible and suspicious of strangers, Gwothernan, knew his way around a battlefield.

"Or perhaps," Qedrim reflected, "it's that suspicious nature that puts him on his guard."

There was still a vicious bit of fighting. Some of which saw the slingers hand-to-hand with a light infantry force. Slingers, because they carried little in the way of armour or weapons, avoided hand-to-hand fighting. On occasion, though, it was unavoidable. Such as when they'd fallen back among the oxcarts, and some commander wasn't quick enough to close ranks when the slingers had gone through.

Qedrim, armed only with a short dagger in addition to his sling, stayed away from the fighting. The fighting refused to stay away from him, though. Soon, he found himself using his walking stick as a club, warding off thrusts and trying to strike in return.

'And you thought you'd be safer with the slingers than wandering among the camp-followers?'

Gwothernan came to the rescue, with a scratch band of horsemen taken from the main fight. He was roaring curses as he laid about him with a broken spearshaft. He seemed oblivious to personal danger. That seemed to protect him, for he came through with only a few scratches and nicks on his right arm.

As if it were fated, his eye fell on Qedrim, who had taken a few nicks of his own. "No betting game this, is it?"

Nettled, Qedrim drew himself up. "Five silvers I survive as long as you!"

The commander pushed his helmet up and back and looked Qedrim over. "You have guts, don't you? But be careful. Your own side can be enemies if you press them too hard."

He rode away.

Because Qedrim had been paying more attention to the enemy than to the countryside, he didn't realize at once that they weren't headed straight back to the city of Higfrod. In fact, he only found out when, one evening after supper, some other slingers were discussing where they might be going.

The consensus had been that they were headed off into the hills somewhere. But no one knew, however much they claimed to, exactly where in the hills. Everyone knew that some of Annavristi's Lords had holdings in the hills, most of them quite defensible.

Qedrim, a little stunned, said aloud, "We're not heading back to the city?"

One of the company, a fair-haired young fellow on his first campaign, sneered. "Don't pay attention, do you? We were beat back there, for all we stayed a night on the field. They say those magic warriors of B'tlas', they did a fair job on our lot. I heard about half the rest deserted overnight. So if we do a fighting retreat to the city we come there battered and beaten, to a city not ready for a siege. So the sensible thing is to head for the hills, and hide out until we can get another army together."

"I see." Qedrim did see. He suspected that rumour had increased the size of their losses. Fuelled by the indisputable fact they were retreating. It had made their situation to look worse than it was.

Still, he didn't really see himself marching off into the hills. Cities were where he belonged. The Arndal Hills were far back in his past, and he had no desire for that sort of life any longer.

On the other hand, he had no real idea of the country. Did he want to go off overland in the hope of finding a city? Preferably not Higfrod, which was about to be under siege?

No, the hills were not what he wanted. But it seemed a short stay in the hills would be better than any alternative he could discover.

Next day the enemy's harassment slackened off. One of the slingers said around the campfire, "They're probably having a hard time finding anything to eat in the wake of the army."

To which Qedrim nodded. The best strategy for Annavristi's army was to drive off all the herds, scoop up the grain in the bins and burn what stood in the fields. Leaving nothing but ashes for the pursuers. He had seen the smoke of fires off in all directions as they marched.

People in these parts would have little good to say for the Kharmista for the next ten years or more. Peasant memories were long and peasant grudges bitter.

He shrugged.

Before going to sleep, he practiced lifting and moving a rock the size of his head. In the dark, nobody could see what he was doing. As long as he only muttered his commands, the worst that could happen was someone yammering at him to shut up and let them sleep.

It seemed that calling his stones to return to him in the evening had helped build up his ability. He himself was very tired at night, and he slept soundly.

He had little time to even work out games for this new ability. Lifting contests might be one method, where he bet on himself to lift more weight than some muscular lout. Given his own build, he'd probably find a lot of people to bet against him.

For a while.

LORD HAMALTIK'TA HAD a seat, high on a hill. It was a walled town. In the nature of things, it was a sprawl of jerry-built houses and shacks had sprung up outside the walls. The site was named Lakvos'ta, a word from the local tongue. Which the Common Language was replacing more and more. It was a word that had the rather grand meaning "Eagles' Eyrie."

The walls themselves were grey fieldstone, fitted and joined, though not with mortar. There was a rumour that the latest Lord had been rebuilding sections of the wall, as ground settled and parts of the wall began to fall. In the sections he replaced, he had dug a foundation and put the stone together with mortar.

The army camped outside the walls, even outside the ring of houses. While Annavristi, Gwothernan, and a small party went in to discuss matters with the Lord. Qedrim had a bad feeling about that, though he didn't share it. There might be an advantage to be had in killing off the Kharmista and presenting her head to B'tlas. He understood very well it wasn't only lame slingers who looked out for their own personal interests.

For three days there was no word whatever, though rumours abounded. On the fourth day, a party of horsemen came out, wearing Lord Hamaltik'ta's insignia, a blue scorpion on a red field. Among them was a herald, who rode a little forward from the rest of the party, and called for the army commanders to assemble.

This took a little time to accomplish, but at last most of them gathered to hear what the news might be. Qedrim managed to work his way close enough among the onlookers that he could hear what they said.

"Commanders of the Army of Lady Annavristi, Kharmista of Higfrod! Your Lady has agreed to accept the hospitality of the Lord Hamaltik'ta for the present. She bids you return to your homes!"

"Why doesn't she come out to tell us so herself? Or at least Lord Gwothernan?" The phalanx-commander spoke the words that were in Qedrim's mind, and probably in others as well.

The herald merely looked at the phalanx-commander. "Are you suggesting I lie? Your place is not to question orders, but to obey."

He turned, and the party rode back into the city. The phalanx-commander shouted something that was on the minds of a number of people as well. "We haven't been paid in a week or more! We'll need something to get food for ourselves!"

The herald neither turned nor answered.

THE COMMANDERS' MEETING was long and vigorous. They all knew, even the rank and file knew, that something was wrong. The Kharmista was not likely a guest, but a prisoner. But there was no consensus on what to do.

The phalanx commander was the commander of the senior force. Therefore as near to an overall commander as they had. he took it upon himself to pronounce some truths obvious to most of the others. "We're nothing like a full army, and we've been marching for a long while, with little for food along the way. We haven't the resources to storm a walled town, especially not one situated the way this one is."

Qedrim managed to find a spot from which he could listen in on the deliberations. It was a sign of the confusion among them that they hadn't set sentries to keep out such listeners. From what he was able to hear, they were on the point of deciding not to decide. Such non-decision would have the army sooner or later wandering off, in bits and pieces. Until what was left could hardly do anything useful here.

That left the Lady Annavristi, through treason and indecision, all by herself against her enemies. Well, that was the way of it, wherever or whoever you were.

He stood up and walked into the council.

He used part of their moment of stunned surprise to pull five stones from his pouch and balance them on his fingers.

The phalanx commander was just on the point of demanding a reason for Qedrim's intrusion when Qedrim spoke. "I have a few abilities with stones," he said to the gathering. Then he spoke to the stones. "Here, go over and fly around the commander's head."

The stones circled around the commander's head like small round birds.

"Now light on his shoulders," The stones then moved to the commander's shoulders in a formation where they almost touched his shoulders.

"Softly, softly!" Qedrim gently coaxed them so that the stones didn't hit the commander.

He looked around at the group. "This could all possibly be just some illusion. But—-Ah, yes, there we are. Stone, come up out of the ground!" A stone as large as his chest ripped itself free of the ground, dropping bits of detritus as it went. "Now, float over our heads!"

Qedrim turned his attention back to the commanders. "All right, gutless wonders. You were about to decide not to take any decision right now and leave your Kharmista for Hamaltik'ta to hand over to B'tlas. Would it alter your decision if I were to pull down a piece of the wall? D'you think you could summon enough guts among you to go through the hole and take the town?"

He looked around once more, and spoke over the mutter of sound that was beginning to come from them. "I'm going to go over to pull down some wall. Come along, or stay."

'And by the Old Woman's Apron, I hope I can make my deeds match my brag!'

He walked away, with the boulder following him.

The wall was solid, cut stone and mortar much of the way round. At last, however, he came to a section of the old, rougher, sort. He looked it over.

"All right." He turned to the people, a mixed bunch of various sorts of troops, who were following him. "After I do this next bit, I won't be worth much for a while. Making stones move from where they're sitting takes a lot out of a man. I'd appreciate it if you'd have someone throw a blanket over me, maybe have them keep watch on me."

He didn't bother waiting for an answer. All this was as new to them as it was to him, and he didn't want them to go have a conference over exactly who and how many should watch him. Whether they should stand, or be allowed to sit?

He looked up at the wall. "Topmost course of the wall, come down! Come down! Second courses of stone, fall away! Stones in all your courses, lift in your places and roll away!"

There was a grinding, clashing sound, and a whole section of wall, wide enough to admit at least five men, fell apart and rolled away.

"Almost too close!" he thought as the stones rolled and clattered down, forcing him to skip a few steps backward.

Then his vision closed in. There was a vicious stab of agony in his bad knee, and his legs refused to support him. He felt his knees hit ground, tried to throw out his hands to break his fall.

He went down into blackness before he knew whether or not that attempt was successful.

Chapter 5

Qedrim woke, and drifted back to sleep, repeating the process several times before he would wake up enough to wonder where he was. He knew he was on a pallet of some kind, knew he was in a room, and that sunlight was streaming in through a small window.

Something moved. Qedrim noticed there was a man beside him, dressed in a dusty-grey tunic and trousers with a powder-blue sash. Qedrim's mind vaguely recalled that sash as being a sign of one of the Gafrodi healing sects.

His mind was juggling memories. He was in the Kharmista's palace, after having been battered by the mob. No, there was something wrong with that.

"Here," said the Healer gently. "Have some water."

He was—-where? He drank some of the offered water. Though his hand shook so badly the Healer had to hold his head up and hold the cup to his mouth at the same time. The water was almost cool, with a bit of sour wine in it, and he drank it down thirstily.

"Where am I?"

The Healer, a muscular young man with an open face, said, "You're in the town of Lakvos'ta. There are several people here who would like to speak to you, whenever you feel up to it."

Which brought back another memory. He had been standing before the wall and looking up and—-nothing. "The wall fell?"

"Yes." The young face turned grim, "And soldiers stormed through, slaughtering anyone they came across. Not a fine thing, save perhaps in warriors' minds."

He spoke the word 'warriors' as an epithet of deepest disfavour.

"But you're taking care of me."

"My Oath does not allow me to discriminate. Nor does your Kharmista, for all of that. Do you wish visitors?"

"I suppose I'll have to see them sometime. Might as well be now."

The first to come in was Annavristi, Gwothernan close behind. She smiled at him. "You've rescued me again, Qedrim. You're adding to the debt I owe you."

All of which made him very uncomfortable. "I'm no hero, Lady."

"What is a hero but one who sees a need for action at a dangerous time, and carries out the action? They say you tore the wall down with your bare hands, and wore yourself to rags in the process."

Which was near to a request for an explanation, and of course, he'd already told the army. His secret, such as it had been, was out. "I've discovered in myself a bit of power with stones, and have been practicing it. Pulling down the wall was just about more than I could manage."

"So the Healer said. He declared you were near worn down to skin and bones. You will have to be my guest for a little longer."

"Thank you, Lady."

She looked at him in silence for a bit. "We'll have to do something more for you than make you a simple freeholder. Not to mention that your present freehold is now under the rule of B'tlas."

"I wasn't looking for a reward, Lady."

'You're lying scum, Qedrim. You'll take any reward you can get.'

"Of course not! All the more reason to reward you fittingly. Now, we've promised the Healer not to fret you unnecessarily. Gwothernan wants a private word with you, but we'll be visiting you again later." She walked out.

"She is a fine young Lady, isn't she?"

Qedrim pulled his eyes from the doorway, and turned to Gwothernan. "Yes."

"I may have been wrong about you. But she's my Lady, since the time I watched her take her first steps, and I'll see no harm comes to her. And I suppose it sounds like a threat, which is unfortunate.

"Both the Lady and I owe you, for more than simply pulling down that bugger's wall. I understand the army was all in a dither when you walked in and dared them to come along.

"So there are debts to be paid, now. But I've seen more than one young buck come dancing in, hoping to romance the Kharmista into making him great. It's never worked. She's too smart for that, and I stand behind her. No, it doesn't mean I rule through her. I carry out her orders. Sometimes, I do things she doesn't know about. Because it's better someone else take the blame.

"What I'm telling you, in long and roundabout fashion, is to watch your step. I'll be watching it as well."

Qedrim looked into the stern old face, meeting Gwothernan's steely eyes, "You don't trust me yet, do you? You're right about that, you shouldn't trust me. And you should trust me even less if I swear great oaths about how loyal I am. I'll just say she's my Lady, for so long as she'll have me around."

It made him feel better somehow, that Gwothernan still glared at him distrustfully. Without another word, Gwothernan nodded, then the old Commander strode out the door. Qedrim felt a little better, knowing there was someone else looking out for the Lady's interests.

His next visitor was the grim-faced phalanx-commander, Belsando. "So, you did everything just as you said you would, and we did our part. Now, could you take these confounded stones off my shoulders? D'you have any idea how hard it is to explain them?"

Qedrim swallowed his laughter, knowing full well men such as Belsando make bad enemies. He called his stones away, noticing a trace of slowness in their response. Pulling down that wall had certainly left its effect on him. Would he be able to build his ability back up again? He half-wished for Shapak-ailesh to show up and explain it to him.

HE WAS RELIEVED TO find, as his physical strength returned, his ability with the stones recovered. It did not recover quite so quickly as his physical strength. But as he continued to practice with the stones, it came back bit by bit.

Now that his secret was known, and known so widely, there was no longer any point in exercising in secret. This brought another result. He'd heard a rumour going around some people thought he was showing off. He took to practicing secretly again, but no longer made quite such an effort to remain hidden.

After another week with the Healers, they declared him sufficiently well to be kicked out of his bed "to make room for someone who actually needs it."

They had arranged quarters for him in the Palace. Though Lord Hamaltik'ta's home was nowhere near to the Kharmista's palace in style or size. Qedrim was well-fed and clothed, though he saw Annavristi only from a distance.

Qedrim was privy to most of the rumours, and the rumour with most persistence said B'tlas was headed up to Lakvos'ta deal with them. The stories differed in details. B'tlas had a thousand of those invincible soldiers or, that he had only twenty left. That he would arrive in two days, in two weeks or, in two months.

Then one day a page came to summon Qedrim, "The Lady Annavristi and the Lord Gwothernan wish you to be present for their council, sir."

"Me? Why on earth do they want me?"

This threw the page into a fluster. He was used to delivering messages, not discussing the reasons behind the messages, "Sir, they didn't tell me that! They just request your presence!"

And Qedrim, realizing the truth of this, said, "I'll be there, thank you."

He mused to himself as he went along the corridors. This was not likely some reward for saving the Kharmista (*twice!*) but more like a summons because no one actually understood his ability with stones, and they probably hoped he'd be able to use that power in her service.

Could he? Well, most of his notions had been on the lines of making money, betting he could do this or that with stones.

Pulling down the wall had been a desperate act. He wouldn't be able to do the same thing again soon, not without killing himself.

It appeared the answer to the question of what he could do for the Kharmista with his ability was "I don't know."

They didn't ask that question straight off, though. Gwothernan announced the first order of business, news about the military situation.

"B'tlas is coming this way at last. There's a story about a large stone knocking him off his horse during the battle, and he's had difficulty riding since.

"However, he has entrusted his army to a commander by the name of Losibalson, and ordered Losibalson to come up and deal with us.

"We have a little good fortune. He has trusted Losibalson with only two hundred of those invincible troops. Likely for fear Losibalson might turn against him.

"On the other hand, we have a small force, daily getting smaller. The long retreat was wearing, and men have been slipping off because they see us as a lost cause.

"We might attempt to fight Losibalson. But I dislike the thought, unless we have a superior position. Lakvos'ta is only minimally so. A siege is possible, stripping the countryside bare, but how long could we hold out?

"Myself, I favour pulling back deeper into the hills, and harassing their advance the same way they harassed our retreat. There we will regroup and work toward reconquering the Kharmosat.

"I am willing to listen to other plans."

It appeared to Qedrim that while Gwothernan was willing to listen to other plans, he was equally willing to dismiss them once heard.

The phalanx commander spoke up. "How do we feed an army back in the hills?"

Gwothernan nodded. "A good point. We will be dismissing the bulk of the army before we go. Part of our work in the hills will be to gather as much in the way of supplies as we are able. So that next campaigning-season, we will be able to support an army. At least for long enough to win a victory."

"If B'tlas leaves us alone to survive, let alone gather supplies."

Qedrim thought the phalanx commander was speaking a little more boldly than was safe. But there seemed to be a bond of some sort between him and Gwothernan.

"B'tlas has difficulties of his own. His army was badly battered too, and he has little time left for campaigning this year. I feel sure we can depend on being left alone for most of the winter."

"You've made all the decisions, then?"

"Barring some unusual circumstances, yes."

"I see our Master of Stones is with us. Is that not an unusual circumstance?"

And did the two of you work out that bit of talk between yourselves?' Qedrim wondered.

"It might be," Gwothernan answered, "But I know altogether too little of Qedrim and his abilities. Qedrim, what can you do for us?"

Qedrim stood, gathering his thoughts. He did not want to appear unhelpful, but neither did he want to make rash promises he might be unable to fulfill.

"The best answer to that, Lord, is 'I don't know.' I have only recently discovered this ability of mine, and it grows with practice. Furthermore, pulling down that section of the wall left me unconscious and weak, and I am only gradually recovering the powers I had. I can do a few things with small stones, but as for larger tasks, not yet.

"I don't really know enough about this gift, yet. Will I ever be able to do some task as large as pulling down a wall without collapsing afterward? Perhaps. When would it be? I have no idea. Am I willing to put myself at your disposal? Yes, with one condition; if you ask me to do something which I think may kill me, I may refuse."

Gwothernan's scowl said clearly he didn't like conditions on obedience. But there weren't great bands of people possessing power over stones. So executing Qedrim as an example would not be a useful notion either.

Annavristi laid a hand on Gwothernan's forearm. "Go easy, my old friend. He has an ability, he's willing to use it for us. If he uses it to the extent which it kills him, then we no longer have his ability to depend on. You won't fault him for that?"

Gwothernan turned to look at her, and Qedrim knew his thoughts, "You don't know what I know about him."

'No, she doesn't, and that's just fine. If she did know, I wouldn't be allowed this close.'

Revelations of that sort didn't belong in this sort of council, so Gwothernan went on to matters of available food stores. Qedrim found it a tedious business. Food came, food went. If it was short, you worked out a game to get you the money you needed to buy it. If it got too short in the place you were at, you went off somewhere else. But even Qedrim could see the matter was not so simple when you were trying to feed an army, let alone a small army. So, he tried to pay attention.

Still, he was glad when the break came. A page, either the same one who had fetched him, or one who appeared very similar, slipped in the door and walked up to speak quietly to Gwothernan. Gwothernan nodded to the page, then glanced up at the group and said, "It appears we have a visitor, a Thawrd Wizard."

This brought sudden a silence to the group, followed by a buzz of conversation. Qedrim considered what he knew about Thawrd Wizards. The popular tales said they were intent on spreading their own philosophy. He'd heard it described as either "natural justice," or "the greatest good for the greatest numbers."

Kings and rulers tended to dislike them. Thawrd Wizards seemed to be against arbitrary use of force, against crushing people by heavy taxation, and so on. On the other hand, it seemed to take a great deal to force a Thawrd Wizard to use his magic, save in self-defence. Nor, indeed, were they all-powerful. People told more than one story of a Thawrd Wizard, in this place or that, killed by a more powerful magician, or even by a dagger in the back from an unexpected assailant.

Qedrim doubted this supposed lack of self-interest. Everyone had some self interest, everyone was out for themselves. Of course, a person might put themselves at the disposal of someone whose interests were not their own. Even that seldom lasted long.

The wizard came in. He wore the usual brown robes of the Thawrd Wizard, the usual flat fur hat.

Other than that, there was not much really 'wizardly' about him. He was short, stocky, heavy built, and the hands protruding from the sleeves of his robe were more like those of a labourer. The right hand grasping the staff was in clear sight, allowing Qedrim to notice the tiny scars on the knuckles, the scars of a brawler. Furthermore, on his right cheek was a scar which indicated a close acquaintanceship with a dagger point.

He walked up and bowed to the Kharmista and to Gwothernan. "My name is Kassibanio, and as you will have heard, I am a Thawrd Wizard." He smiled. "Many of you will certainly be doubting my qualifications. I will not give you any great and fearsome threatening signs, only a little one, no threat at all. Sadahhi!"

At this word, a small purple flame appeared on his palm. It lept off his hand, dividing itself into many as it went, each of which danced in front a single member of the council.

Qedrim had a chance to observe one of these flames up close. There was no sign of what was burning. Indeed, there was no heat at all, merely a small purple flame flickering in front of him.

Kassibanio spoke again. "Eisha!" The flames disappeared, as if they had never been.

He surveyed the gathering. "I hope I have disposed of all questions regarding my being a wizard. If any more definite sign is required, I might provide it later. At the moment, let me say merely that I am here to give advice and counsel."

"And your advice?" Gwothernan was scowling.

"First, let me explain. I do not make bargains. I offer to help the person who seems most likely to appreciate my work, and make suggestions. After you have come to power, you may indeed invite me to leave, but I can hope that you will carry out my suggestions."

Gwothernan's face twisted sardonically. "We should believe you will be so accommodating?"

Kassibanio smiled. "Consider this: If I require a certain concession of you for my aid, but after I have aided you, you decide the concession is too great. You will then refuse the concession, leaving me with no choice but wreaking some horrid vengeance on you, or fleeing away, a failure. You might even make an attempt on my life, fearing lest I wreak that horrid vengeance.

"It is much better if I merely depend on your honour and gratitude, with no threats from either side."

"This sounds extremely fuzzy-minded and idealistic! You help us for nothing but a promise to consider your conditions afterward! No one does that sort of thing!"

"I do, Lord," answered Kassibanio mildly. "And I do so because what I know regarding you and the Kharmista you serve leads me to believe you will show your gratitude after. There are some, one might even say most, rulers whom I know it would be futile to approach thus. I am not a complete naïf, Lord."

"And a little flattery won't hurt, of course?" Gwothernan smiled sardonically. "Very well, what are these conditions we are to consider?"

Kassibanio smiled. "A simple one, really. You should choose a council to advise you. The council would give advice, but you would not necessarily be bound to accept their advice.

"And further, common people would be allowed to put their grievances to this council, which would in turn bring these to you, or such of the grievances as the council considered to have any merit."

"There is a rumour," Gwothernan said, "that you Thawrd Wizards are intent on overturning society. That seems to be the case!"

The wizard smiled gently. "No, we do not look to overturn society. A society overturned turns into a chaos, with everyone struggling to better his lot. At the end, such a society usually finds itself being ruled by the strongest and the most ruthless.

"I do not claim this change I ask for will have no effect on your society, for it will. The changes, however, are those my order considers to be desirable."

"Indeed! And if a neighbour who happens to be one of those strong and ruthless men decides to add us to his dominions. We might be conquered while the council was trying to make up its mind whether or not there was actually a threat."

Kassibanio shook his head. "I hope we are not that foolish. No, the Kharmista still rules, she still makes decisions. And if it comes to be a case where a decision needs to be made instantly, she will still do so.

"It might even be that I, or one of my order, will stay in the Kharmosat to continue to give advice, regarding just such things as neighbouring rulers who might have designs on her land."

At this point the Lady Annavristi took over. "Lord Gwothernan, I think we can use any help offered to us, right now. And the cost, it seems to me, is not extreme. And as to upsetting society, I believe B'tlas has done that already, so far as our own people are concerned. Kassibanio, I agree to your request. What advice can you give us?"

"Thank you. Lady. My first advice is that you should take care. I believe the Kharmost of Daura has been showing himself as mediocre at best in regards to magic. The better to take his enemies unaware when they begin to feel safe."

"Those invulnerable warriors of his?"

"A fair example," Kassibanio gave a small bow to the Kharmista. "So far as I can determine, he has not intentionally built any of them to fail. He has, however, rushed through the building process, so that as many as a third of them will break down in battle.

"But there will be a certain core who will be partially invulnerable. A commander might observe them on the battlefield and believe them for tough fighters. But remember watching them smashed on other fields. So he may make allowances, augment his line where it faced them, and go to battle. Only to find that they smash through his formation with little loss"

There was silence in the room.

The phalanx commander stood. "You tell us this, and it is useful to know. But can you do something really useful, such as dealing with these fellows yourself?"

"A fair question. The simple answer is 'not at present.' I shall have to do some research, look into the methods used to make them. And then try to find a method which would counter them, seeking out the one likely to work the best."

"Why not make some for us? Without the vulnerability?"

"Ah, straight to the point, as befits a professional soldier. While I do not understand the exact method B'tlas is using, I do know that most such makings involve the mixing of blood of men with clay, while speaking certain spells. And the blood must be that of freshly-slain men, men slain within moments before the mixing.

"Now, it just might be possible that, in the last extremity, your Kharmista might countenance such work. But I will not cast such spells for you." He paused. "Or anyone, for that matter."

Gwothernan was scowling fiercely now. "How long till you are ready to deal with them, then?"

Kassibanio's brows rose. "How long is a rope? How high is up? How far is down? Some questions cannot be answered until one has more knowledge. Six weeks? Six months? Several years? I'm sorry, I will do my best for you, but any answer I attempt to give to your question this moment is bound to be wrong."

"So we retreat into the hills, with these invulnerable men coming after us, until they finally corner us and destroy whatever's left of us?"

"The situation need not be so grave, Lord. In a few weeks, the winter rains will render taking an army into the hills near to impossible. And even the invulnerable soldiers cannot be everywhere on any battlefield. If you move your troops to where they aren't, you can do a great deal of damage."

"I see." Gwothernan smiled, with little mirth. "A fine state when I must take lessons in basic tactics from a wizard, no matter how wise."

He cast an eye over the crowd. "So near as I can determine, the decision of this meeting has been taken. We will withdraw into the hills. I believe we must leave at least some garrison here in Lakvos'ta, if only to give a little more delay to Losibalson."

THE NEXT FEW DAYS INVOLVED a lot of rushing around. They were getting what supplies were readily available in the locality. Then there was the paying off the soldiers who were to be sent home, and setting up a garrison for the town.

"It must take a cold mind," Qedrim reflected to himself, "to order men to a place where he realizes they're going to die. Not to merely have a hard fight of it, but die defending the city to give the important people time enough to get away.

"And what of the men themselves? Some of the least ignorant must surely know what's coming. And yet they stay, they don't sneak off somewhere."

A sardonic smile came to Qedrim's face as he continued to ruminate. "And you're not sneaking off somewhere safe, either, Qedrim! You're heading off into the hills with the rest of them, and hoping winter weather will keep Losibalson from following all the way."

In the midst of all the hustle, Qedrim saw Kassibanio approaching. No, the wizard wasn't headed off on some unknown errand, he was coming for Qedrim himself. "I'd like a word with you, young Qedrim."

"Regarding what?"

"Birdsongs and blueberries, of course! Come on, there's a wineshop here where we can talk in more comfort."

Since he couldn't think of any good reason to avoid talking to the Thawrd Wizard, Qedrim followed.

During the evening, darkness would have covered most of the faults of the Black Bush. Even the minimal light which made its way into the place during the daylight hours, revealed it as dingy, grey, and greasy, smelling of old smoke, old food, and stale bodies.

The wine, though watered strongly, was mildly palatable. Better still, the wizard paid for them both.

"Now, then, Qedrim, tell me how you come by this power over stones."

A part of him wanted to tell the fellow to mind his own business, but the basic secret, that he had the power, was out. Qedrim found himself telling the story. A version of the story, at any rate, leaving out Shapak-ailesh. Instead, simply making it a matter of finding out what he could do with his special stones, then going from there. He also left out his games, and the stone he'd thrown on the battlefield to knock B'tlas out of the saddle.

He finished up with the tearing down of the town wall, and what it had cost him.

The wizard smiled, though the smile did not appear to make him look any more friendly. "A more complete version than I could get from anyone else, at any rate. I'm sure there are other things you could tell me, but never mind. So you have decided to throw in your lot with the Lady, have you?"

That last question, a sudden shift of direction which caught Qedrim unprepared, brought out the answer before he could think through any positive or negative implications. "Yes, I have."

The next question should have been "Why?" and Qedrim was rapidly preparing a response to that. But the Thawrd Wizard merely nodded. Then the wizard went into a long inquisition over the earliest time Qedrim could remember recognizing his ability with his special stones.

"When I was a boy, very little, I found out that with certain stones, I could always hit difficult targets. And I couldn't tell which stones would work, except by touching them, nor could I describe the way they felt. They just felt 'right,' if you understand that."

Kassibanio nodded. "I believe I can understand. And before you ask, I have no power over stones myself. I have, however, some understanding of such gifts in general."

Qedrim continued. "So of course I took to making sure I always had a lot of special stones with me."

"And after a bit you discovered you could do other things with these stones as well?"

"That's right." He wasn't going to get into the whole affair with Shapak-ailesh. Even if he ended up impolitely refusing to answer questions.

The Thawrd Wizard seemed content with Qedrim's terseness. "And from there, you extended your ability to other stones?"

"Yes."

"Hmmm. And you're on our side, are you?"

"Been talking to the noble Lord Gwothernan, have you?"

"No. Ought I to have been?"

"Well, the two of you could have a fine time sharing suspicions. I near killed myself pulling down a wall to help rescue the Lady. Does that ease your mind at all?"

"I had known that already, of course. It's simply that I felt the need to talk to the one who had such powers, if only to satisfy my curiosity.

"Now, tell me truly, what do you think of the Lady's chances of success?"

"Me? Qedrim the Disreputable Slinger? You want an opinion from such as I? If you doubt the chances of success, why are you here at all?"

"Too many questions. Suppose I answer the last first. Yes, there are chances of success, but there are a number of factors involved. And I will answer all the other questions in one. You are part of the Lady's party, and possibly more important than you think. I wish to know how all her people feel about your chances, nor are you the first I have asked. Now, I have given you several answers, will you favour me with one?" There was good humour in his voice as he spoke.

Qedrim nodded. "The answer is, 'I don't know.' And before you ask me 'Why are you here, then?' the answer to that one is the Lady seems to have too many people against her. So I'm going to be for her."

He realized this was the truth; not only that, it was opposed to his attitudes. His former attitudes, rather. What were his present attitudes? That was too deep a thought for him to consider long.

Kassibanio smiled at him, sympathetically this time. "So. Well, your help will be well-received, Qedrim."

At that moment someone came to the table. Both of them looked up, ready to dismiss an interloper, but Qedrim recognized him. "Thaldo! You're here?"

It was indeed the young farmer, recognizable despite his light infantry kit.

"Oh, yes, I managed to get along. And being a seasoned veteran by now, I have ways of dodging fatigues and the like."

"And I hear you've come up in the world, smashing down fortresses and all."

"Just did a bit of this and that," Qedrim said, embarrassment creeping over him. "Sit down, I can buy you a cup of wine for old times' sake. Kassibanio, this is my friend Thaldo, the first friend I met in Higfrod. Thaldo, this is Kassibanio, the Thawrd Wizard who's come to help the Lady."

Kassibanio appeared to have little disinclination to share a table with a mere light infantryman. "And what do you think of the Lady's chances?" he asked Thaldo.

"We'll mash 'em, of course."

The smiling blue eyes fixed on him. "And now that you've told me what you've been told to tell everyone, what do you think, yourself?"

Thaldo took a sip of wine. "I think we've got our work cut out for us. Those Morrkerr-eaten pottery men of B'tlas' (That's what they're made of, you know? Pottery!) they're bloody hard to kill. If he had a whole army of 'em, I doubt anybody could stand up to him."

"We're doomed, then?"

"Didn't say that. I thought we were doomed, I'd've lit out long ago. And we've got Qedrim."

Kassibanio heeded Qedrim, smiling even more broadly. "Well, young Qedrim you seem to have become the army's hope. Can you live up to that?"

"Old woman's Apron! I can move stones around, that's all! I don't think I'm anybody's hope!"

Thaldo chuckled. "You looking for somebody to bet against you?"

Qedrim drew a deep breath, but held back his immediate retort. After all, that had been him, back when he first arrived in the country. He was out for himself, like everyone else. He pushed up a smile.

"Maybe I'd best get B'tlas to bet against me. Lay his kharmosat on how many stones I can balance on my finger."

He recalled Gwothernan having said something similar.

"I don't know about being anybody's great hope, but I've put myself at the Lady's disposal. If I, or anyone, can figure a good way to use my powers, I'll do it."

He grinned at Thaldo. "You can bet on that."

"Bet you a cup of wine at <u>The Copper Bowl</u> back in Higfrod you can't do it!" He was grinning too.

Qedrim shook his head. "Too low. Say two cups and you're on."

"Two it is, then." He turned to Kassibanio. "You'll be witness to the wager, of course?"

Despite the good humour the Thawrd Wizard had shown hitherto, Qedrim was sure that such foolishness would rate a frown of annoyance, at the least. His smile seemed only to have broadened. "Of course."

Thaldo swallowed the last of his wine and stood. "One thing we seasoned veterans know is when not to push our luck. I've got to get back before Ten-leader Nedisalsen notices I'm gone, or he'll have my guts for a waistbelt."

And with that, he was gone.

Chapter 6

The road wound up into the hills. An early morning rain had laid the dust, presaging the coming fall and winter rains. The army could be seen slogging along, until the tail of the force faded away behind the shoulder of a hill and curtain of rain.

He was important now, Qedrim mused. Which meant he rode up near the front, not back at the tail end. Not that he rode well, but he could manage to stay on a horse. Most of the time. He'd had enough experience for that. It was going to take much more experience before his backside became accustomed to it.

They'd already shed most of the army. A part of it to the doomed garrison of Lakvos'ta and more dismissed to their homes.

'How did those men accept their fate?', he wondered.

What remained was a small, solid core.

He was near the front, yet not at the front, so he was still some distance from the Lady Annavristi. Which was just as well. He didn't belong up there with all the Lords looking down their noses at him. He didn't lack for company. Several of the lesser Lords were interested in him, and for some that interest went beyond what would be shown for a strange animal.

Kassibanio also rode with Qedrim. The skirt of Kassibanio's robe hiked up to allow him to sit a horse, revealing a pair of hairy, brawny legs matching the rest of him.

Their talk was not the sort of serious talk they had had in the wineshop. but much less serious. Kassibanio was interested in many things, plants and trees native to Qedrim's homeland, and even the old stories they told there. This last reminded Qedrim of that evening of storytelling with Shapak-ailesh.

UP INTO THE HILLS THEY wound, day by day. The weather was cooler now, decidedly on the edge of autumn. The showers which soaked them from time to time were now cold, chilling to the bone.

"The only good fortune," muttered one of the lesser Lords, "is that there's no pursuit."

In fact, a messenger on a worn horse had come to tell them Lakvos'ta had fallen again. But that Losibalson appeared to have no intention of advancing beyond there.

Reports said that upward of three hundred people of the city had been marched away to the lowlands in chains. Rumour also said that the Lady had declared "We will free them when we return." Qedrim could well imagine her saying something of the sort. He also felt he recognized a statement which was expected. Though the speaker had no way of knowing whether it could be carried out.

This not being his country, Qedrim had no idea where they were headed. Even the name of their goal, The Wooded Budaba, was nothing more than a name. Many other askars were in the same boat, as the rumours that went around could attest to. It was over the next hill, it was three days away, it was another weeks' march, and so on.

Qedrim decided they'd be there when they got there, and stopped fussing about it.

Along the way he practiced with his stones. While there was the problem of people thinking he was showing off, Qedrim also knew that he needed to find out what the limits of his power were, and work to improve it.

Kassibanio approached him in the evening. "You know, men are a bit leery riding near you when you have stones flying around you. It seems a bit risky."

Qedrim looked at the wizard. "It doesn't bother you."

Kassibanio laughed. "I'm a wizard, remember? I'm fairly sure none of your stones would hit me by accident. Others aren't quite so sure."

After that, he settled for stacking the stones on the saddle in front of him in various patterns, such as diamonds, circles or inverted triangles. It was all practice.

Then they entered a dark wood, mostly thick stands of willow, but did not appear much different from any of the several woods they had marched through. Word came back this was the Wooded Budaba, though no one, not even Kassibanio, seemed to have any idea of what a Budaba was.

Here they set up a camp, which they then set about turning into a permanent camp. Fatigue parties set to work building quarters for the Kharmista and a selection of the Lords. Other parties set to work building shelters for the army itself.

Building material consisted of wood and sod, and stone.

When they had finished building the shelters, the Lady Annavristi expressed her thanks for the work the men had done on her behalf, "I would like to thank everyone for their hard work and their generosity, for without it, this encampment would not exist. Thank you."

Lord Gwothernan, had no compunction about going to work with the lifting and hauling, as well as directing the camp's layout and the work in general. He grinned through his grime and sweat and responded, "The least we could do, Lady."

Qedrim and two minor Lords, Malsan'to and Genilabas, had put together their own shelter. Qedrim, a little more knowledgeable about what they needed, oversaw the matter, made sure the north and east walls were as windproof as could be.

After that came the problem of food. They had brought considerable grain with them, picking up a few bushels here and there along the line of march. While the building was going on,

Gwothernan sent parties out to find any farms in the area and gather some grain, in the Kharmista's name.

Qedrim had heard the orders were, "Don't take everything. We need these people to be at least willing to put up with us. If we grab their last bushel, they'll likely head off somewhere else, and if we're still here next year, what have we got? So be careful."

Furthermore, parties of men familiar with the hills went out looking for any edible roots. It was late in the year for any berries anyone knew of. Some people, who knew the good from the bad, were set to collecting mushrooms.

Qedrim went with the hunting parties, using his sling and special stones to take down deer. Deer-hunting was something an ordinary slinger wouldn't try. But Qedrim was no ordinary slinger. In addition, he was able to knock down the more common game for slingers, rabbits, quail, and the like.

Then the fine, cold rains of winter settled in, and men were kept busy plugging leaks in roofs and walls.

It wasn't the kind of living Qedrim liked. But he tried to make himself feel content with the knowledge no one else among the army was having it any better.

THEY HAD GOTTEN THEMSELVES well settled in their encampment, when one evening, Kassibanio came to the door of the shelter which Qedrim shared with Malsan'to and Genilabas. "Qedrim? I need to talk to you."

Qedrim turned, as he paused, mid-sentence in the middle of the story he was telling to Malsan'to and Genilabas, "Here I am."

Kassibanio stepped closer to Qedrim and spoke quietly. "The Lady and some others are making a trip to talk to the King of Dai'vlash. I want you along."

"Me? Talking to kings? Doesn't sound likely."

Kassibanio's teeth showed in the gloom as he grinned. "And you're not likely to talk to the King. But I've spent a long time thinking it over. Even looking into omens, chancy things that they are. And I think we'll be better off if you come."

"Omens? What kind of omens you been consulting? The ones at the bottom of a wine-jar?"

Kassibanio only continued to smile good-naturedly. "No, omens were the least of it. All they told me was 'Qedrim may be a help.' I've spent a bit of time with Gwothernan and the Lady, telling them that if we're going to King Faldisen as supplicants. It might be best we have some proof that we have a possibility of winning. Your powers, though they may not be fully developed, are one thing in our favour.

"Particularly as Faldisen himself is new, and his own position slightly unsure."

He paused. "Previously, there was a blood relationship, no matter how tenuous, between the Lady and the King of Dai'vlash. Now, however, we are calling on aid in the name of the relationship which had existed. A tie which, set against the needs and political necessities of kings, is so tenuous as to be invisible.

"So you see, the least little thing which might favour us must be considered. Even Disreputable Slingers." The smile removed any sting in that epithet.

"Like that, is it? All right, I'll come. I suppose you'll tell me what I have to do to help. And when."

"If I know myself. Just have yourself ready to set out tomorrow."

SO HE WAS READY. THE day began in cloud and mizzling rain, making for a miserable cold day, if it were to be spent outdoors on the trail. "Is this an omen of how the weather for our trip will be?" he grouched to Kassibanio.

Kassibanio chuckled. "Weather predictions are not my specialty, but it is winter, you know. Would it surprise you to discover that the weather for the trip isn't likely to be much different than this?"

"Huh. You could lie a bit, just to make me happy."

The Thawrd Wizard laughed.

HUMOUR WAS HARD TO come by on the trip. The trail was narrow, and often slippery, so slippery that on some slopes, the horses had to be led. The wet eventually soaked through all garments, so they were never warm.

Their route took them deeper into the hills at first, as a precaution to allow them to slip round any towns which B'tlas might have garrisoned. After two days they reached a cross-trail which, for all Qedrim could see, was no different from the one they were on. But they turned to take the right fork. It took them deeper into the hills as well, then tended off leftward, and eventually they began to come back out of the hills.

The weather, aside from a few breaks in the rain, did not change. The trail was still bad, and by now every stream and river was in spate. Fording streams was hard and fording rivers was treacherous. Twice they lost men to the raging waters. One was swept away when his horse stepped into a hole, and another was caught by a tree swept down from higher up, hitting the rider and his horse like a battering ram.

Still, they went on.

ONE EVENING THEY CAME upon Shapak-ailesh, camped for the evening, with his mule close by. Gwothernan and the men making up Lady Annavristi's guard were suspicious. A suspicious nature was a prize trait in a bodyguard. Qedrim stayed away from Shapak-ailesh, and acted as though he didn't know the little man.

However, the little man refused to play his part properly. While Shapak-ailesh did act as though he and Qedrim had never met, he didn't stay away. After a long discussion, and the display of the contents of his mule's packs, Gwothernan and the guards were satisfied that he was probably harmless. Despite that, they did not let him near the Lady.

After a while, Shapak-ailesh casually dropped by the fire where Qedrim was sitting alone.

"Ah, my young fellow, I believe I might have something to interest you."

"I doubt it."

"Ah, but I have." The merchant's voice lowered. "I am going to talk to you, in the guise of selling you a Fire lighting Talisman, guaranteed to light a fire on even the wettest wood. And we have to discuss the matter for so long because you must bargain me down from an exceedingly excessive twenty silvers to five.

"Now I have a hint for you, one which may be of use in days to come. It is this: Consider what a king might be thinking about anything."

"'Consider what a king might be—-!' What kind of Morrkerr-eaten gibberish is this? If you have some advice, tell me straight out!"

"If I tell you straight-out everything I believe you need to know, we will be sitting here all night, and your companions will be rightly suspicious. And this is not some obscure hint. You and your party go to ask a favour of a king. Think about what the King is going to want, what he knows, what he fears. Use your head a bit, and you'll be the better for it."

"This sounds like the kind of advice you should give to the Lady. Or Lord Gwothernan."

"O Caller of Stones, how much heed will they give me? You, at the least, are acquainted with me."

"All right, then, I'll do it."

"Fine. Now give me my five silvers."

"Give you—-!"

"We were bargaining, remember? If you give me no money, everyone watching will know you were lying about buying anything from me. That would not be good, for either of us."

Qedrim dug into his pouch, brought out five silver pieces and passed them over.

"And here is your talisman. And a good night to you."

Shapak-ailesh left them the next morning, heading off in the other direction. Qedrim wondered if Shapak-ailesh knew more about what faced them than he had said. Qedrim wished Shapak-ailesh had stayed around a little longer so he might get more out of him.

THE GREAT CITY OF GA'TUITOS was surrounded by stone walls. It was, Qedrim reflected, probably a Great City in this region, but it wasn't all that huge. After all, he'd seen Suragos.

Qedrim knew, though, that mocking what his fellow-travellers considered a Great City would win him no friends among them. So, he rode through the winding, zigzag streets, admiring with them the statuary and the fine buildings.

Some larger buildings had marble facades, making it appear as though the whole building were built of marble. Some buildings, however, had places where square sheets of marble had fallen away, to reveal the rugged stonework underneath which ruined the effect.

A boy had gone running ahead of the Lady's party from the gate where they had entered. So there were servants waiting at the main door of the palace to greet them.

"Greetings, Lady," said one of them, a tall man, though now slightly stooped, leaning on his staff. "In the King's Name, Greetings! We will direct you to your quarters, and the King will summon you at an appropriate time."

All of which, Qedrim felt, was a polite way of saying the King would call for them sometime or other. Most likely the King didn't even know they were there, yet.

The servants showed them to a suite of rooms in the palace. The walls of which were stone, worked into vaguely squarish shapes, and put together with a minimum of mortar. Woven hangings, usually portraying historical scenes, covered much of this expanse of stone. Qedrim recognized few of the scenes.

One exception to this was an excessively stylized version of Thogor Peacemaker's Great Victory. Even that seemed a little unusual to Qedrim in that Thogor and all his commanders had been portrayed wearing high tiaras. Something he'd never heard of before. Nor were the tiaras the kind of thing you'd wear into a battle.

'But you're not here to decide whether there are faults in the palace hangings.'

The party washed up, changed clothes, warmed themselves at charcoal braziers, and waited.

No one expected the King to see them immediately. Even supposing he really wanted to talk to them, doing so too soon might give the wrong impression. That he was at the disposal of a mere Kharmista.

However, servants supplied them with good and plentiful food, as well as new clothing. Which was a sign the King was, at the least, not ill-disposed to them.

KING FALDISEN OF DAI'VLASH was a strong-looking handsome man. He wore a fawn-coloured tunic and trousers with a light scale-mail cuirass over top.

"Of course," Qedrim thought. "He's just managed to take the throne, in the face of other claimants. Armour would be a necessary safeguard."

He continued to look at the sovereign. This was the man whose mind he was supposed to read, or something. Well, what <u>would</u> a king think?

It came to him, not as a magical reading of the King's thoughts, but a flash of insight into the situation. This was a new king, who had taken the throne in a contested succession. He was still shoring up his support, rewarding supporters, giving gifts carefully to those who might offer him something. If only a promise of no trouble.

This was not a good time to come to him for the kind of help the Lady needed. It had to be tried; at the very least, they had to be sure that no help would be forthcoming from King Faldisen.

the King spoke. "Welcome, Lady Annavristi, Kharmista of Higfrod! This is cheerless weather to travel in; I trust your quarters are dry and warm?"

Even for kings, basic courtesy must be maintained. A sovereign did not greet anyone by simply demanding "What do you want?" In fact, a sovereign usually had some well-informed advisors to suggest to him just what any supplicant wanted.

So Annavristi, being courteous in turn, said, "Thank you for your hospitality, King Faldisen. You have been very generous to us. And I thank you in the name of the ancient bond between my house and yours."

This last, of course, overstated the case. He was only tenuously, if at all, related to the Kings who had been related to her by blood. But it might be taken as a hint that she hoped he would accept for himself the bond those who had previously held his place had acknowledged in their time.

"I do what I am able," said the King. He paused. "Tell me, what is this news I hear from your land, of B'tlas and his incursion?"

"It has been a tragic business, Highness. After making demands no person could accept, he resorted to war. We met him on the field of battle, and at the end of a day's fighting, though we held the field, we felt it best to withdraw. We have withdrawn to the hills, and are making preparations to return."

"Ah, the battle. I have heard of it, though what I have heard has been distorted by being transferred from mouth to mouth, as it were. Tell me, how did it go?"

Qedrim half-expected Annavristi to call Gwothernan to speak to this, but she did not. Clearly and concisely, with little elaboration, she described the main movements and the results of each. When she was done, the King was silent for a bit.

"I would know more of these invulnerable soldiers," he said, finally. "What can you tell me of them?"

"They are produced by magic. A sort any thinking person would call foul. And it appears they are a sort of pottery, bounded together and animated by spells, so that they are almost invulnerable. From what we have heard, B'tlas has some five hundred of them. We have a wizard with us who could tell you more about them."

"Ah, the Thawrd Wizard among you."

His tone of voice spoke of wariness. Kings and rulers were usually wary of Thawrd Wizards, having heard tales, often outrageously expanded tales, of their works.

"And what can you tell us, wizard?"

Kassibanio spoke, as though he hadn't noticed the coolness of the King's tone.

"These men are made by mixing freshly-shed human blood with clay, and moulding it into the shapes of men. With spells being used at all points in the manufacture. I am of the opinion that B'tlas is being deliberately careless with their manufacture so as to produce a larger number than usual. But leaving the invulnerability of an unknown number of them incomplete.

"This is intended to lead others to underestimate them. To find themselves suddenly facing a core of perhaps a thousand who cannot be killed."

"I see," said the King, slowly. "Are they are truly invulnerable, as it appears?"

"Nearly so, Highness. You understand, I have no first-hand knowledge of the making of such, only an understanding of their power. It would seem to me, from what I know, that at least a hundred of them could withstand several, perhaps even several score, of hard blows before the invulnerability was overcome."

"And with a thousand such, or perhaps more, as you say, a man could sweep a battlefield with them if he used them well." the King was thoughtful.

By now Qedrim had realized something more. the King was not likely to put himself in the position of offering support to an enemy of B'tlas. If B'tlas, with his pottery warriors, should take great offence at this. He might extend his war to encompass the overthrow of the King.

"So, Lady Annavristi, what would you desire from me?"

"Highness, I ask that you give me aid to drive B'tlas from my land."

King Falsiden nodded. He would have foreseen that as the least of Annavristi's likely requests.

"I must discuss this with my counsellors. If you will accept my hospitality for a time, I will call you again to tell you my decision."

"I thank you for hearing me, Highness."

She would not have expected an immediate response, Qedrim realized. Indeed, she would have been greatly surprised if such a response were forthcoming.

"Be free of my palace, Lady, and be free in my city. I would only ask that, if you go out into the city, you do so in company of a party of my guards. My city is quite safe, but it is not impossible that your enemies, or my enemies might have found their way inside."

"You are very gracious and generous, Highness."

IT WAS THREE DAYS MORE before the King recalled them.

Qedrim, listening carefully, found out that most of the others, especially the Lady Annavristi and Lord Gwothernan, had reached the same conclusion he had. There would be little help to come from this quarter.

The King was still smiling as he greeted them. After all the courtesies were done, the questions as to their quarters and rations asked and answered with the standard polite phrases, the King spoke to the question, "With regard to your request, Lady. I have prepared a letter to be sent to B'tlas of Daura stating my disapproval over his actions. A copy shall be provided for you."

The Lady did not let her face betray the depth of her disappointment. She did say, though, against all tradition of polite and indirect speech, "I thank you, Highness. I had hoped for something more tangible."

the King's expression did not flicker at this impoliteness. "I do have another small token here."

the King snapped his fingers and a servant stepped forth. The servant was carrying a small chest. It was a little less than a forearm in length, by half that wide, and a palm-breadth in depth. The servant brought it to the Lady, then opened the lid to reveal a mass of gold coins. One of the Lady's servants stepped forward to take charge of the chest.

"You may be my guest, Lady, until the weather improves sufficiently enough to travel."

"Your Highness is very generous, but I must return to my people."

"No, I must insist you stay. It is altogether too dangerous out on the roads at this season."

Qedrim read a little more into the situation. the King would, indeed, send his letter of protest. With one excuse or another, he would keep the Lady here as a guest, letting B'tlas secure his hold on Higfrod.

the King clearly hoped this would keep B'tlas from reaching out for the crown. At least until such time as someone discovered a solution to the problem of the pottery soldiers.

The Lady bowed, though. "I thank you for your concern over our welfare, Highness."

There were more guards to escort them back to their assigned quarters.

'Just so we won't go rejecting his hospitality.'

The door to their suite of rooms was not locked, but a pair of guards took their places outside the doors.

Chapter 7

The party moved to one of the suites' interior rooms to discuss matters more privately. Even then, they discussed the situation in low tones. There was no way to prove that spies were not listening from hidden places above the ceilings.

"It's Hamaltik'ta of Lakvos'ta all over again!" declared Annavristi. "More politely done, no locked doors, but the same!"

Gwothernan was frowning. "I'm afraid you're right, Lady, but we'll have to think carefully about what we do here. It will be difficult to escape, and impossible to do so without the King's men following and harassing us all the way."

"You have any thoughts in the matter?"

"Not yet, Lady, but I will consider it."

Qedrim, after listening to this exchange, went to the doorway where he began taking stones out from around the door-jamb, stacking them carefully beside him.

"Stop! What're you up to now?"

Qedrim turned to Gwothernan. "I'm pulling stones out of the wall. And when I get done here, I'll go do the same at the corridor wall. And at that time, it would be helpful if you were to put on your most Lordly face and demand the guards escort you to the king, because our rooms are falling apart."

"And what good is that going to do?"

Qedrim was working it out for himself as he went along. "They'll know there was nothing wrong with these rooms, and they'll know nobody could do this sort of thing without tools. They'll ask the king, maybe even take us to see him again. And if stones keep coming out of the walls, he might decide it would be best to let us go."

"Or do away with us altogether!" snapped back Gwothernan.

"And if it looks like that's happening, I'll make stones fly. How many guards d'you think I'll have to knock down with flying stones to make the rest unwilling to touch us? Not to mention how the King will feel if his palace continues to fall apart."

Kassibanio spoke up then. "It's an idea, though. I might even be willing to suggest that something dislikes our party being held here."

"How long can you keep on manipulating stones?" That was the Lady Annavristi, concern in her voice.

"Long enough, Lady. I'm just moving one stone at a time, not a whole city wall."

He was beginning to work out a technique, which stones he could pull without the whole lot coming down. There were times, of course, when several came loose, but he was always able to catch them and lower them to the floor.

When he had a hole large enough to step through, he went to the outer chamber and began to remove stones from the wall there.

In this case, however, he did not go on for very long before the door flew open.

"What's happening in here?"

The stones continued to fall from the wall, drifting down to stack themselves on the floor. Qedrim, while dismantling the walls, held himself ready. Everything depended on the guards' reaction. They might, just possibly, try to use their weapons, and if they did, he had to be prepared to react.

Gwothernan stepped forward. "I'm sure the King did not intend to insult the Lady Annavristi by assigning her to dilapidated quarters, where the stones fall from the walls as we speak."

One guard stared at the other for guidance. The senior man spoke. "Lot'ifon, go fetch the Captain. Tell him it's an emergency!"

He then spoke to Gwothernan as the other guard's footsteps went hurrying down the hall. "Lord, I have no authority to alter or change your quarters. If you will be patient, I'm sure matters can be worked out to your satisfaction."

His voice was steady. Though his eyes wandered now and again to where the stones were drifting down from the wall, seating themselves with a light 'click.'

The captain was not long in coming. He was a squat and burly man. His helmet was slung at his belt and his broad dark face was without expression.

Until he saw the stones coming down.

He stiffened. "Dark destroyer's teeth!" Then he mastered himself. "What's going on here?"

Kassibanio chose that moment to speak. "I believe, Captain, that there is some power at work which causes the very stones to protest at keeping the Lady here."

"You're doing this, wizard? I've heard about your sort! We can deal with you!"

"I promise you, Captain, by the vows I have taken, that the power which moves the stones has nothing to do with me."

The Captain glared at him a moment longer, then nodded sharply. "So." He turned to his men, and his eye fell on Lot'ifon. "You! Lot'ifon! Go tell the Chief Servant what we've got here! He might want to roust out a magician."

"Sir!" With the barest flicker of annoyance at being sent off running again, Lot'ifon was away.

The Captain, much less steadfast than the senior guard, said to Gwothernan, "Lord, we'll have to have the Chief Servant out to see to different quarters for you. I don't have the authority. Destroyer's teeth!" His eyes kept drifting to the steadily stacking stones.

The Captain continued to wait, by turns clutching his sword-pommel and wiping his palms on his trousers.

At last the Chief Servant came up. In his tow, followed a tall man (by Gafrodi standards) who wore a loose jacket and grey leggings, along with a little round hat. He also had a lean and ascetic look, and a beak of a nose. He assessed the situation, made a hand-gesture which ended with a snapping of fingers, and a blue light surrounded Kassibanio. A moment later the light turned brilliant green.

The wizard nodded. "He is doing some things, small workings such as a magician has in operation most times. But he has nothing to do with the walls."

Qedrim had already decided he would be best simply standing with the rest. Not doing anything to call attention to himself. He was waiting for the magician to do the next step, to try to discover exactly where the power came from that was moving the stones. When he did that, Qedrim would have to think of some way to deal with him. The fellow had evidently already decided to check the only wizard in the group, however. It was a reasonable decision. But one indicating a nature which was not sufficiently suspicious.

The Chief Servant, a well-fed man with a harassed air, said, "Then you believe this story of theirs? That some power causes the stones to object to the presence of the Lady?"

The magician made another gesture. Which was similar to but slightly different from the first, and the blue light surrounded the Lady. A moment later the light changed to pink, then faded again. "She is undoubtedly the cause of it. Though there is something unusual in her—ah, relationship, shall we call it?—to the action being undertaken. But yes, I'd say that the underlying cause is rooted in her presence."

Again, Qedrim noted, the fellow was not asking the right questions. It was true, though, the Lady Annavristi's presence was the cause of the removal of the stones.

The Chief Servant frowned, as though this were all part of some grand design to make his life difficult. "Well, this must go to the king."

"Lady, Lords, I ask that you be patient a little longer. The King must make a decision."

"Of course," the Lady answered.

So they waited, and the stones continued to move out of the walls and stack themselves. The guards tried not to stare at the sight, but their gaze continued to drift in that direction.

Qedrim was a little worried over how many stones he could pull out of the walls before the roof fell in. He varied his choice of walls and positions of stones within the walls as much as he was able. But unless something interrupted him, there would come a time when the chambers were unsafe.

Luckily, the Chief Servant came hustling back in a short time. He bowed to the Lady, appearing more harassed than ever, and said, "The King wishes to speak with you. If you will be so good as to follow me?"

"Certainly."

So once again they went trooping along the hallways, with guards—a larger number, this time—to the right and the left. Qedrim, improvising as he went along, brought with him two ranks of stones from the walls, floating at head-height, between the party and the guards.

The guards held their discipline in face of this, though it was clearly a near thing. The Captain stomped along muttering quietly "Destroyer's Teeth! Dark Destroyer's Teeth! Bloody Dark Destroyer's Teeth!" as though the words were a litany to ward off evil.

The King continued to smile and be welcoming. Though his smile grew strained at the sight of the stones floating along, as if in escort.

"What is this, Lady?" he demanded brusquely, ignoring the usual courtesies and belying his smile.

The Lady bowed. Taking her cue from Kassibanio's hint, she said, "It appears, Highness, that the stones of your palace wish to be rid of us." She made her statement short, with no demands that they be set free at once.

The King gazed at the sight, the gathered visitors, the servants, the guards, the floating stones. "What sort of trick is this?"

"A trick, Highness? Did not your magician explain it to you?"

"Magicians? Bah! Something is going on here, Lady, something I do not care for. Not at all, Lady!"

Qedrim thought it time to push matters just a little. There was a grating sound. A stone in the wall of the Great Hall pulled itself free and joined the others in their lines.

The King lost his smile then. "Kill them all!" he shouted, face pale with anger and fear.

The guards turned to do their duty, but Qedrim had not lost his awareness of armed men all around. The stones moved, ringing on helmets and thudding on flesh. A moment later there wasn't a guard standing.

The King was standing, though, standing and staring. The Lady spoke again and Qedrim admired not only her coolness but her quick thinking. "I believe they want us gone, not dead, Highness."

The King's smile was gone, replaced by a snarl. "So, if that is to be the way of it, let it be so! Go, all of you, back to your hills! And don't think to have heard the last of this! Chief Servant, see them gone!"

They went, as quickly and as carefully as they were able. Qedrim wondered if the others were thinking, like him. Of whether the King might change his mind, and have them ambushed on the way out of the city.

Just have to hope he stays a little unsure of the situation for long enough. Might that 'power' tear down his Great Hall around him if he goes against it?'

Qedrim kept his escort of stones until they were well out of the city. Then, rather than merely discarding them, he set them in a low, two-course wall barring the road.

Gwothernan raised an eyebrow at Qedrim as the stones rattled into their places. Qedrim shrugged. "Merely another little hint for the King."

Later that evening, with an extra blanket wrapped around him, he drank cup after cup of soup and shivered. The whole thing had been tiring, very tiring. Only the fact that he had been practicing daily and getting more and more used to his ability had kept him from collapse.

Kassibanio sat beside him. "Quite the effort, young Qedrim. I might have made a change or two if I'd been in charge, but it did have its effect."

"We were lucky," Qedrim mumbled. "That magician should have been able to spot me."

Kassibanio shook his head. "Not luck, or at least not altogether luck. This power of yours, whatever it is, does not seem to relate to most forms of magic. He was searching for ordinary forms of magic, and of course, did not find them."

"It is possible," the Thawrd Wizard went on, "that if he'd asked the right question, 'Is someone here causing this?' he might have gotten an answer involving you. But as it was, he asked if I were doing it, and I was not. Then he asked if the Lady were doing it, and she was not. At that point he decided I was probably correct. As I said, luck, but not luck only."

A shadow fell over Qedrim, and he glanced up to see the Lady standing in front of them. "Kassibanio, I would like a word with Qedrim."

"Of course, Lady."

She settled gracefully into the place he'd left. "Thank you once more, Qedrim. I'm afraid this journey was a failure. We've turned the King from a friendly neutral to an enemy."

She waved down his beginning protest with a slim hand. "No, I don't fault you. He would have held us until Higfrod was totally under B'tlas' power, and we would have ended our days as landless hangers-on at his court.

"What you've done is to set us free from that. And he probably won't bother us, expecting B'tlas to finish us in the spring.

"But we're free again, and while we're free we have some hope. And you shall be rewarded."

Her gentle voice was relaxing him. He was barely able to mutter, "No reward necessary."

She looked at him again. "I'm sorry!" You're worn to a stump, and here I am nattering at you! Sleep well, true friend!"

She kissed him lightly on the cheek and was gone.

No matter how much he would have preferred to stay awake and enjoy that moment, his eyes insisted on falling shut.

THE RETURN JOURNEY to the Wooded Budaba was marred by winter weather. While it was not uneventful, at least they didn't lose any more men or horses.

There were nightly discussions, to which the Lady Annavristi expressly required Qedrim's attendance, where future plans were discussed.

The first such meeting began with Lord Gwothernan declaring. "The situation is against us, and will be so as long as B'tlas has the initiative. If we continue to lurk in the Hills, he can ignore us until our support has faded to nothing, then hunt us down."

"Do you have any thoughts as to how we can take the initiative?" the Lady asked.

"It will have to be an attack into the lowlands. Not only that, it will have to be a credible attack. At present we haven't the force for that."

"And we have sent most of our army home. Do you think they'll come back?"

"Perhaps a handful, little more, until we have shown that there's something to come back to. But you will recall, it was necessary to send the army away. We couldn't have kept them fed in the Wooded Budaba for the winter.

"This means we deal with what we have, not what we wish we had. Qedrim, would your have the strength to pull down Lakvos'ta's walls again?"

"I might. But much depends on what they've got in there. If I make a breech, and they jam those pottery men into said breech, where are we?"

Gwothernan frowned. "There's a question. Will B'tlas have sent for the pottery soldiers to return to him? Or, will he leave them with Losibalson in Lakvos'ta for so long as we're free, and a possible threat? I'd suggest we count on them being in the town until we have credible evidence to the contrary.

"Which still leaves us with the question, what shall we do? We don't have the numbers to storm Lakvos'ta. Even if we get a fair number of men coming back to us in the spring, the casualties we'd take in storming the town would make further recruiting difficult."

So the discussion went on, evening after evening. One topic was how many troops were likely to rally to them, another was possible ruses to take Lakvos'ta. Most such ruses were too complex to work. How many engines, rams, catapults, and towers, would be needed to take the town? What effect would all this have on gaining troops to fight B'tlas in the open field?

Even by the time they had reached the Wooded Budaba, there was no real consensus on most topics. As far as Qedrim could tell, a positive thing which emerged was Gwothernan was now accustomed to considering him as a useful member of the group. Though perhaps not a friend.

"AHA! HE'S RETURNED from the big city!" cried Genilabas, as Qedrim entered the shelter. "And what news? Is the King going to lend us troops?"

"Not for me to say," Qedrim answered. "The Lady will make her announcement when the time's right. Folk like me oughtn't to be spreading tales and rumours."

"But you were there!" Protested Malsan'to. "You know as much as any! And it wouldn't be spreading tales, you'd be telling the truth!"

"She'll tell it all, in her own time. Not for me to be messing about with the news."

When the rumour-mill had received the tale, they were doubly annoyed with him, as friends might be. "'No, I can't say anything about it,' he says, and all the time he's the one managed to get them out whole! Not one little word, not even 'I had to do some tricks with rocks.' No, not Qedrim; he keeps his good friends in the dark!"

"You'd prefer me to be a blowhard like you, Malsan'to?"

"We'd think you could tell your friends a little bit, Qedrim. It's not as though we'd go blabbing through the camp."

"Someone did, Malsan'to. And I doubt the Lady will be happy to know everything which went on. Down to the colour of the King's shoes, is running round the camp already."

"If the Lady is surprised at the news, she's incredibly naïve. Did she strike you as incredibly naïve?"

Qedrim smiled at that. "No. I just didn't want it to be my fault."

A mischievous grin crossed Malsan'to's face as he looked over to Genilabas. "Hear that, Genni? No wonder the Lady plans on making him a Lord. Probably take precedence over us, too, and have us bowing every time we see him."

"Oh, Yes, Lord Qedrim of the Big Stones! And won't he Lord it over his former companions!"

"Old Woman's Apron, you're insane, the both of you. Nobody's going to make a Lord out of me!"

"Listen to him, Malsa! You'd think he, of all people, would have a little notion of what's really in the wind!"

WITH THIS SORT OF WARNING, unofficial and flippant as it might be, Qedrim was not totally surprised when the Lady Annavristi asked him to come take a place next to Gwothernan and thus nearer to her. She stood and spoke to the group.

"By now everyone has heard what Qedrim has done in my service. I think it is time, and past time, that I declare him to be a Close Friend of the Kharmista."

Still smiling, she surveyed the assembly. "Now, there are certainly some here for whom a certain seat at a table is of great importance. Let me assure you, because Qedrim is sitting nearer to me, you have not fallen in my esteem. Rather, he has risen."

She sat, and Qedrim heard Gwothernan mutter, "Won't work, Annaki. You've rubbed some noses out there in a bad smell."

She smiled at him and answered in a quiet voice, "I did something which had to be done. I'm sorry if it's made your job harder."

Qedrim could feel animosity, mostly towards him. But there was some towards the Lady herself. Yes, Gwothernan would have a harder time looking out for the Lady's welfare. Perhaps he, Qedrim, should do some watching out as well. Yes, he was able to look after himself. But she shouldn't suffer on his account.

He set certain faces in his mind. Certain people whose attitudes he was fairly sure of, who might do something wrong.

The meeting was the usual statement of strategies. Then of resources, both actual and potential. There was a lot of talk regarding stratagems to take Lakvos'ta, without the necessity of storming it.

"The bare fact is," Gwothernan told the assembly, "we have to do something. Some specific and telling deed, to prove we're still a force to be reckoned with. A beacon to call men back to our force who might otherwise be loth to come forward.

"Taking Lakvos'ta will be such. It is far enough from the centre of things to allow us time after taking it to send out our summons. Far enough that B'tlas can't have an army marching on us before we can get any benefit out of taking the town."

Some made suggestions of sending in men disguised as shepherds or merchants. who would kill the guards in the middle of the night, then open the gates to let the main army in. Others made more complex suggestions. So complex as to render them impossible to carry out without some of the complexities causing the plan to fall apart.

One man, a tall, broad-shouldered fellow, whose beak of a nose appeared as though it had been the model for that horrible coin, said, "Could Qedrim not use his stone magic to pick men off the walls, and allow us to go up and over them safely with ladders?"

Everyone looked to Qedrim for an answer. "The honest truth is that I don't know. It is possible, perhaps, but I would have to do considerable practice. I doubt if I could clear a whole wall, and keep the wall cleared. I suspect the men going up the ladders would still catch some arrow-fire, though it might be less than usual."

Qedrim noted that the fellow who had brought the matter up was one he had already marked as likely to make trouble.

"I see," said the fellow, with a definite hint in his voice that Qedrim did not seem to be as magnificent as he had been portrayed.

Qedrim himself did not bother to respond, knowing how useless it would be. Qedrim also noticed that Gwothernan had his hand on the kharmista's arm under the table. He had been restraining her from coming to her feet to defend him.

As he did so, Gwothernan said, "Sobeldanser, Qedrim's abilities are new to us all, and not thoroughly tested. Be sure that he" (there was a slight stress on the pronoun) "will be working through the winter to discover how best to serve the Lady."

'Not the best method altogether, Gwothernan. You've sort of asked him whether he's going to do anything useful. And if all he can do is swing a sword, he might just feel a little more testy.'

WINTER WORE ON. THEY held general meetings, whose primary purpose was to pass on news from people who had gone down to spy out the situation in the town.

A man going down with a pack of hides to sell might learn a lot if he kept his eyes and ears open. If he were careful not to ask suspicious questions, or try to look at things a trapper ought not to look at, this man might find out a good deal.

If he were careful who he approached, he might set up the beginnings of a spy system in the town. People who already knew a great deal, and who knew others who knew and who could find out information. Information to be passed along to the next man who came along who could give the proper password. All this meant there was a stream of intelligence coming out, in bits and pieces, to the Lady's camp.

Such reports were not always a reason for calling a meeting. But as the winter wore on, sometimes a bit of news which might have been considered small was used as a reason to recall them to the purpose of their existence in the wilds.

With winter's cold and damp came other visitors, diseases which ran through the camp like fire. Kassibanio proved to have an extensive knowledge of herbal remedies. Including herbs found practically nowhere else but in the hills. He was kept busy tramping from sickbed to sickbed, mixing up doses, and overseeing the unwell.

Neither Qedrim nor his two companions fell ill. But Malsan'to declared, "You know, without that wizard, I swear we'd've lost a third of our number. I've seen illness and despondency take people off before."

"You, Malsa? You make it sound as if you've been in hill camps with the Lady in desperate straits a dozen times before!"

"No, it was three years back. My Father and some of our men got caught wrong side of the Dishballin River chasing outlaws. We had to camp on the bank until the river went down far enough for us to get back, and that meant most of the winter. About half of us made it."

Qedrim often went out with the hunters. It became a known fact that if Qedrim could see something, he could kill it with a sling stone. It was seldom he came back from a hunting trip without something, even if it be only a few quail or rabbits.

Also, with the advance to Lakvos'ta coming up, Qedrim continued to practice with stones. Continuing to strengthen his abilities. Thinking about how one man, using stones of whatever size, might carry out a town's conquest.

He thought on occasion it might simply be a little easier if he was able to go down and convince Losibalson to bet his town against Qedrim's ability to do something with a stone or two.

By spring they had a fair notion how many soldiers were in Lakvos'ta. Well within a margin of error of twenty-five to a hundred. There was no consensus on the numbers of pottery men, which Qedrim felt was an important omission.

One story said the pottery soldiers had been returned to B'tlas in the city of Higfrod. But another said that, since they needed neither to eat nor drink, and since their inability to do other than follow literal orders unsuited them to garrison duties, they had been stored away in a warehouse. One enterprising fellow even claimed to have seen them, stacked floor to ceiling like cordwood.

Gwothernan stated to a meeting, "We'll proceed as if they were in the town, and available for immediate use. Not an endearing prospect, but one I feel we must accept." That statement eased Qedrim's mind; they weren't going rushing in and hoping for the best.

Sobeldanser asked, "What of our Thawrd Wizard? Can he tell us whether they're present or not?"

Kassibanio himself answered. "There has been a spell put over the town to prevent just such spying. I have made some strong efforts to penetrate that spell, and have gathered no more than vague notions.

"There is something inimical in the town. Whether it is pottery soldiers or something else, I can't say."

Sobeldanser scowled, "We are going near blind into a dangerous enterprise, and our wizard seems unable to breach magical protections, or to defend us against magical warriors."

Gwothernan turned a fierce gaze on him. "Are you defeated before you start, then, Sobeldanser? Perhaps you had best turn your command over to another."

Sobeldanser straightened. "Turn my command over to someone else? Not likely in this world!"

"Then perhaps you could come up with some positive plans rather than merely moaning over all the difficulties we face?"

Next day Kassibanio found Qedrim, who was whirling some stones in a circle in front of himself. The stones swooping down to near his feet and then bringing them back up above his head. "I'd take it as a kindness if you'd set those stones down for a moment, so I can talk to you without fear of being brained."

Qedrim landed the stones and smiled. "Will you say anything which might make me want to brain you?"

"I hope not. It's only that I understand you to have some ability with making talismans."

Qedrim scowled at this reminder of his past. "A few of the easier ones, yes."

"That's really all that's necessary. You see, given the state of our forces, and the forces against us, I'd like something to hearten our men."

"I see. So what do you want from me?"

"I'd like to build some talismans, some rather powerful ones, and you could help. No, I don't expect you to build them yourself. But if I give you instructions, I believe you could make some simple talismans which I could embed in other talismans, to produce something of a different order."

Qedrim frowned. "I learned about such things, but Old Freyollach was vague on the theory. He could do more than I, but not much."

"Are you willing to learn this?"

"If it'll help, I'll do it."

He learned a great deal in the next few days. He'd never known before that if you take a Talisman of Water Purification, then altered the talisman just so, it was no more than a collection of bits and pieces of material. If one took that as a starting point, though, one could make something powerful with it.

He also discovered, though Old Freyollach had mentioned it a time or two, that with the more powerful talismans there were limits on how many one could make. These limits had little to do with the availability of materials. For some of the most powerful, a person could make only one per year. Even making several different talismans, if they were of the same order, was not possible.

"I'm not going to teach you all about the orders of talismans and their relationships and limitations, young Qedrim. Just enough to get by here.

"Is that the way you were taught to make a Talisman of Water-purification?"

"Pretty much, yes." Qedrim scowled, trying to recall exactly how Old Freyollach had taught him. That is before Qedrim had taken to cutting corners.

"And it would work, too, for a while. Now go back at it from this point here," a rough finger pointed at a place on the Talisman, "and follow my directions."

It only made Qedrim feel worse when he himself recalled, as soon as Kassibanio pointed out the first error, the way things ought to have gone.

His annoyance with himself came out in snappishness at Kassibanio, who only smiled gently at Qedrim's snarls.

A few days later, Kassibanio called a meeting. It was a fairly short meeting. Kassibanio got up and announced, "I have, with some assistance, produced two talismans. One is a Talisman of Hiding, which can shelter up to one hundred men. It is not invisibility, more a matter of strongly suggesting people look elsewhere. Of convincing them that there was no movement there, and so on. The moment a person under that protection touches a person not under it, the effect of the talisman is lost for all. The talisman cannot be made to operate for another ten days, and once the talisman is used, cannot be used again for six weeks.

"The second talisman I have here is one of Wound Healing. This one can heal any cut or gash, though the talisman cannot reattach severed limbs. It has other limitations, such as being able to do no more than one thousand one hundred and forty-four healings, great or small, before it must be put aside. The talisman can recover, of course. For instance, if it is used up completely one day, it may be used once, or perhaps twice, the next day. Twice or perhaps four times if it is left two days, and perhaps up to five times if the talisman is left for a third day.

"However, using the talisman up too often can remove the magic altogether."

Kassibanio paused and eyed the crowd. "Even with the limitations, these Talismans should be useful."

"Very useful indeed. Their mere presence will be an encouragement to our army," Gwothernan replied,

"There is one thing further; we move on Lakvos'ta in a week's time. Make ready."

LAKVOS'TA LOOMED ABOVE them as they crept around to the front gate. Somewhere back behind them, the main body was coming. But the advance party—if Qedrim was a fair sample—did not brood on the paucity of their own numbers. They consisted mostly of light infantry, with a score of archers. Qedrim had been interested to find his old acquaintance, Thaldo, among the light infantry. Though they hadn't had a chance to do more than exchange a greeting, what with the forced march and all.

The Talisman of Hiding sheltered them. And every one of them hoped the thing would work as they had been told it would. A fair number likely had their doubts.

Now the advance party were facing the gate. It was locked and barred as usual. If the town had been under siege, the garrison commander would also have put a barricade in the space behind the gate.

Gwothernan glanced at Qedrim. "Your plan. You start off."

Qedrim took a deep breath. It was his plan, though Gwothernan had done a good deal of emendation and smoothing out. In the starlight it was difficult to see much, but Qedrim was able to make out stones here and there on the ground. He hauled one up, about the size of his torso, and hurled it against the gate.

Hardly waiting to see what damage he might have done, he hurled another, and another. At that time it became difficult to make out stones of the appropriate size. So he took two he had already used, and brought them up to smash against the gate with all the strength he could manage.

The gate began to give. Massive though the gate was, the continual battering was more than it could endure.

The alarm inside had gone up an age ago it seemed, and there was shouting and the sound of trumpets. Men on the walls cast down torches to be able to see who was outside, and there were more shouts of alarm when those on the wall were unable to see any people. There was nothing but the two boulders moving back, and rushing forward to smash at the gate.

As he continued to move the stones, Qedrim realized he ought to have thought of that. The sight of two stones, with no human agency, battering at the gate, would surely also batter at the defenders' morale. Gwothernan had certainly thought of that.

Then the gates smashed in. With a shout, the small party rushed forward. Their sudden appearance, seemingly out of nowhere, caused more dismay on the walls. Qedrim took stones from his pouch and slung them at whatever he could see in the light of the torches still on the walls. Whatever hindrance he could be to establishing order up on the wall would be all to the good.

The garrison-commander managed to get some troops formed inside the gate. Then there was a roaring battle going on almost at once. Qedrim left off slinging stones at the men on the walls and moved in under the arch. He then went to work with the same two stones he'd used on the gate, but this time he was battering the enemy ranks.

With that assistance to the previously invisible troops, the enemy were soon dead or fled.

Arrows were coming down from the walls now. Qedrim took one of his special stones, whenever he saw any sign of movement up on the wall, he let fly. Nor was he the only one fighting back. The Gafrodi archers were also shooting through the dim light.

Then the Gafrodi archers went swarming up the walls, to take and hold the section over the gate.

The advance party's first objective was, to open the gates, and second, to hold the gates until the main body arrived. To that end they held their position just a little way inside the gate. That way, no one could come in behind them without taking a circuitous route from one of the other town gates.

After having driven off the first enemy force, it seemed the Gafrodi were given five heartbeats' respite before another force of Dauri came shouting round a corner and charged down the street at them.

Qedrim sent the two large stones down to plough through their ranks, then brought them back again. The Dauri broke and ran before they came to close quarters with the invaders.

Qedrim leaned against the wall, breathing deeply.

"Are you hurt?" Gwothernan was eyeing him with concern.

"Just a bit tired. Heaving those things around on top of a night march is a bit much for me."

"Rest while you can. They'll be back."

Qedrim wanted to ask how much longer before the main body could be expected. But he wasn't going to ask Gwothernan. That would only earn him a look of scorn.

He surveyed the area. Was the sky lightening, or was it his imagination? If it wasn't his imagination, then where was the rest of the army? He'd known this was a dangerous enterprise. But he didn't want it to be a futile one as well. Him and this little band wiped out, and the gates swung to and blocked against the rest of the kharmista's army.

"What have you got yourself into?" Qedrim wondered to himself.

"Here they come!"

Here they came, indeed. This time it was the pottery soldiers, three abreast, spears presented. Given what he'd seen of them in action, Qedrim knew a mere hundred men—less than that, now—couldn't possibly hold them.

It was now too late to do anything but try. It wasn't as if they hadn't been warned. Kassibanio had told them "It's likely the pottery soldiers are stored, and it will take a little time to reactivate them. There's a chance that 'little time' will be less than we would like, but we can't eliminate every risk."

Qedrim didn't waste time fretting. He was still able to throw stones, maybe slow them down a bit, at the least. Even as he flung the first rock down at chest height, he realized there was a better method. If he sent the stones at ankle height, they could cause more confusion. If it were possible for pottery soldiers to be confused.

In fact, the plan worked better than he could have expected. The first ranks went down with a clatter, and others fell over them before they were aware of the situation. Once down, they seemed unable to rise again quickly. Although it was not a terrible disadvantage for invulnerable warriors. It did give the advance party that little extra time.

Further, many of the pottery soldiers had broken legs and were unable to rise at all.

They were just beginning to organize themselves once more when Qedrim brought the stones hurtling back. Once more, pottery men were upended, some with legs broken, some smashed entirely. They managed to rise and come on again, though, and once more the stones came plunging back. By this time the pottery men were at close quarters with the Gafrodi.

Qedrim hesitated. Then he sent the stones up and brought them smashing down from above. What had Kassibanio said? Something about any one of the pottery men being able to endure only so many blows without smashing. With no way of discovering how many, save to continue to strike.

Well, if he dealt as many blows, and as hard as possible, could he use up their invulnerability?

So the stones went up and down, up and down, again and again. With each blow, it seemed, one pottery man broke. Did sending one stumbling into another count as a blow? Have to ask Kassibanio. Have to survive to ask Kassibanio.

He'd been heaving stones, and heavy stones, for a long while, a very long while, and he was beginning to feel it. How much longer could he manage to go on?

Then shouting broke out from from behind. Qedrim's first thought was that the garrison of Lakvos'ta had managed to take them from the rear. Then pikes went slipping past them, striking toward the pottery men, driving through the desperate remnants of the advance force.

The phalanx had arrived.

It was still too soon for Qedrim to be able to rest, though. There were still enough pottery men to hold the phalanx. Perhaps, to hold the phalanx long enough for the garrison commander to bring up reinforcements.

It seemed an awfully long time before the last pottery soldiers were withdrawn. Qedrim thought hazily, that the commander had probably decided there were better uses for the pottery soldiers than being smashed to powder bit by bit defending a street.

The phalanx surged on down the street, shouting, thrusting with their pikes, and driving toward the middle of the city.

Qedrim slowly lowered the stones to the ground, as far out of the way as he was able to. He leaned against the cold stone of the gateway and relaxed. Between one breath and the next, he was asleep.

Chapter 8

Qedrim woke in dimness. He felt the softness of a bed, or at least a cot, beneath him. The thought of 'I keep doing this' ran through his mind. A quiet figure raised his head and gave him a drink. He wondered, dimly, if this were the same Healer who had cared for him after the last fight for the town. He slept again.

He wasn't sure how long he slept. Though he later discovered it had been a day and a night, with waking periods from time to time.

When he really woke, the Lady and Gwothernan were sitting beside his cot. "You've done it again, Qedrim," Annavristi said. "We've taken the town."

He shook his head, causing a sudden wave of vertigo. After that had passed he said, "Wasn't just me, Lady. There were a lot of others out there too."

"And we'd've been slaughtered if you hadn't dealt with those pottery men. We lost heavy enough as it was." Gwothernan was looking at him, an expression on his face as though he'd only just seen Qedrim for the first time.

"Did what I could," Qedrim muttered.

"And you did it well. What gave you the notion to use those rocks the way you did?"

"Just figured I could slow them down by aiming at the legs. And when they got too close for that, it appeared using the stones from above would do better."

"And you need to rest." Annavristi looked at Gwothernan. "Gwothernan, stop pestering him. Just say he did well and let it go at that."

Gwothernan nodded, his stern look returning. "You did well, Qedrim. Now rest, as the Lady says. We still have a war to fight."

His two erstwhile housemates also visited him, breezing in and making low mocking bows to "The Lord Qedrim of the Big Stones."

Qedrim couldn't help but smile a bit. "And I see you two are mad as ever. I understand we did well enough?"

"Oh, well enough indeed," said Malsan'to, "It appears the pottery men, what were left of them, collapsed and died, if 'died' is the right word, when Losibalson died. I heard Kassibanio say that was most likely a precaution taken by B'tlas, so Losibalson couldn't lend them to anyone else."

"B'tlas would've had to be mad to turn troops like that over to any of his commanders, without some safeguard," Genilabas said, "Imagine having your own invulnerable warriors show up facing you on a battlefield?"

"So, will you be up out of that bed in time for us to march, Qedrim?" demanded Malsan'to.

"I should be. I wasn't hurt, you know. Merely tired myself out a bit more than I ought."

Thaldo also came by. He had a bandage on his left thigh and he limped along, but he seemed to be in good spirits. "They say I'll be back in shape before the march."

"March?"

"Oh, yes, the Lady sent word to her people to gather here for the summer campaign. Sent word before we left the Wooded Budaba, which shows her confidence. People are starting to show up already, and while Lord Gwothernan for certain doesn't tell me what's in his mind, it makes sense that we'll be marching soon."

"How soon?"

"Oh, don't worry, you'll have plenty of time to get back on your feet again, lift some stones, that sort of thing. Might even be able to make some money with your sling, if you give the right odds."

Thaldo said that with a grin, but Qedrim found himself wincing inwardly at the thought of how he used to make his living. He managed to find a grin of his own.

"The Lady rewarded me for saving her life, way back there last year in the city of Higfrod. I haven't spent all that yet, so I don't need to go running games on the side. If you want, though, you can lay bets I'll be out of this bed in good time to march with the rest."

"Won't find anyone to take that, even at big odds. But I 'd better get along. I've got a twenty-Captain doesn't like me at all, something about a woman, and he's looking for a way to get me into trouble. Even for a lame and wounded hero, he finds little chores to be done."

Qedrim chuckled. "But you're a real veteran now, you know all the tricks."

"Perhaps not all, but just enough. I'll be by to see you again, later."

QEDRIM NOTICED FEW other Lords dropped by. Not that he'd expected such visits, having a fairly objective notion of his popularity in that quarter.

'Just see Sobeldanser dropping in to see if I'm all right!'

Even before he'd thrown in his lot with the Kharmista with all his games in all those towns and cities, what he called 'friends' were more like 'friends of the moment,' joining him for this endeavour or that.

He still at times had trouble accepting Malsan'to and Genilabas didn't really expect to gain anything by their association with him. Or perhaps if they did, it would be on a basis of a favour for a favour.

Kassibanio came to see him, sometime after he'd been released from the Healing House. I'd've come sooner, young Qedrim, but I've been doing a lot of studying. You've heard about the last pottery men? How they died when Losibalson did?"

"Yes, I'd heard about that. Seems like a sensible precaution for even B'tlas to take, assuming he's as foolhardy as the tales say."

"Yes. But the fact they were so connected with Losibalson would appear to say B'tlas had managed to transfer complete control, not merely command, of this body of pottery men to Losibalson. It's another little bit of information about them. Though I'm not sure what help it will be to us. Save in the sense any little bit of information we gain is another piece of information we didn't have before."

"I used your notion of each of them only being able to take so many blows when I used the stones on them."

"Aha! Do you think there was something to it?"

"I was too busy keeping the stones moving to try to keep count, but it appears to me there was more to it than wishful thinking."

"It will help, even if it's only minor comfort to our soldiers, that the things can be beaten, eventually. Staying around to hit at something you know can in time be killed is a different thing from staying around to hit at something that is unkillable."

"A minor comfort, for sure."

"Yes. But you, I assume from your present state of health that you'll be ready to do your part if we fight them again?"

"Yes. But you say 'if.' Is there some chance me might not fight them again?"

"I wish I could say yes or no. But in war, there is always a chance this or that will happen. For certain, there is an intent on our part to fight."

Qedrim drew a deep breath. From the time he'd been able to stay awake for any time in the Healing House, he'd been training with his stones. The ability was coming back steadily. But for all his positive outward attitude, he wasn't at all certain how long it would take to build himself back up to where he had been before they'd stormed of Lakvos'ta.

WORD CAME ONE DAY, with a dusty messenger from the south, and rumour promptly spread it through the town. B'tlas was marching up toward them.

That much was sure knowledge. The numbers of his army varied according to who was passing the rumours. Such figures as three or four hundred thousand were plainly ridiculous. As were figures such as two or three thousand. Even if the latter included such figures as a thousand pottery men.

There were also persistent rumours Qedrim was dead, or had deserted them. This was foolishness,of course, but it could not go unchallenged.

"Qedrim," the Lady Annavristi said, "would you mind going and showing yourself around town? Do a few tricks with your stones, that sort of thing?"

One of the last things he wanted to do was to go doing tricks in public with his stones. For one thing, how did you do that without laying bets? For another thing, he'd thought that was it the old Qedrim who did such things.

This was the Lady Annavristi looking at him, though, asking him to do this.

"Yes, Lady, I'll do what I can."

SO HE AND LORDS MALSAN'TO and Genilabas went out, night after night, visiting wineshops. After they'd had a bit to drink—nowhere near drunk, just easy—one of the Lords, most often

Malsan'to, would say, "Qedrim! Do us a trick with your dancing rocks!"

So Qedrim would complacently take out some of his stones. No bets were laid. He only put the rocks through some tricks, hopping around the table, stack in an inverted pyramid, or fly around someone's head, things of that sort.

After they'd gotten sufficient attention, he'd keep on doing tricks, then they'd leave. Often as not, some people would follow them. And when they went into another wineshop, the tale would be passed, and he would be urged to show off again. So he would.

He had developed, and kept developing, new tricks with the stones. Which meant he had a fair repertoire, so he was not showing the same tricks in place after place.

He spent freely, though he drank less than he appeared to. Which gave him another reputation, that of a man with a hard head for wine.

"THERE ARE FEWER RUMOURS about your death or desertion now, Qedrim. There are still a few who insist they've seen some fellow in disguise doing clever illusions. That, however, we can live with. Thank you for your efforts."

"It wasn't much. Nothing at all, Lady; and it gave me more practice."

"But I've made you into a sort of performing bear, or the like. And now a lot of people are saying you're a show-off. It's not fair to you; you've done so much more than that."

Any residual rancour Qedrim might have felt melted away. "Lady, I've done difficult things for you; why should I balk at something so easy?"

Which brought a fuller smile. "Lord Qedrim, you have been a real gift to me! Thank you once more!"

"CLOTHES? WHAT D'YOU mean, I need new clothes?"

"Qedrim, friend, housemate, you have perhaps not noticed that your outfit, which was once quite nice, is in sad disrepair? And while I'm not the picture of sartorial elegance that Malsan'to thinks he is, I still manage to keep my knees from showing through my trousers."

"You think I should dress fancy, as if I were some Lord or something?"

"Qedrim, friend, you are a Lord. Or had you forgotten? And while no one thinks you should become an ostentatious spectacle. A little care for your appearance would do well."

"So suppose the two of you come along and give me some advice? I could simply order another suit like this one was when it was new, but I suspect you have something different in mind."

When he showed up in his new suit, he was pleased to see Lady Annavristi smile at him.

"WE NOW HAVE SOME REASONABLE figures for B'tlas' army," Gwothernan said. He looked down at the piece of paper in front of him, then up at the gathered council.

"Eight thousand men. These include six hundred horse. Eight hundred in the phalanx, most of the rest light infantry of various sorts. And a thousand pottery men.

"Most likely estimate for our own force is six thousand. So the odds are against us, and when you include the pottery men, we are badly outnumbered."

He paused and looked around once more. "However, there is no denying we took this town, Lakvos'ta, against bad odds. Without deluding ourselves, we could see this as a possible victory. Qedrim, are you capable of using your stones for us?"

"Capable, Lord Gwothernan. But in this town we had a fight limited to the width of a street, bounded by walls. A battlefield would be a different matter."

"Yes, indeed. The main question is deployment. We could have you fight against one section of the enemy line, perhaps two. Or, given a fast horse and rapid judgment, perhaps three. I would prefer to have you opposite the pottery men. Knowing you were supporting them would hearten the men in that sector.

"That sounds wise, so far as I can see. I'm not a military man; I'll go by what you say."

"Fine. Now, are there any other questions?"

"Yes, I have one," declared Sobeldanser. "This man, who has been given Lordship and precedence, will skulk behind the lines, safe from enemy blades?"

"What would you have, Sobeldanser? Put him up front, where some fool archer can put an arrow in his guts, and prevent him from giving us any help at all? Surely you know enough tactics to see he must be protected in order to serve best?"

Sobeldanser sat, glowering quietly. Qedrim could tell he wouldn't have been satisfied. Not even if 'this man' were out in front of the line in some 'honourable' position. In fact, if Qedrim were in such a position, Sobeldanser would find it to be an insult to his own honour. On the other hand, if he were behind the lines, he was "skulking," manifestly a coward, unworthy of the trust being put in him.

For Qedrim to point this out to him would only make him all the angrier. He reminded himself that he had already marked Sobeldanser as a man to be watched.

THE ARMY OF HIGFROD was marching again.

This time, Qedrim was near the front, in the same vicinity as Lady Annavristi and Lord Gwothernan. His rank as Close Friend meant he could no doubt ask for the Kharmista's time, and be able to talk to her.

That was a nice thought, but he did not avail himself of the chance. What had he to talk to her about? The paucity of the crop from the land he owned?

Nonsense! He was a lifter and mover of stones, little more. He did not have the military expertise Gwothernan had. Not even as much as Thaldo—wherever he was back there in the column—that he should have anything useful to say to her. Come to think of it, he had less military expertise than she did herself. No, he had nothing to say to her, much as he might wish to have.

One advantage to his present status was he heard news shortly after it came to the Lady. Which relieved him of the necessity to sort through two dozen rumours to work out what was most likely. This, in turn, meant he heard, every night, of the likely position of the enemy. And also, the probable time before the Gafrodi were facing the enemy on a battlefield.

Since his knowledge of local geography and landmarks was minimal, none of this news meant much to him except the time-estimates.

Then one evening they found themselves camped with the enemy over the next rise. Sentries ringed and guarded their camp, while parties of light horse scouted forward. While a night attack was not likely, it was still possible.

Qedrim also knew that, though the Gafrodi had picked up a few hundred more men in the course of the march, they were still badly outnumbered. It was now confirmed that B'tlas had a thousand pottery men with him. Their mere presence was worth a larger number in terms of morale.

Qedrim took advantage of his status to speak in the planning session the night before the battle. "Lady, I have a notion. Well, more like an expansion on your notion of juggling stones in the wineshops of Lakvos'ta."

She looked at him with interest. "Go on."

"Suppose we collect an assortment of the men, and I do some juggling for them. Not sling-stones, real boulders. Then we send them back to their regiments, let them pass the word as to what they saw. It may only help a little, but a little is better than nothing."

She looked at Gwothernan. It seems like a good idea. Lord Gwothernan?"

He smiled slightly. "Yes, as he says, whatever little help it might be is still help."

THE FIRE LIT THE SCENE, groups of men, of all units, sitting or standing and waiting. The stolid men of the phalanx were marked by their calm patience. There were others, such as the light infantry. Some were even painted with the body paint they would wear into battle tomorrow. The whole group was a selection of the army which would be fighting next day.

"First thing," Qedrim said to them, "I want you to be sure there's no trickery here, no fake stones, no wires. Pick ten or so among yourselves to come up here and look at these stones, feel them, make sure it's all on the up-and-up. Go ahead, make your choices."

"First thing," Qedrim said to them, "I want you to be sure there's no trickery here, no fake stones, no wires. Pick ten or so among yourselves to come up here and look at these stones, feel them, make sure it's all on the up-and-up. Go ahead, make your choices."

He waited with patience as they talked among themselves. He could have picked out some by pointing at them. But having them pick their own representatives made the tests that much more persuasive.

Of course there might be some who would think the choice of witnesses had been rigged, and there were ways he could have done that. However, Qedrim hoped most reasonable men would be convinced. He further hoped they would take that conviction back to their units, and pass the word.

At length several pikemen and a larger number of light infantry, archers, and slingers came forward. They hefted the stack of head-sized stones Qedrim had gathered, felt them all over for wires, and finally pronounced themselves satisfied there was no deceit here.

"Now," Qedrim said, "I hope none of you have been foolish enough to bet against me. And if you have, I hope you've made it a big bet, because it'll serve you right when you lose!"

There was scattered laughter.

"Off we go, then," One of the stones lifted and flew, swooping around Qedrim. One after another, they lifted and soared, until six of them were flying around him, just above the level of his head.

He waved the stones into a line. Although no hand-gestures were really needed, and had them swoop down abruptly at the audience. The stones sweeping by a little over their heads, forcing them to duck wildly. A moment later the stones came back again, higher this time, and resumed their flight around Qedrim's head.

"You notice, I'm not laughing at you. You saw stones coming at you, and you ducked. Any man of sense would. Just think how B'tlas' men will be ducking when these things come at them.

"Now, does anyone want to see any special tricks?"

"Stand 'em up on your head!"

Qedrim brought the stones up to stack just over his head.

"Anything else?"

"Stick 'em up B'tlas' arse!" called a rough-voiced slinger.

Qedrim grinned. "That's for tomorrow's show."

There were other calls, for other maneuvers. So Qedrim obediently brought the stones into various formations. He marched them and counter-marched them through the air, stacked them and spun them.

He heard one of the phalanx-commanders call out, "Too bad your lot aren't that good on drill, Basaldo!"

Finally he set them down. "That's it, lads. I've got to save some strength for tomorrow."

By the time the men had left for their units, Qedrim was sweating.

"You haven't worn yourself out, Qedrim." Qedrim looked up at Gwothernan. He heard in the words not so much concern for Qedrim himself as more a concern for a weapon Gwothernan was going to need the next day.

"Let me sleep until dawn, I'll be fine."

IN ACTUAL FACT HE WAS still groggy when they woke him at dawn. He had a bit to eat, then got his horse.

The army was falling into position, making ready to advance in the formation in which it would meet the enemy.

Fatigue parties had filled two ox-carts with stones the size of his two fists. Boulders were fine for some purposes. But Qedrim, thought he could do as much damage with smaller sized stones and was able to keep them moving longer.

The oxcarts bumped and creaked behind him, and he kept his eyes open for when they had their first sight of the enemy. He was just a little left of the centre of the line. It had been arranged that light cavalry patrols would go forward, and hurry back to say where the pottery men were in the Dauri battle-line. Then Qedrim could move there, as quickly as his horse could go without him falling off.

'And those oxcarts aren't going to be able to move very fast. I might have to grab some stones as I go.'

A light horseman was galloping up from the left, now, along the front of the line. Guessing this was the man who was to direct him to his proper place, Qedrim turned his own horse in that direction.

Sure enough, the man, a tough-looking grizzled old fellow, pointed one hand toward Qedrim's left, and cupped the other hand round his mouth.

"They're about a bowshot that way!"

"Right!"

'Just like an archer to say things in terms of the range of a bow! How far will a bow shoot, anyhow?'

He turned his horse and began to trot down the line. No, the ox-arts weren't going to be able to keep up. He whisked some stones out of the nearest one, and brought them over with him, a score or so. It was feasible for him to send each one separately, but that might wear him down too soon. His best plan was to get them into a line and send them back and forth through the enemy as many times as he could manage.

Now the enemy were in sight, coming this way as rapidly as the Gafrodi were approaching them. Yes, the pottery men, moving in their deceptively clumsy fashion, could be made out. He was still not quite there. The pottery men were on left flank of a force of light infantry, spear and shield, with a hatchet or short sword for when things got too close.

An idea came to him. Not part of the plan, but still...

He swung his score of stones out into a line and sent them into the Dauri light infantry. Not head on, but angling back to his right.

He saw the light infantry fall into disorder, men went down, others stopped, a few even fled altogether. Now the Gafrodi were nearing close quarters—-

"Old Woman's Apron!"

He turned back to his right. The pottery men were still a short distance away, but he had wasted more time than he'd thought. He whipped another score of stones out of the nearest oxcart, flung them into a rough line. Then sent them over the heads of the Gafrodi, diving for the shins and ankles of the pottery men.

He brought them whipping back, again at shin level, and had to pull them up rapidly to avoid hitting his own men. Now he brought them down again. This time to shoulder height, slamming down hard on pottery heads and shoulders.

The Gafrodi light infantry, despite all promises and demonstrations, were having trouble dealing with an enemy who, even without armour, absorbed stroke after stroke without obvious harm.

He could see another flaw in the Gafrodi plan. Dust.

The field was mostly grass, but even so, that many feet moving, stepping stamping, caused dust to rise. In short order it was difficult to see far down the line, see if there was a section which needed help more than this one.

Should he go look? No, his tomfoolery had already cost some small part of the advantage his ability gave them. Best stay here and pound, up and down, up and down, watch the occasional pottery man crumble to fragments.

Abruptly the pottery men's line was too thin. The light infantry were surging in among them and striking hard. Too many blows for the enemy to absorb.

Qedrim trotted further to the left, and came on a spot where the Gafrodi were starting to give way in front of the continue press of the enemy. He paused, and began crashing his stones down on heads and shoulders.

Urgently, as though by sheer force of will and hammering of stones he could throw the pottery men back, he went to work. His breath was coming in gasps by the time the pottery line was weakened enough for the Gafrodi to come through.

When he moved again, he found himself in a spot where the Gafrodi had either been killed or driven away. Leaving the pottery men to swing in against the exposed flank.

Again Qedrim went to work wildly, using his stones and his strength with abandon. He wouldn't be able to keep this up much longer. But if the Gafrodi, attacked front and flank, gave way, the battle might well be done.

There were horsemen in the dust beyond the pottery men.

Old Woman's Apron! All he knew about battle tactics was the bits and pieces he'd picked up. But it was sensible for B'tlas to send in cavalry to exploit a gap in the Gafrodi line.

Then things changed in the blink of an eye as the cavalry struck into the rear of the pottery men, swords rising and falling. The enemy spinning and falling away, some of them even breaking up.

Raising and lifting the fist-sized stones was becoming an intolerable burden on him. He paused for a moment, and felt himself begin to fall. He grabbed hold of the reins, turned the fall into an clumsy sprawl.

Qedrim found himself sitting on the ground, without the strength to rise again. Somewhere over there his stones were lying on the ground unheeded.

He found another one and began to raise it and bring it down. The arrival of the Gafrodi cavalry from behind the Dauri line suggested that they were victorious off on the right flank. But the pottery men here were still fighting. They would do so until the last of them were smashed, or until their master called them off. Or until he was killed.

The stone slipped and fell, and he lacked the strength to raise it again. Qedrim did not lose consciousness this time. He only lost the will to do anything but sit and watch the fight. Meanwhile, idly wondering if some shift of the battle would find him sitting in the midst of the pottery men, one of whom would surely finish him off.

Even when the fighting was done, the pottery men marched off, ignoring the cavalry harassing them, he continued to sit there. He thought of many things he might have done better. None of this brought him any comfort.

Chapter 9

"Lord Qedrim?"

Qedrim looked up. It was a light horseman. He was little more than a boy, with bow in hand, and a quiver at his saddle still containing a half-dozen bright-feathered arrows. From the look of his face, battle had not been what he'd imagined, nothing at all. Yet he was up and following orders. Or perhaps it was because he had orders to carry out that he could and would go on.

"Lord Qedrim, the Lady sent me to look for you. Some feared you might not have survived. Are you hurt?"

"No, I'm not hurt. And I suppose I survived, if this might be called surviving."

"If you wish, Lord, you could ride with me."

"Ride with you? Well, that's a thought. But I'm still holding on to my horse, and I suppose if I can get myself up and onto him, I could manage. Just give me a moment. No. Don't bother getting down, I should be able to do this myself."

His horse, which had stood calmly hitched to the reins in his hand, sidled a bit as Qedrim tried to mount. He sprawled across the animal's back, hauling himself bit by bit into a more or less proper seat in the saddle.

The next difficulty was staying in the saddle as they moved. They went at a light canter. Qedrim held on with his knees as tightly as possible, and shortly came to the fire where the Lady and all the other commanders were gathered.

Gwothernan frowned slightly at Qedrim, then turned to the Lady. She had removed her armour, but it was clear she had taken part in the day's battle. Her expression was only a little less dazed than that of the young light horseman who had fetched Qedrim.

"Lady, I believe we are all present or accounted for."

"Thank you Gwothernan. Lords, we have come through this day, and B'tlas is driven from the field. There is no question this time of a drawn battle.

"However, our own losses have been severe. Definite numbers are not yet available, but we appear to have lost between a quarter and a third of our troops.

"We cannot afford another battle soon, and preferably we will not fight again until next year. But then again, B'tlas will not be fighting soon either. He appears to be retreating toward Daura. He will not wish to shut himself up in Higfrod, deep in hostile territory.

"I understand that it's very soon after a terrible battle to make plans for future moves. But I am led to understand that B'tlas has left a large garrison in the city of Higfrod. But what effect the outcome of today's battle will have on them is not yet determined.

"However, whether the garrison fights or surrenders, I believe we can muster sufficient force to take the town."

She paused. "Lords, gentlemen, soldiers, all, I congratulate you."

Worn, weary, battered and used up, they could still manage a cheer for their Lady.

"YOU BUGGERED IT UP, Qedrim! Not quite badly enough to lose us the battle, but you buggered it up! All you had to do was concentrate your work on the pottery men! But you had to go for the flash! Throw a few rocks down at the enemy who were out of your territory. You gave the pottery men time to get at the men you were supposed to be supporting."

Gwothernan was blazing angry. But, Qedrim, who had not yet had a chance to sleep, was barely capable of staring at him blankly.

"Destroyer's Teeth! You don't have anything to say? You don't even realize how badly you've buggered it up! Say something, Morrkerr eat you!"

"Seemed like a good idea at the time," Qedrim muttered. The trouble was, he'd known he'd buggered it up. Known from the instant he turned from admiring the confusion he'd caused among B'tlas' light infantry to see how close the pottery men were. All the time that he was frantically trying to make up for his error he'd known he might be the cause of their defeat.

"Seemed like a good idea?! You Morrkerr-eaten little gamester! You were gaming with men's lives! with the Kharmista's life!

"You're not supposed to have good ideas! You're supposed to carry out your part——!"

A fist-sized stone landed with a thump at Gwothernan's feet, and he stopped to look at it.

"I was wrong," Qedrim admitted. "I was wrong and we all nearly paid for it. But I'm tired, and I don't need you to dress me down as though I were one of your troopers who'd showed up on parade with a rust-spot on his sword.

"In case you want to know, I'll have to live with what went on out there, and I know it. And I'm tired, so save your words. I'm going to find a bed."

IT DIDN'T MAKE HIM feel that much better to know that the losses taken against the pottery men, while a considerable part of the total, were nowhere near most. He'd still made a mistake, been just a little too confident about what he could do.

Qedrim considered asking for an interview with the Lady. He was willing to offer to give up his titles as punishment for his error. The Lady was already too busy with planning for the next move, seeing to the state of the army, and all the things that went with being the Kharmista. She had no time to grant him absolution, even if absolution would have helped him any.

He managed a more or less calm interview with Lord Gwothernan. Gwothernan had managed to compose himself enough to realize that Qedrim had an ability no one else possessed, and therefore could not be summarily dealt with. Better to work matters out so that difficulties didn't happen again.

"There's a difficulty with our battles. So much dust gets stirred up that in time you can't see where you ought to be. I'm not using this as an excuse; it wasn't until the battle had been going on for a while that the dust became a problem. We'll want to think about that for the future."

Gwothernan nodded. "It should have occurred to me before. We'll have to take that into consideration."

That was that. "Well," Qedrim thought, "perhaps we simply weren't fated to become drinking-companions."

The army camped there for several days, just off the battlefield. Their light horse patrolled for miles around them. One party was shadowing B'tlas' army. The Kharmost was surely heading for home, but Gwothernan was not about to take the chance of him deciding to do something else.

Another party of light horse went off to the city of Higfrod, to inform the garrison of the battle's result and to call them to surrender. "We don't expect much to come of that," Gwothernan told the assembly. "It's merely a matter of doing the standard things. Who knows, the garrison just might surrender to a party of horse-archers."

A chuckle arose from the group.

Qedrim thought the party might have had more luck if he had accompanied it. The rumours would have come to Higfrod regarding the fall of Lakvos'ta, and of the flying stones in the recent battle. If he were to throw a couple of stones at the walls, the garrison <u>could</u> surrender to a party of horse-archers.

However, he had still been in a state of deep depression when that party had been sent out. Besides, he suspected Gwothernan, was still too angry to trust Qedrim on such a mission.

SHAPAK-AILESH APPEARED in the camp. He came trudging over a hill, leading his mule, looking as though he had travelled several leagues that day. Qedrim, who happened to be nearby, suspected he had come by his Hidden Ways to somewhere. Perhaps just over the hill. Perhaps over the hill just beyond that, and trudged from there.

There was nothing especially unusual about his coming to the army. Several other peddlers and merchants had made their way out to the camp since the battle. Shapak-ailesh's only distinction was his size.

He sold nothing out of the ordinary. Merely a selection of simple talismans, a bit of wine, whetstones, this and that.

From all Qedrim could tell, he did not appear to deal in any considerable magics at all, only little things. Finally, of course, he ended up outside the tent Qedrim shared with the two Lords. Having become used to each other's company, they had continued to share lodgings. At this particular time, the two Lords were elsewhere, so Qedrim greeted his visitor alone.

"Ah, most noble slinger, hero of stormings and battles, hurler of great rocks! Your firestarter still performs well, I trust?"

Qedrim, still touchy about the battle and his part in it, took the greeting as a jibe. But the sudden change of topic took him by surprise.

"Firestarter? What firestarter?"

"Ah, he has forgotten, so soon! In the midst of winter rains, on the rough trail out of the hills towards Ga'tuitos! This humble soul sold you a talisman guaranteed to start a fire even with the wettest wood."

Qedrim had indeed forgotten. He did not feel disposed to be polite and friendly, though. "Oh, yes. And overpriced, too, as I recall."

The little man put on a hurt expression. "Only the best of quality, O Lord, and for the best of quality one must expect to pay."

"And so I did. Now what do you want?"

"Ah, he has become so brusque and rude, the young slinger on the road, living by his wits alone! Perhaps it is that the reward has not been completely paid."

Qedrim held back a scathing retort about the fact that the prospect of a marriage the Kharmista with himself was extremely unlikely. Though there didn't seem to be anyone in earshot, he knew you didn't say things in supposed privacy in camp that you didn't want to want to hear coming back dressed up in various styles.

"No, I think I've messed things up quite well on my own. Or do I blame you for all this?"

"Ah, he seeks someone to blame! Tell me, if, as one presumes, the world goes on tomorrow, and the next day, and the day after that, what will you do? And how?"

"I suppose I'll have to go on as I have been," Qedrim muttered, grouchily.

"As you have been? Ah, but which of you? The lame but canny gambler with the eye always to money, or the one who has found someone besides himself to care for?"

Qedrim almost reached out and shook the little man for saying such things in camp. What kinds of rumours would be going round after this?

The little man only looked at him. "Ah, he worries! Do not fear, O nervous young slinger. Do you think one with my resources would allow my words to be overheard and reported? If anyone who passes by is asked what we talked about, all he will have is vague memories that it was 'the usual thing.'

"Now, as to my question?"

As Shapak-ailesh spoke, Qedrim was thinking of how he'd failed the Lady. Then a thought occurred to him. This burden he felt, what must she feel, with the whole of the army, all its losses, all on her back? So if he moped around feeling sorry for himself, what use would he be to her or to anyone? Yes, he'd messed things up, and badly. What now? Go through the rest of his life with this one battle as a weight on his shoulders, or take a lesson from it and go on?

He looked at Shapak-ailesh with suspicion. "Have you done something to me?"

"I? Do something to you? Never, O great and powerful Lord! All I have done is to speak words. That you listened and heeded was all your doing."

"It was you who brought me to Higfrod, you embroiled me in all this!"

"Ah, well, yes," admitted Shapak-ailesh. "I took the liberty of bringing you to Higfrod. However, all your embroilments, as you call them, were done by yourself. Taking decisions of your own, with no one but yourself directing those actions."

"So. Well, suppose we go back to your question. I will go on. The Lady has come to expect certain things of me. I will not disappoint her. As for ridiculous notions of marriage, leave that aside. I'm a foreigner who's been granted noble status here for some things I've done, but that's all."

"Ah, and now the Great Lord is modest as well!" The little man held up a hand to forestall anything Qedrim might say. "No more! I have in my pack a jug of fine wine, one which I guarantee will not have been seriously harmed by travelling. I had planned to sell it to some Royal Court for ten gold coins. I am willing, however, to part with it for a mere ten silvers."

"Ten silvers? Is it, too, guaranteed to start a fire with the wettest wood? Five silver, if it's drinkable at all, and not the sort of vinegar that goes to the soldiers."

"You wrong me, Most Noble! Wrong me most terribly! This is a wine the like of which you have never tasted. I am cheating myself to offer it as low as eight silver."

The final price was six silver and four coppers, on condition that Qedrim had satisfied himself that the wine was acceptable.

Shapak-ailesh went rummaging in his mule-packs. Muttering as he did so, about merchandise that went into hiding when it was most needed. Even when it was sold for a terribly low price. At last he brought out a wax-sealed jug and handed it to Qedrim. Qedrim tasted it, and agreed that it was indeed an acceptable wine. Better than anything available in camp, save perhaps at the Kharmista's own table. He paid over the coins and took the jug inside.

He had a few sips of it, and saved the rest to share with Malsan'to and Genilabas that evening.

"Where did you come by this?" inquired Genilabas. "Have you been raiding the Kharmista's stores?"

"Bought it from a little pedlar. Good, isn't it?"

"'Good?' That's like saying the Kharmista's palace is 'a big house.' Wouldn't you say so, Geni?"

"At least. But consider this, Malsa; he's sharing it with us. This means we'd best stay friends with him. He can share all sorts of things with us as he rises in the Kharmista's favour."

"Hah! I'm about as high in her favour as I'm likely to get. Don't hold your breath waiting for me to share everything with you, you greedy sot."

AT LAST THEY MARCHED on the city of Higfrod. The army were in bright spirits, for all the losses they had taken. They were now the twice-victorious army of Higfrod, despite B'tlas and his pottery soldiers.

"From the sound and look of them, you'd think they need only make an appearance, give a shove of their hand to make the city gates swing open," Gwothernan said.

"Perhaps they do. Or perhaps they expect All-Powerful Qedrim to juggle a few stones for the garrison and have them open the gates." Qedrim muttered darkly.

Gwothernan glanced at him. Relations between the two continued to be strained.

The Lady spoke up, as though she didn't realize she was stepping in to prevent argument between her commander and his very important weapon. "Better to have the men in good spirits than bad. And the garrison may well be in the mood for surrender when Qedrim gives them a show. They'll have heard overly inflated tales of him. To know he is real might just be the incentive they need to surrender."

Qedrim limited himself to thinking that the reality behind the stories was much different. And, likely much less impressive, than the stories.

THEIR LIGHT HORSE BROUGHT back the word that the Dauri garrison in Higfrod had refused to surrender.

Gwothernan merely shrugged. "Well, that was never more than a vague hope. I wonder what they'll make of Qedrim. Will you be ready to give a demonstration for them, Qedrim?"

"Oh yes, I can do that for sure. We'll have to see how impressive I can be."

TWO DAYS LATER THEY were before the walls of the city itself.

"You have some idea what you want to try to do, Qedrim?"

"Oh, I think I can manage something."

He was almost a little disappointed when Gwothernan merely looked at him sternly, nodded, and turned away.

So he rode down with a herald for company, to a place within clear sight of the walls, but out of bowshot.

The herald went a little further forward, to be sure of being heard from the walls.

"Soldiers of Daura!" the herald called. "You will know that your Kharmost has been defeated, and has withdrawn to his own city!

"The Lady Annavristi, Kharmista of Higfrod, calls on you to surrender! Before you respond, however, please watch the following demonstration!"

Qedrim had brought no stones with him. This for the same reasons that he had invited the Gafrodi soldiers to examine the stones he used when he'd demonstrated his abilities for them. He couldn't exactly invite the garrison to inspect the stones he used, so he did the next best. As they had approached, and as the herald spoke, he had made note of several usable stones. Now, one after the other, he wrenched them from the earth, and held them floating over his head.

That done, he set them to moving. The stones forming and reforming patterns, marching and counter-marching, whirling, dancing around him.

Finally he sent them flying over to the city walls, and landed them softly beside the wall, and left them sitting. They would be reminders for the people who manned that part of the wall, a reminder of the sort of thing they faced.

He looked at the herald. "Ask them now."

"Yes, Lord." The herald turned back to the walls and called out, "Men of Daura, will you surrender? The Lady promises you will be allowed to depart unhindered!"

Silence lingered for a long while.

Then an archer stood up and launched an arrow, well off to their right. It was only a signal of refusal, though a strong one. Attacking a herald or a member of a party coming to parley would result in a slaughter the defenders if the city were taken.

"Hah!" Qedrim took his sling from his belt. Then dropped one of his special stones in it, and slung the stone toward the wall, close to the now-hidden archer. It was an impossible distance for a sling, and the watchers from the walls would know that. When the stone hit the wall, flinging up a spray of stone chips, sparks and mortar, he felt the lesson would not be lost.

"Now," he said to the herald, "let's get back."

"SO NOW WE ATTACK. OR do we try to starve them out?" Sobeldanser was grim. "They seem not at all impressed by rock-juggling."

Gwothernan frowned, but ignored the gibe at Qedrim, and spoke to the actual statement. "A siege is possible, but not desirable.

We want the city reasonably whole, with as little harm to the people as possible.

"And further, though I hope it will go no further than this assembly, there is a small possibility B'tlas might send out an army, if he hears we're sitting siege here. It's not the sort of risk he takes. But to depend on your enemy to continually follow a certain pattern is to invite surprise and defeat."

He paused. "Now, we know that the garrison is little more than a thousand, and we are fairly certain there are none of those pottery men inside. They are not suited for garrison work, and B'tlas likely took all of them out when he came to meet us. We already have parties making onagri and ballistae, as well as towers and ladders. We will assault the walls as soon as is practicable."

"What do we need for catapults?" asked Sobeldanser, keen to have his taunts noticed. "We have Qedrim on our side."

"Oh, don't fear, Lord Sobeldanser, Qedrim will be doing his part. You see to it that you do yours."

QEDRIM STOOD AT A SUFFICIENT distance from the wall that no arrow could reach him. He unwound his sling, put one of the special stones into it, whirled it three times round his head and let fly.

There had been a head barely showing at that point, but the man had ducked down again. It might be possible...

As the stone went over the top of the wall, Qedrim reached out to it. He then curved its path, and brought it back to hit the wall where he guessed the man might be. It was all done against an unseen target, but he thought it likely he'd hit the man. After all, the fellow would most likely duck down, not move to the side as well.

If, after a while, everyone up on the wall got used to having to not only duck, but move as well, it could only be to the good for the army of Higfrod. He did the same thing twice more. Though he could never be sure of a hit, he knew he had given them something to think about.

Then there was movement up on the wall, and he saw them setting up a ballista. It was much like a bow, but the arms were powered with twisted ropes, not springy wood. Depending on how it was built, it could shoot either large arrows or stones up to the size of two fists.

They were having some difficulty setting it up without any of them revealing themselves, and he figured he'd gotten two men. Though they had each ducked below the wall.

This ballista had a sort of shield built on the front, making it a bit unwieldy, but a little safer for its crew. It occurred to him that he could hit the crew, now and then. But they would merely replace the men and continue to work the thing.

At about that moment, the ballista launched an arrow. He moved over a little, and saw the thing bury itself in the dirt, just off from where he'd been standing. That was another thing about the ballista. It was most effective against masses of men, when aim at one particular person wouldn't matter.

He looked down at his sling.

'You only got the one trick, Qedrim?'

He looked around, spotted a head-sized stone, and sent it at the wall, speeding it up as it went. The crew could dodge, but the ballista couldn't, nor could the crew move it quickly enough. Wood splinters flew, twisted ropes spun free, broken pieces of wood went in all directions.

"There!" Qedrim said, "Take that!"

"I HAVE A NOTION, BUT I'm not sure I've got it all worked out."

"Yes?" Gwothernan's tone of voice indicated willingness to listen, at least.

"Suppose I get some stones up there, go after anyone who shows themselves along a whole section of wall. At the same time, we get the rest of the army going up against that wall with ladders. I might just be able to give our people a chance to go up and over."

"I suggested something like that for Lakvos'ta and you rejected it."

"I wasn't sure, then, what my abilities might allow. Still not, really. But I'd be willing to do some trials, see what works."

A VAST PART OF THE Gafrodi army advanced in columns toward the walls of Higfrod. The advance parties carried scaling ladders.

Ballistae appeared on the walls, and Qedrim went to work with some fist-sized rocks. Sending the rocks flying toward the walls, each aimed at one of the engines. The ballistae barely got into action when the flying stones reduced them to wrecks of wood and rope.

There were still men up on the wall, though, and some were armed with bows and slings. They could also still topple scaling ladders.

Qedrim assembled five big stones, each about the size of a man's head, and sent them floating toward the wall. The relatively slow approach was deliberate, to allow the men on the wall time to see the stones approach.

He held the stones up there, equally spaced, about five feet above the wall. A few men on the wall stood stupidly staring at the things, while Qedrim brought the stones down hard on the inside of the wall. Then he moved them from right to left about a foot below the wall, then back again, and up to their previous positions.

"Got a few, taught the rest to keep their heads down," Qedrim thought.

It would have been nice to have taught the lesson once, and had it hold long enough for the first of the Gafrodi to come over the wall. But he knew that was unlikely. When the ladders hit the walls, the defenders would be up to deal with them.

So it proved. When the ladders hit the walls men stood to deal with them. Again, Qedrim brought the stones down hard. He moved them rapidly four feet over, then six back, keeping this motion up inside the wall.

When the Gafrodi reached the top of the ladders, he lifted the stones and held them. With any luck, the Dauri would be so confused and intimidated they wouldn't rise fast enough to face the men who were coming over.

Mostly that seemed to be the case, but Qedrim muttered "Old Woman's Apron!" as he saw a ladder full of men pushed out and away from the wall.

He had been holding his stones in place just in case he saw an opportunity, and he used this chance. Qedrim brought all his stones over to this section of the wall. Then he brought the stones in fast and hard toward the wall. Bringing them out, and back in again. He continued to do this, preventing the Dauri from standing to attack men on the other ladders.

Though they managed to topple the one ladder, that was the only success, partial though it was, on the defenders' side. As more Gafrodi took to the ladders and swarmed up the walls, the outcome became more and more certain.

At last came a shout, "They've opened the Dog's Head Gate!"

More Gafrodi went forward shouting, heading toward the gate, and in. After that it was only a matter of waiting.

Smoke began to rise in various parts of the city. Someone muttered, "They've set fire to it rather than let us have it."

Gwothernan snorted. "I'd be willing to bet a few of those fires have been started by our own loyal soldiers. Seems like when men get their blood up, setting fires is one thing they like to do. Even if it means their own countrymen will be burned out because of it."

About mid-afternoon, a man came hurrying out of the gate. As he approached, he could be distinguished as a light infantryman. Sweaty and smeared with dirt and blood, he flung himself down at the Kharmista's feet. "Lady, Higfrod is yours once more!"

"Thank you, soldier." she looked around. "Someone find this man a drink of wine."

Gwothernan was already giving orders to the commander of the infantry reserve. "Get some parties fighting those fires! We don't want to present the Kharmista with a charred ruin."

"Yes, Lord."

Qedrim stood there, breathing deeply. He hadn't worn himself out this time, not nearly. But he'd still be glad to find a bed. He had a sudden feeling he'd like Gwothernan to say, "Well done, Qedrim," but he knew there wasn't much chance of that. Probably the best he could expect was that the Commander would not make any specific mention of the ladder that had been knocked over despite Qedrim's efforts.

Even losing one ladder full of men was somewhere around ten times less than usual, perhaps better.

It wasn't for several hours that he decided he might as well go into the city. "All the fighting's done, I'm not likely to catch a sword by accident." he thought.

He had no commander to forbid him, save for perhaps Gwothernan. And since the battle was done, the only reason Lord Gwothernan would interfere with Qedrim's movements would be sheer perversity. Whatever Lord Gwothernan's other faults, that was not one of them.

A great deal of the city had been untouched by the battle. The fighting had been restricted to certain districts, where the garrison had gathered, or rallied, in their attempts to hold the city, or to try making its taking too expensive for the Gafrodi.

Qedrim found his feet taking him on the route to the Copper Bowl, the wineshop where he had run his first games back when he'd first come to the city.

Though much of the city had shut and locked itself up pending the final results if the Gafrodi attack, the Copper Bowl had already opened. This was no big surprise to Qedrim. It had struck him as the sort of place that might have stayed open during the battle itself, were the proprietor not certain soldiers roused by battle would likely take what they wanted with no thought of such petty matters as payment.

The owner would, however, cut what corners he could and run a few risks just to make a bit more money. Qedrim felt this line of reasoning uncomfortably close to his own, about a year or so ago. It was not so uncomfortable as to prevent him from having a cup of wine, though. He was almost glad he was the only person in the place.

The wine was exceptionally poor stuff, thin and sour, with an aftertaste of some sort he couldn't identify. But it was wine, and it was what was available.

Whatever else its properties, on top of his labours of the morning, it relaxed him almost to the point of falling asleep right on the spot. He wondered if he should show up at the palace, expecting to be fed and housed there. The Kharmista would just be settling in, though. Finding out what had been lost or ruined in her absence. Finding new or old servants too, most likely.

No, going to the palace was a foolish thought, to say the least.

Best he should go back to his tent outside the city. If the Lady desired his presence, she'd send for him. His two tentmates were already in the tent, sleeping, when he arrived. Being as careful as possible not to disturb them, he found his own place and fell asleep himself.

THE NEXT DAY SAW A lot of rushing around. The army, save for some parties kept in the city to maintain order, was returned to its encampment outside the city.

There was much coming and going, with the Lady arranging—or rearranging—affairs in the city. Men who had been part of the rule of the town, the entire state, for all that, under B'tlas' rule, had been cast out of their places. If the people who had served under the Lady could not be found, other worthy persons must be discovered.

"Lord Gwothernan will find it a little more difficult to deal with the place-hunters than with a besieging army," Malsan'to said. "With a besieging army, he can use his sword. With this lot, though they may not be picked for any particular task, they may be necessary for efficiently running the city. And a favour of some kind may be needed some time in the future, from even the least likely of them.

"So their presence must be suffered, at least until the Lady has all the scribes and magistrates she requires, and the rest politely dismissed."

Qedrim found himself a little cheered by the thought of Gwothernan faced with that sort of difficulty.

He himself felt at loose ends. There wasn't much call now for a lifter and hurler of stones. Though he was certain his service would not be forgotten. The Lady was not that sort. Even Gwothernan, for all his faults, would not ignore someone whose services he would need in the future. If only as far off as next year, when B'tlas tried them again.

However, Qedrim had gone through much of the money the Lady had paid him as a reward last year. At some time or another, possibly before she was ready to entertain guests again, he would need more. His only method of earning money was running some sort of game. But without various tricks to make the betting all one-sided, a gambler's living was not likely to be prosperous in the long run.

Not to mention gambling, even without cheating, was not work Close Friends of the Kharmista engaged in.

Second best would be putting on shows for money, making stones dance and the like. But that didn't seem right either.

As he was thinking these sort of morose thoughts, Malsan'to stood. "Come, Lord Qedrim! It's too fine a day to sit in a cool old tent growing mushrooms round the ears! Come on, let's go walk in the city."

"City's still a wreck, Malsa! Not much to be seen."

"Oh, and you know all this without looking? Come along, most Grouchy Lord Qedrim of the Big Stones, or we'll cut the tent ropes and drop it on top of you."

At which Qedrim, despite his dark mood, managed to force a grin. "All right, then, let's go, since you seem intent on pestering me. We can go find a wineshop and I can beggar the both of you by betting I can make stones dance on my fingers." He felt a twinge, recalling times when he would have done just that.

'Close Friends of the Kharmista can't hoodwink their friends. Well, fact is they can actually have friends.'

"But you forget, we know all your secrets! We'd be betting on you, not against you."

"Oh, if we get you drunk enough, I think I can manage to talk you into betting against me."

THE CITY WAS VERY NEAR back to itself again. The dead had been carted outside the city and buried. The markets were open, and there was even some activity in them, with people beginning to trickle in and browsing the tents as the merchants began to set out their wares. Shapak-ailesh had set up shop in one of the markets, selling mostly herbal remedies of one sort or another.

"Look, it's the little pedlar who was selling things in the camp. Where on earth d'you suppose he's from?" wondered Genilabas.

"Hard to say. I've never seen his like. What about you, Qedrim?"

"I've seen him, I've bought a thing or two from him, but I have no idea where he came from."

'And I don't want to know.'

He'd just as soon have gone on by, even if it meant heading right to the Copper Bowl and its poor wine. But Malsa insisted otherwise.

"You, little fellow! Where d'you hail from?"

"Myself, O great Lord? I come from a far country, one which I doubt your grace has heard of."

"What's it called? I'll tell you if I've heard of it."

Shapak-ailesh bowed. "I'm led to believe the name of the place is Ohaza."

"You're led to believe—-! Don't you know?"

Shapak-ailesh bowed again. "Lord, my people travelled a great deal."

"Got you there, Malsa," Geni said with a grin. "Come on, let's go."

"If it is on any interest to you, Lords, I have a skin of wine, of very good quality. Which I am willing to sell exceedingly cheaply."

"Hah! Come on, lads, I've bought 'cheap' things from him, and they weren't cheap." Qedrim steered his friends away from the little man. He heard behind him protests of how he was maligning the name of a poor merchant.

They went off and found a wineshop, not the <u>Copper Bowl</u>, and had several cups of mediocre wine. Despite some urging, Qedrim refused to show any tricks with stones.

They returned to their tent wearing the cheery mood found in the bottom of a wine-cup.

OF COURSE THE LADY had not forgotten Qedrim. Or perhaps she finally remembered him, and a servant came to the tent. Qedrim did not immediately recognize this rather slender man as the Fallash who had served him so long ago. But the first words reminded him, "Qedrim of Arndal, the Lady Annavristi invites you to be her guest at the palace."

"It's Fallash, isn't it?"

The servant looked a little startled. Lords did not usually go out of the way to remember servants' names.

"Yes, Lord."

"Yes. You've changed a bit."

"It's been a difficult year for some of us who served the Lady most closely. I, in my good fortune, had an uncle who had a place in the market, so I was able to eat."

"Yes. Fortunate for you."

'Clearly you didn't eat as much as you were used to.'

"If you will allow me, Lord, I will gather your effects and carry them for you."

"Thank you. I don't have much. I'll carry the sling myself." He grinned at the remembrance of the to-do over the sling and stones last time. But Fallash either did not remember, or chose not to appear to.

When he got to the palace, he did not see the Kharmista, save from a distance, and then mostly at mealtimes. Whatever went into running the kharmosat, apparently there was still more to it when recovering one from someone else's rule. There were scribes here or there, people taking notes. People were writing letters in the Kharmista's name. The Kharmista or Lord Gwothernan or other high-level functionaries people were dictating letters to people.

Three days after having been re-installed in the palace, a servant came to speak to him.

"Lord, there is a businessman named Etchihral, wishing to speak to you, regarding your land."

It took Qedrim a moment to recall exactly what land the man might be referring to, then he recalled the land the Kharmista had awarded to him last year. "Have him sent in." he said, curious as to what this was all about.

The man who came in was short, even for a Gafrod. He was sturdy built and dressed like a merchant. Though seeming well-muscled for a merchant, "Lord, I understand that you own a certain parcel of land, outside the city."

"Yes," said Qedrim, a little warily. "It is mine, but it cannot be sold." Just in case this fellow was some sharper intent on doing Qedrim out of his land.

"Ah, no, I did not wish to purchase it. I wish to inquire, if you'll favour me by saying, is the land being worked at present?"

"No, not as yet." The thought of giving the truthful answer, "I have no notion as to how one goes about farming," was too embarrassing. In the Arndals, one would usually buy a few sheep to run on any land they owned.

"Ah, fine, fine!" Etchihral went so far as to rub his hands. "Suppose I were to offer you forty silver per year for the right to cultivate it?"

"That sounds like an interesting offer, but I wouldn't want to make a hasty decision. Could you come back in two days' time?"

"This is not a proposal to be put off for long, Lord."

Qedrim, recognizing an effort to push him into making a hasty decision, said, "If I must make a decision now, at this moment, the decision would be that I would not deal with you, nor any agent of yours. Will you be willing to wait two days?"

"Yes, Lord, I will wait."

THAT EVENING QEDRIM went searching for his two friends, and tracked them down to a wineshop.

They were both a little merry, but when he explained the offer he'd been given, they seemed to sober up immensely. "Forty silver! He knows you're a foreigner, or he wouldn't even try an offer like that. Push him up to a hundred, and go as low as sixty. Lower than that, he's taking advantage of you." Malsan'to was adamant.

Genilabas agreed. "He's right, Qedrim. The fellow's trying to take advantage. Unless the land is really atrocious, even seventy per year isn't too much."

The day after next when Etchihral appeared, he had clearly decided that Lord Qedrim, though he might be a foreigner, had likely gotten reasonable advice. He did try for forty silver, but when Qedrim countered with a hundred, it took very little effort to close the deal at sixty-five silver per year.

Malsan'to and Genilabas served as witnesses for Qedrim, and two other people, farmers from the look of them, witnessed for Etchihral. They wrote up the contract, then sealed and deposited it for safekeeping in the God's house near to the Main Gate.

Chapter 10

The winter rains came. As the Kharmista's council had done last year in the hills—save for being more comfortable this year—they made plans for the coming year.

"I doubt there are any of us so deluded as to not expect B'tlas to be knocking on our door next year." Gwothernan announced. "We'll want to be ready for that. We have spies working their way into Daura, seeking any information they can discover. We can expect B'tlas is at least building more pottery men.

"This means we will have to gather every soldier we can find."

Lord Gwothernan turned to where Kassibanio sat. "Kassibanio, do you have anything to offer to this group?"

Kassibanio rose. "Not as yet, Lord. I have in mind a notion to find out what B'tlas is up to. If this notion has any success, I will let you know."

"You said once that you distrusted divinations."

"And so I do. What I propose is not really divination, but the plan will take some days, more likely weeks, to put into operation. I would prefer to say nothing more until I have discovered whether or not my plan works."

Gwothernan was silent for a moment, and Qedrim had the impression he was on the verge of demanding to be told just what Kassibanio planned. Then he shrugged. "Very well. Be sure to inform us the moment you have something to tell us."

After the meeting, Kassibanio approached Qedrim. "Young Qedrim, I will need your help."

Qedrim, a little nettled at the immediate presumption that he had nothing better to do—as, indeed, he hadn't—responded, "What if I tell you I'm otherwise engaged?"

The Thawrd Wizard smiled. "I should have to accuse you of shameful mendacity. In this winter season, there is not much else to do save stay out of the rain and gamble your living away. And you do not gamble, do you?"

"Not any longer." Then, in order to prevent any discussion of gambling as it related to himself, he hurried on, "What did you need me for?"

He saw the slight change of the Thawrd Wizard's expression which suggested Kassibanio had noticed his determination to avoid the subject. Kassibanio merely said, "We need to build a new talisman, a Talisman of Uncovering Secrets. I have a feeling B'tlas is preparing something more than simply more pottery soldiers. I would like to find out just what.

"A Talisman of Uncovering Secrets? Does such a thing really exist?"

"Oh, yes, The Talisman of Uncovering Secrets is one of the Higher Orders of Talismans, very tricky to make, and almost as tricky to use right, but it can be done."

"If such a thing is really possible, I'd think you'd carry one with you from-—Wherever you come from."

Kassibanio grinned. "From Askos. But unfortunately the talisman does not work so. The Talisman of Uncovering Secrets must be made in the exact place the talisman is to be used from. I understand there may be allowances of four to five arm lengths in any direction. But if it is moved beyond that, the talisman must be disassembled and remade."

"Why did you not make one back in the Hills? We could have had some notion of B'tlas' plans, then we could remake the thing here."

"Because there are certain items necessary for the talisman's production, such as a freshly-cut emerald. Such things were in short supply in the Hills. Even in Lakvos'ta, asking the Lady to spend some of her already stretched resources on an emerald would have been taken poorly.

"And even now, with the city in her hands, the expenditures we must make will certainly require come convincing and persuasion. I can only hope the end result will justify the expenditure."

A suspicion came to Qedrim. "You aren't simply recruiting me for this so that I can ask the Lady for money to build your Talisman, are you?"

"No, Not at all! I am the one proposing this, I will take the responsibility to see to the funding. I need you because you understand a bit about talismans, and we have worked together on them previously."

"Oh."

QEDRIM FOUND THERE was more to the matter of the emerald than just the stone itself. The emerald had to be one which had not been worn before.

"We're unlikely to get one that has absolutely never been worn before, but the fresher the better. We'll still have to use some purifying spells on the gem. The longer anyone has been wearing the emerald, the more extensive the purification must be. And we will not want to take more time on that than is absolutely necessary."

Even when they had gathered the materials, progress was not swift. Sometimes they had to let the thing sit for a day or more. "To let the materials bond themselves together," Kassibanio said.

"I've never made a talisman that required such fussy work," Qedrim said, realizing as he spoke, he'd never taken pains with making a talisman. Slap the talisman together and sell it, that had been his method.

"Ah, but there are worse ones. I've never made a Talisman of Cool Light, but I understand they require up to six months to build properly. And everything has to go just so. The length of this in proportion to the width of that. So a good deal of work is involved in selection of material, and even more careful trimming."

"I've heard of them. I've heard they're so expensive only Kings can afford them."

"True. And they're expensive because they're so hard to make. Now, have you got that bundle of straws done?"

"'Thirty of them, thumb length, the total, without the cord to tie them, weighing no more than a copper coin.'" He repeated the requirements. "Yes, I've got them done."

AT LAST THE TALISMAN of Uncovering Secrets was ready to use.

"I'd offer to allow you to try the talisman, but it tends to attune itself to the first one who uses the talisman. And we'd end up with me trying to give you instructions as to how to make the talisman seek the things we want."

"Just fine with me. If you mess it up, I can't be blamed. Though Gwothernan might find a way to blame me."

"So," said Kassibanio. Then, looking at the talisman and laying a hand on it, he said, "Talisman, I would know what secrets B'tlas of Daura hides from the world."

There was a small flash of light, and just over the talisman appeared a picture. A small boy, perhaps five summers, carrying a small lap-dog which squirmed in his grasp. He was at the gate of the Royal hunting hounds' compound. He was too small to reach the latch for the gate. But with one hand and his feet, he climbed up a bit, and tossed the lap-dog over the fence.

The throw overbalanced him, and he fell on his buttocks, then scrambled to his feet and ran away.

The hounds, large and fierce, rose up to look at the pampered little intruder.

Kassibanio raised his hand, and the picture faded out.

"So, his great secret is that when he was a small boy, he tossed a pet belonging to his mother, or sister, or whoever, to the hunting hounds."

"I suppose you'll have to be more precise."

"Ah, yes, precise. And if I am too precise, asking the talisman exactly what magical weapon B'tlas prepares against the Lady, I may be shown exactly nothing. Because his preparation is more broad, perhaps aiming at the King, with the Lady only a step along the way."

"Ah, well, one must try something." He put his hand back on the talisman.

"WHY ON EARTH DID THE talisman refuse to respond at all until you asked that particular question, 'What magical weapon does B'tlas plan to use against the Lady next year?' You'd already asked that same question in different words!"

Kassibanio shrugged. "Now, if I knew the answer to that, I'd be able to sit quietly in a little house by the gate and become rich charging a copper to solve anyone's problems for them. I know how the talisman is built and the essentials of how to operate it. But how and why the talisman chooses to show what it shows are far beyond me."

GWOTHERNAN PONDERED. "You cannot show this to the meeting, you say?"

"No, Lord. The Talisman may not be moved, without spending another six weeks remaking it. I doubt if we could crowd the whole of the council into my chambers, and bringing them in a few at a time, until all have seen...."

Gwothernan shook his head. "So. Can you show the talisman at least to me? It would be best if the Lords had the word from someone they know well."

"Yes, I believe that can be done."

KASSIBANIO LAID HIS hand on the talisman and asked, "What magical weapon does B'tlas plan to use against the Lady next year?"

There was a flicker, then the picture leaped up above the wizard's hand. The picture displayed a large beast. The beast had four legs like tree-stumps and large ears which flapped as the beast lumbered along. Long tusks protruding from its mouth, and a trunk which rippled and moved like a snake.

On top of the beast, just behind the head, sat a man. While he was a small figure when compared to the beast itself, the man directed the beast with shouts and pokes from a goad which he held in his hand.

"That is the beast?" demanded Gwothernan.

"Yes, Lord," Kassibanio removed his hand from the talisman, and the picture died out. "I know of it. This beast is called the elephant, and is native to the lands to the east. This, however, is not a real elephant. This beast has been produced in much the same manner as the pottery men, and likely has less intelligence than an ordinary beast. "

"How much intelligence would the beast need? If it is as invulnerable as the pottery men, it could stamp its way through the phalanx, without heeding the pikes."

"The beast has a weakness, Lord."

"And what would that be?" demanded Gwothernan. "The Morrkerr-eaten thing does not even require grain or hay to live on!"

"The weakness is that the beast needs the man on the top to guide it. Kill the man, and the beast is not so dangerous."

"The beast will stop and stand still if the rider is killed?"

"I wish I could say that. No, the beast is most likely to continue walking in a straight line until it falls in a river or a pit somewhere. But if your men know this, they can open ranks and let the beast go through."

"Yes. And all it needs is some lot to be a little slow closing up ranks afterward, and whoever follows, infantry or cavalry, will be able to cut a hole through us and destroy us." He stared at the wall for a bit, then sighed.

"Well, better a small hope than none at all. You're quite sure Qedrim couldn't destroy them with his stones?"

"I doubt it, Lord. By this time, B'tlas will no longer be playing games, attempting to delude us. His forces will be just what they appear to be."

"Including whatever pottery men he may have left?"

"Most likely so. Further, they will have been cut down to those who can't be stopped easily, if at all."

"I see. So we are facing an almost impossible battle?"

"I wouldn't say so. If B'tlas could be killed, or driven from the field, it is likely all his magical constructions will fail there and then."

"Ah," said Gwothernan thoughtfully. "So our tactic for the first battle would be to avoid coming to grips with any pottery beings, man or animal, while trying to reach B'tlas. Or at least drive him from the field."

"Though not a military man, I would say that seems to be a fair assessment of the situation."

"Huh! You would, would you? Well, I'll deal with that. You be ready to tell the council what you've shown me here today."

THE COUNCIL WAS NOT at all happy. They were not happy with the fact that they had not seen, and were not going to witness the revelation Kassibanio had produced for Lord Gwothernan. They were not happy they had to depend on the word of a foreign wizard, and a Thawrd Wizard at that, that the talisman had been operated properly. They were least happy that next year, they would be facing a Dauri army containing not only near-invincible pottery men, but also invincible elephants as well.

Gwothernan, however, was well-practiced at handling a fractious and cantankerous group of nobles, "It will do us no good at all to weep and wring our hands because things are as they are. I have already formulated a tentative plan to take advantage of the enemy weakness. And we will have some time to work at this before we gather up our troops from their farms and villages and march away.

"At that point, it will be up to you to pass on the battle plan to your own troops, and see to it they are ready to follow it."

"What is this plan?" demanded Sobeldanser. "Tell us how you plan to deal with this invincible enemy!"

"The plan is merely a notion, at present, which I will refine before issuing orders. Simply put, we will refuse the flank facing the pottery men, rushing our other flank forward to come to grips with the Dauri. Then we fight our way through, and kill or drive away B'tlas.

"I am told that when B'tlas is killed, or even driven far enough from the battlefield, his pottery creations will cease to move."

Sobeldanser was not pleased. "This is a very simplistic plan, for such an ambitious undertaking!"

"The plan is simple because it needs more thought, which I intend to give it. And I will say nothing further now, unless someone has something concrete to propose."

Sobeldanser opened his mouth to speak, saw Gwothernan's expression, and remained silent. None of the others even hinted at wanting to speak.

"THE LADY REGRETS NOT being able to deliver this in person, Lord Qedrim. But she desires you not live as a pauper after all you have done for her."

The servant was a willow-slim young man, with a studiously blank face. Qedrim suspected he knew what was going on behind the blank face. And while he, himself, disliked the notion of the Kharmista keeping him. He knew the other option, going back to underhanded gambling, was not possible.

So he accepted the money.

AFTER THE THIRD TIME, he found Shapak-ailesh conveniently in his path when he went out. He sighed and approached the little merchant. "And what have you to sell me today?"

"Ah, so terribly fierce and gruff! And never have I sold him anything which was not worth the price and more!"

"Oh, for certain! And never have you approached me without some reason. What is it this time?"

"I'm sure it has occurred to your Lordship that the most mighty and terrible Kharmost of Daura is aware of the presence in the court of the Lady Annavristi of one with the power to hurl stones. And it would be most convenient for the Kharmost if the stone-hurler were removed."

"You're warning me that I'm in danger?" In fact, it had tended to slip Qedrim's mind someone might kill him and claim a fair reward from B'tlas.

'Or maybe even from Sobeldanser.'

"Ah, but of course your Lordship needs no warning! His Lordship is thoroughly alert!"

Qedrim scowled, mostly at himself, and said wryly, "My Lordship is often so concerned about one thing or two, that twelve or more others escape his attention. Shall I assume you have some certain word of an attempt?"

"Ah. Unfortunately the word is not so specific as 'a killer will try to slip a dagger between your ribs on the Leatherworkers' Street at the fourth hour after noon.' But it is certain. Certain enough to wager a great sum on, that an attempt will be made on the life of your Lordship, be it soon or late."

"So. And what do I owe you for the warning?"

"Ah, the warning is free of all charge. But I have in my pack here a shirt you might wish to purchase. This shirt has a charm worked into it sufficient to turn aside most blade-strokes, possibly even an arrow."

"So I should wander about in armour? Even if I could afford it?"

"Ah, this is no metal armour, with its clinking metal, weighing like the mountains! This is a mere shirt of leather, fine and soft, but embroidered with a charm."

"Indeed," said Qedrim, warily. "And for this shirt, a mere hundred gold pieces, I assume?"

"Do you have a hundred gold coins, O Lord? No, no, I will not make rude inquiries. For this item, I ask a mere five coppers."

"Five coppers!" Qedrim was instantly suspicious. "Five coppers would scarcely buy the leather to make a shirt for me. And if one adds in the cost of the magic you say is involved, I couldn't understand how you could possibly afford to sell such a thing for such a price!"

Shapak-ailesh cocked his head to one side. "And are we not taking the wrong parts now? Am I not the one to set a price, which you stigmatize as too high, and make a lower counter-offer? But you are telling me that my price is too cheap." Then he put up a hand to forestall any rejoinder from Qedrim.

"This offer is in the nature of an attempt to win your favour, or goodwill. You would then be more amenable to bargains I might offer in the future. And mostly the shirt is meant to help you stay alive."

"And you care so much that I am kept alive?"

"Ah!" The broad face showed an exaggerated expression of dismay. "But it would be altogether a terrible thing if your Lordship were to die before I had completed the paying of my debt to you."

Qedrim continued to regard the little man. A gift such as this was certainly something more than a mere attempt to gain goodwill. Yet the little man had never before done him harm. It required a very twisted mind to conceive of Shapak-ailesh having done all this merely to make Qedrim less wary.

'And you have just such a twisted mind, don't you, Qedrim?'

"So, then, let me see the shirt."

"Ah, fine, fine! The great Lord is willing to accept this gift! A moment, now!"

Shapak-ailesh began rummaging in his mule's pack, muttering to himself. "Where are you hiding now? No, no, not the Magic Mirror, nor the Sleep potion. No. What is this behind the Bag of Sheep...? Ah, here it is!"

He pulled forth a soft leather bundle and shook it out, revealing a shirt which looked as though it had been tailored specifically for

Qedrim. The dark brown leather was covered with embroidery in a tan thread which showed up well against the background.

The embroidery was curling and interlaced vines, with small flowers spaced regularly along the vines. The vines ran up the front, down the sleeves and back, then all over the back as well.

"Highly decorative."

"Decorative indeed. There is no rule to say that anything must be plain and ugly to be effective magic. Here, put it on."

Qedrim looked around. "To hear you, one would think every third person on this street is a Dauri assassin, bought and paid for, determined to put a knife into me."

"O, assuredly not every third person. Perhaps only every fourth person. No, no, don't take on so, I was joking. But I will declare that you will be safer wearing this shirt, and the sooner you are wearing it, the better I will feel."

So Qedrim pulled the shirt on, then paid the little man his token payment.

"Ah, the shirt fits well, and it looks quite striking! A good day to you, then, until we meet again." Shapak-ailesh went off, his mule ambling pliantly behind.

Qedrim found himself extremely wary. All afternoon, even when he had returned to the palace, he was expecting an attack.

None came, of course.

IT WASN'T UNTIL THE fourth day that it happened.

He had become accustomed to wearing the shirt, and often forgot it was there. Though every time he caught sight of the embroidery on the sleeve, or happened to look down the front, it reminded him he was in danger.

He had tended to avoid crowds, which was sometimes difficult. Such as when one was purchasing a bunch of grapes at a fruit-vendor's stand. When several other people might drift over and stand by. These always turned out to be people waiting their turn to buy something, or merely looking at what was on offer.

This time, however, he was concentrating on counting out the appropriate number of coppers, when he felt a blow on the side. The attack caught him by surprise, and knocked him off balance, though only momentarily. He whirled and swung a fist at the fellow, who was surprised that his knife scraped along the surface of a leather shirt as though the shirt were iron.

Hired assassins do not gain the sort of experience allowing them to ply their trade without also possessing an ability to think and move quickly. Even in strange and surprising circumstances.

The man writhed away from Qedrim's blow, stared at the leather shirt or whatever it was, while thinking better of a second attempt, and then leaped away into the crowd.

Qedrim, without pausing to think, pulled one of his special stones free from his pouch and tossed it after the man. "Get him!"

The stone whipped away, just over the heads of the crowd, causing people to duck and flinch away. A moment later the assassin, still fleeing, was hit on the back of the head and brought down.

Qedrim went over to look at the fallen man. The people who had seen what had happened shrank away from him. The rest did the same when they heard muttered comments about what had happened.

"Dead as a stone. Well, it doesn't matter much. Questioning him would only have confirmed he came from B'tlas." He called his stone back to him and put it away. "Or maybe," he grinned crookedly. "Lord Sobeldanser is happy to have the man failed and dead."

THE WATCH DID NOT ALL know him, but they all knew of him. Despite the habit of years spent avoiding dealings with the City Watch, Qedrim forced himself to stand still as the watch came pushing through the crowds, using the butts of their spears in a less than gentle fashion.

Qedrim said, "My name is Qedrim, and I'm a Friend of the Kharmista." He thought it best to get the important information out up front. "This fellow tried to put a knife in me, but missed his stroke." He wasn't about to get into discussions of magic shirts and all. "He took off running, and I threw a stone after him and got him."

"I see." said the senior man. He looked around at the crowd. "Any of the rest of you lot see it?"

This produced a sudden fading away of the crowd, since it was not only petty gamblers who avoided dealings with the Watch. However, two fellows, both of them short and red-faced, spoke up. "It was him!" the one declared, pointing at Qedrim. "He flung that great boulder at this fellow, killed him dead. Could have killed more, too! Just lucky it was only the one fellow got brained!"

"Yes!" agreed the other. "The gods' own luck only the one poor fellow got killed!"

The senior man of the Watch turned to him. Qedrim imagined that he was now supposed to offer them a little something for their trouble, to prove that he needn't bother himself with all this. Instead, taking for granted that his reputation would have gotten around, Qedrim held out his palm with the stone resting in it.

"I'm certain you gentlemen have heard of me. Qedrim, the man who throws stones for the Lady?" he set the stone to dancing from one fingertip to another.

The men of the Watch looked at the dancing stone, then looked at the two accusers. "You two! You've some nerve, trying to make trouble for the Kharmista's friend! Lord Qedrim, you're free to go, your word's good enough for us."

As he went wandering off, remembering to take his grapes with him, Qedrim heard the Watch beginning to threaten the pair of "witnesses." The pair would probably be let go with the payment of a small "fine."

That was not, however, the end of the matter.

TWO DAYS LATER, QEDRIM found Fallash waiting at the chamber door.

"Lord Qedrim of Arndal, the Lord Gwothernan requests an interview with you."

"Does he indeed? You're certain the message did not say 'demands an interview?'"

Fallash' expression did not change one whit. "No, Lord Qedrim, he said he requests an interview."

"Very well. Will you tell him I'll be there shortly?"

A request from that fellow is the same as a demand.'

He wondered to himself, as he walked the hallways of the palace, just what Gwothernan wanted with him now.

Gwothernan sat at a table, and he was apparently not angry. Yet.

"You asked to see me, Lord?" There was no sense in not at least trying to be polite.

"Yes, I did. I understand someone attacked you in the marketplace the day before yesterday."

"Yes. Nothing much. The fellow tried to knife me, then ran. I threw a stone and brought him down."

"And you told no one?"

"Outside of explaining to the Watch, no. It didn't seem worth the trouble. He tried, he failed, he died. There was no more to it than that."

"No? I understand there are magical means to discover who sent such a man, though the magic must be used as soon after death as is possible."

"So we'd find he worked for B'tlas. But we know that."

"Do we? There are others, though I dislike to have to say so, even here among our loyal Lords, who would be glad to see you done away with. You've come from nowhere. You've advanced more rapidly in the kharmista's favour than any of them could dream of. They'd even risk losing a war against Daura to be rid of you.

"If we could catch even one of them, it might make all the others think a little more carefully before they try anything drastic.

"And there is one thing further. Yes, B'tlas probably paid the man, but not directly. There is probably a local intermediary, here in Higfrod, who carried out that function. And that local paymaster is someone we would dearly love to catch. If only to remove him and destroy that much of B'tlas' espionage establishment."

"Oh. So it's not enough to kill an assassin?" a smirk spreading across Qedrim's face "I have to bring in his body. Perhaps have him skinned out and prepared for a hearthrug?"

Something about Gwothernan's usual demeanour called forth levity from Qedrim.

"If you're trying to aggravate me, you'll be happy to know your mere presence aggravates me. You'll probably be even more happy to hear that I fully realize I'll have to endure that aggravation for the foreseeable future. You do understand, don't you, that your ability will be needed, even after we deal with Daura?

"There will be others who seek to fight us. Either out of fear of what a victorious Higfrod might represent, or a feeling that a war-weary Higfrod might be easy prey."

"I hadn't thought of that," Qedrim admitted. "I had thought, however, that King Faldisen might still be ill-disposed toward us."

Gwothernan scowled. "I hadn't forgotten that, either. It would be nice if we could send him some kind of large gift to placate him. I could hope—-. No, that's nothing you need to bother with. The Lady Annavristi and I will deal with the King."

Qedrim, who had been listening with interest to Gwothernan's idle musings, was disappointed the Lord had caught himself when he did.

"So, was that all you wished to talk with me about?"

"Yes. Just keep in mind that so many actions have consequences, small though those actions be. And see to it you stay alert; whoever paid for that killer might well pay for several others."

EITHER THE PAYMASTER had not paid for others, or no others found an opportunity during the following weeks.

Qedrim whiled away the winter visiting wineshops, though he didn't gamble. He did meet Thaldo several times. The young man was still in the army, and said he had a promise of a position as Ten-leader when the summer recruitment began.

At last, when the farmers brought in their crops, the army of Higfrod gathered itself and prepared to march. Gafrodi spies, along with a judicious use of the Talisman of Uncovering Secrets, had revealed that B'tlas was also preparing to march.

Chapter 11

A fair, fine summer day found Qedrim with the other Lords, along with the Lady, leading the army along the road toward Daura.

During the daylight the armed column snaked its way along the roads, trailing a visible dust-plume. During the evenings, the commanders worked out the plan Gwothernan had developed. This time, as last, Qedrim's main purpose would be to deal with the pottery men. Some twelve hundred of them were now with B'tlas' army.

The other Lords and contingent-commanders in the army of Higfrod were still dubious at best about Gwothernan's 'refused-flank' formation. Qedrim recalled one of the recent discussions.

"This business of holding back from battle," declared one Lord. "It seems suspiciously like cowardice to me."

"What foolishness is this?" demanded Gwothernan. "We are long past the days when every man charged forward to be first to come to grips! We know that holding ranks and maintaining formation is the best way to fight. Why should a minor reordering of our battle line make a difference to who is brave and who is not?"

"Well, but, it is the look of the thing."

"The look of the thing? If we go forward in line abreast, in perfect dressing so no part of the line is before or behind the other, those pottery men will eat up our line before the forces on the other flank can come close to dealing with B'tlas. And how will you like the look of that?"

"I still do not care to be ordered to use a formation which displays our fear of the enemy."

"Would you prefer me to order you to take command of the infantry reserve, behind the line altogether?"

The fellow subsided, it was plain they might be ready to use Gwothernan's new formation. However, they were not at all willing.

A PARTY OF HORSE-ARCHERS, dusty and filthy, came riding up. "Lord Gwothernan, our commander sent us back because there is news which he felt best we should bring to you without delay."

"Report."

"Lord, the elephants, their drivers do not ride out in the open. There is a square box fitted on each of the elephants, and in it the driver sits, along with several archers. It may be difficult to get at the drivers, Lord."

Gwothernan frowned. "Thank you for your report. Go find yourselves something to drink, rest for a bit, and catch us up later."

He said nothing until they were gone. "Well, it's too late to make great changes in our plans now. Our archers will just have to deal with the matter."

"Lord Gwothernan?"

"What do you want, Qedrim?" His tone of voice said he had no time for idle talk; this news was serious.

"You know I can hit a target as far away as I can see it. If you allow it, I could take a position on some hill or other, and pick off the riders and all before they can get near enough to do any damage."

Gwothernan frowned. "You could, could you?"

"Come, Lord Gwothernan, do you want me to prove it to you? Pick a mark, anything you want."

The Lady took a part then. "Lord Gwothernan, I'd suggest we take his offer. It might just make a bad situation a little less bad."

Lord Gwothernan looked at her, then nodded. "All right, then. Can you deal with the elephant riders and still have time to help at all against the pottery men?"

"Now, there's a promise I wouldn't want to make. I'll do my best. Will that suffice?"

"It will have to."

THREE EVENINGS LATER, they were camped across a valley from the Dauri. Even as unlearned as he was in military matters, Qedrim could see the Gafrodi would have trouble cleaving their way through the enemy ranks to get at B'tlas. It seemed clear to the rest of them as well, given the expressions on the commanders' faces.

He was at the last-minute meeting in the evening when Gwothernan made rearrangements as to which contingents would take station where. The silence, the lack of argument, was very obvious. No one was happy with the situation, but no one had any notion of what to do about it.

Gwothernan had taken a batch of pebbles and sods, lining them up according to how he expected the Gafrodi army to be arranged on the next day. He was lecturing on how they would deploy in order to have their left flank refused when they met the enemy.

Qedrim carefully avoided dwelling on the obvious tough fighting the forward flank would have. Hoping, that by his own force of will he could bring them through.

'Old Woman's Apron! I wonder just what's in his mind for me?'

He opened his pouch, and brought out two handfuls of stones, floating them in the air in front of him. He put them into formation. A dozen of them in three ranks, and floated them to where

Gwothernan had depicted his formation on the ground. At a height of about three palm breadths he let them fall.

They smacked among the pebbles which marked the lines there, flinging them awry. Gwothernan came to his feet, reaching for his sword.

"Before you go chopping me, just think a moment of what I've proved. If you'd had something out there to mark the Dauri forces, I'd have dropped the stones there. Just think about it."

Gwothernan paused with his sword partly drawn, then slipped it back into its sheath. "You have a point? Make it, then, and hurry."

"You have me supporting the forces facing the pottery men, which is all well and good. But suppose I were to drop a load of stones on the right flank, first? The left flank is refused. The pottery men won't reach there right away. And I should have time to make an attack on the right. A serious attack, before I go to my post. And if the right flank hits fast, following the falling stones, they have a better chance at cutting their way through."

"You want to show off more and more, don't you?"

"Old Woman's Apron! I want us all to keep our heads attached to our necks. I don't give more than a clipped copper coin for you, save that you know how to fight, and how to arrange battles. But I want to save the Lady. If you call that showing off, then so I am. The question is, do you want to prevent me from showing off, or do you want to win this battle?"

Gwothernan went still, his face pale, despite the ruddy fire-light.

"Sometimes you push hard, Qedrim. And beware you don't push too hard and too far." He took a deep breath. "I hope I am willing to see sense when it's rubbed in my face. You may well be right, here. This throwing and dropping stones. This is still a new thing on any battlefield I have seen, and I will admit that I'm not altogether certain as to the best use to make of it.

"You feel certain you can do this, and still get back to your assigned position in time?"

"Fairly certain. I won't have to be directly behind the right flank. I think I can manage to do it from the centre. After that, I rush to the left. I don't have to be directly behind the left either, though the farther over I get the better.

"If we have an oxcart of stones stationed behind the left, I should be all right. They don't move very fast, but I can, so it makes more sense for me to move to them than them to move with me."

THE NEXT DAY DAWNED bright and fair. Shortly after sunup there was a shouting and clattering noise as the army of Higfrod fell into its ranks, drowning out whatever might have been heard of the Dauri doing the same thing across the way.

Qedrim mounted up and took his position beside an oxcart. There would be another such cart, if no one had messed things up too badly, way off to his left.

Now the advance began. At least, the right wing, the phalanx, began to move forward. Their pikes held upright like a forest. A screen of light infantry and horse-archers protecting its vulnerable right flank. The rest of the line adjusted its formation. Each section moving just a little later, keeping a steady line. But one which trailed backward from the left flank of the phalanx.

Qedrim was determined this time, though, that nothing should distract him from his main purpose. He turned to watch the phalanx before him, moving along behind it, with the creaking ox-cart following along.

The Dauri line was advancing as well. They held a steady marching pace. Which, when they were close enough, would change into a rush to come to grips, to push home with the pikes, and drive the foemen off the field.

Qedrim's own work would be a matter of judgment. He could see that the later he dropped his stones, the less time the enemy would have to reorder his ranks. On the other hand, leaving it too late might well have some of the stones bounding over to disorder the Gafrodi.

Since it was not something he had been able practice with, he was going to have to go by guess and good wishes.

He pulled the stones from the oxcart, floating them in the air, arraying them into ranks. These were not the small sling-stones he had used the previous night, these were double-fist to head-sized boulders. He lifted them straight up. "Hope Gwothernan has seen to it that these lot are expecting stones to go overhead today," he thought.

Just to be sure, he lifted them further, so the stones went well overhead. Probably unnoticed by men focusing their attention on the enemy to their front. It might have been more effective to swoop the stones down in front of the enemy before making the stones climb far enough that the drop would properly disrupt them. That would be adding just a bit too much flash to it, though, and he wasn't entirely sure how much time he'd have.

So he merely sent the rocks over the heads of the Dauri, some ten feet up, and dropped them at what seemed the appropriate time.

Given the distance and the angle from which he was watching, Qedrim told himself he'd done well. Best would have been to take out the front and second ranks. However, even though he missed the front rank, he had destroyed the second. He further disordered the third for a good part of the thirty-foot length his stones had covered. Not to mention the rocks bounced, often toward the Dauri rear. Which caused further disarray.

Yes, he'd disordered the enemy phalanx, and they weren't going to be able to correct that disorder before the two forces hit. It was up to the soldiers now to make good on that small advantage.

Qedrim turned his horse and rode down to the left rear. Behind him he could hear the metallic clash as the forces came together along with the shouting and the screaming.

The elephants were coming, evenly spaced, just in front of the ranks of pottery men. It occurred to him he'd been thinking too much of one trick. Was the sling-stone actually the best weapon here? He picked a head-sized stone from the ground and sent it down at the enclosure on the back of the nearest elephant. Wood-splinters flew, yellow in the sun. He kept control of the stone stone, and and smashed it against the enclosure again, and once again.

After the third time, the side of the enclosure was wreck, splintered slats hanging from the front and rear posts. Now he could see the driver, and only one sling-stone was needed. The man fell off the sham beast, and the elephant stopped in its tracks.

As he readied his stone to deal with the next, Qedrim wondered if this was the same sort of thing as those pottery men in Lakvos'ta. They moved and fought as long as their commander, Losibalson, was alive, then stopped. It seemed a reasonable notion.

The next elephant was almost at the ranks of infantry already. However, in this case he could see the pale blob of the driver's head. As he had boasted to Gwothernan, anything he could see, he could hit. He used his sling this time. A moment later that elephant, as well, had stopped.

The third elephant was into the Gafrodi ranks already. They were beginning to lose cohesion. One sling-stone took that driver down as well, then Qedrim looked at the last elephant. It was in the midst of the light infantry, stamping and smashing. The ranks were already beginning to give. He killed the fourth driver, rendering the beast immobile. Too late. The Gafrodi were already fleeing.

"Old Woman's Apron! I took on a bit too much, even for the wondrous thrower of stones!" he thought to himself.

He had to try. Qedrim brought a line of stones down from the near end of the force of pottery men. Sending the line as far as he could see through the dust. The stones bowled them all over. The pottery men took their usual laborious time getting to their feet again. By which time Qedrim was ready to bring his stones back.

Qedrim paused beside the stopped elephant, the one which had ruined the Gafrodi line. The archers who had been inside the shelter on the beast's back had already jumped down. Heading back through the ranks of the pottery men to more safe terrain.

Wielding his stones as fiercely as he could, Qedrim delayed the pottery men's advance. He fought them for every palm-breadth of ground. Off in the dust somewhere to his left, Qedrim was fairly sure that at least some part of the Gafrodi left flank was holding. Though he realized this was as much wishful thinking as anything. No Dauri were coming up to attack him from the left, which meant someone down there was still fighting. At least, to his non-military mind, it did.

Abruptly, the elephant began to move. B'tlas must have taken control of them, Qedrim thought. After his first start of fear, he realized the beast was not coming at him, but moving straight forward. Perhaps the control of the beasts was not perfect. Or, perhaps all B'tlas could do was get them moving, in the hope they would cause trouble and disorder over here.

Whatever the reason, the beasts were soon gone, off to the Gafrodi rear. Time enough to worry about them if they came back. The pottery men seemed able to direct their own fighting, at least to some degree, and they were the danger here.

Blows still smashed some of them. Had Kassibanio been wrong about B'tlas and his deep plans? Or, had B'tlas simply been cutting corners to hurry at getting the pottery men made, in the manner of a certain slinger-cum-talisman-maker?

Then, between one step and the next, the pottery men ceased fighting. Many of them were caught in the midst of taking a step and therefore off balance, and they fell. Some fell into their fellows, causing them to fall as well.

Did that mean B'tlas was dead, or merely driven too far from the field?

The next questions were, how much of a victory would it be if things had gone Chaos Away over on this flank? And, Dauri troops were coming up on the phalanx from behind?

He went riding off to the rear, angling to the left, looking for any sign of Dauri troops. He found them, light infantry, in the midst of plundering the Gafrodi camp. Clearly, they had no notion of how things had gone on the rest of the field, and clearly they had ceased to care. He wondered if their ten-commanders or hundred-commanders had tried to call them to order, or they had simply joined in with the rest?

Well, in any case they might be a danger if the Kharmista and her people came back here, thinking the fight was won. Using his stones to strike from above, Qedrim attacked first one band. Then another. And, then another. If they had any sort of organization left, they might have surrounded Qedrim and killed him. Or, at least driven him off. But in this situation, with stones coming from the sky to strike them down. They began to head back to their own lines, in bits and clumps.

Qedrim then took his stones with him and headed back to the main line, or where the main line had been.

After riding some time, Qedrim found the place where the two phalanxes had come together. A row of stones marked that place.

Along with a near-regular carpet of dead, some in Dauri uniforms and some in Gafrodi uniforms.

Just beyond that there were Dauri dead, all of them facing back the way they had come. Obviously killed when they had fled.

Eventually he came on the Kharmista, cantering back in this direction, heavily guarded.

"We've won, then?"

The Lady herself answered. "Yes. B'tlas is dead, and that is one task done."

"It's not up to me to answer for the left flank, but we're pretty badly bashed up over there. I wasn't able to stop the elephants as soon as I'd hoped. I'm sorry."

Gwothernan seemed too tired even to accept this opportunity to criticize Qedrim. "Well, you kept them off our backs long enough. We'll have to spend a bit of time gathering our forces before we march again."

Qedrim apparently let something show in his expression, for Gwothernan spoke again. "What, you thought it was all over with this fight? The next thing, the very next thing, is to take Daura City, before some other of B'tlas' underlings does so. We don't need any more trouble from that quarter."

GWOTHERNAN ORGANIZED a small advance force to march immediately on Daura City and demand its surrender.

Gwothernan asked Qedrim to be present when he reported to the Lady. Then he said to the assembly, "Scarce a contingent that hasn't lost heavy in this last one. But I'm getting together what I can. Qedrim, would you accompany them? Perhaps give the city a further reason for surrender."

"I'll go, but demonstrations didn't seem to work so well against the garrison at Higfrod."

"And the garrison at Higfrod knew that their Lord was free, and hoped he was gathering armies to fight again. This lot'll know B'tlas is dead, and they'll have much less inducement to fight on.

"Just do what you can."

This attitude, packing Qedrim along as though he were an extra cloak which might be of use, though everyone doubted it, put Qedrim in a mood where, if they had reached the city next day, he would have pulled the walls down, stone by stone.

MARCHING WITH THE ARMY to the battlefield had been one thing. The forced march from the battlefield to Daura City was another. Qedrim rode, but this meant only the stress and pain was on his backside rather than on his legs.

On they went, over hill and through valley. Beginning a little earlier in the morning, and halting a little later in the evening than was usual.

The commander of the force was a gruff old Lord by the name of Kw'bel. Though Qedrim's rise had not aggravated Kw'bel as much as Sobeldanser, for instance. He was still not quite sure he wanted this person as a friend.

Also, Qedrim found that though he was with soldiers, he was not quite one of them. They all knew that he was the man who threw stones around, and that he was a Lord, with the favour of the Kharmista.

As everyone knew, it did not do to become too familiar with a Lord, however he had come to be a Lord. And they seemed as though they were never sure when he would have a fit of anger and start throwing stones around.

He wished Thaldo had been one of the contingent picked for this march. But he hadn't been willing to face Gwothernan with such a request. "And besides," he thought, "You didn't know you were going to be so lacking in company on this trip, did you?"

So he had no-one to complain to regarding his aching backside. By the time they had halted below the city's walls, he was heartily sick of the whole business.

Qedrim hadn't pulled down Lakvos'ta's wall, nor Higfrod's, because in those cases, it had been highly likely that the walls would be needed soon after. This time, as near as Qedrim could tell, the war was pretty much over, and Higfrod was still whole. So there seemed no need to carefully preserve Daura City.

So the herald called the city to surrender. "People of Daura! Your Lord B'tlas is defeated and slain! We call you to surrender in the name of the Lady Annavristi, Kharmista of Higfrod!"

There was a time of silence, then a voice called down, "No! We will not surrender! Anyone can come claiming any sort of news, this will not make it true!"

"Hah!" the herald muttered. "I'll wager they've heard the news from other fugitives already. They're only hoping to get preferential terms. I'll warn them, then you can start your demonstration."

Qedrim grabbed the herald's sleeve. "No! I think it'll be better if I go after them with no warning!"

"This isn't the usual procedure—."

Qedrim was in no mood for drawn-out formalities. "I don't give a badly clipped copper for the usual procedure. Get out of the way!"

The first thing Qedrim did was pull several stones down off the a stretch of the top of the wall, just beside the gate they were facing. Wrenching them off and letting them fall might well have served the purpose. But instead he wrenched them off and brought them down and carefully landed them in a pyramid-shaped stack in front of the wall.

"Now, call them to surrender. And if they won't, I'll dump their whole Morrkerr-eaten wall on them!"

"People of Daura!" called the herald. "You have undoubtedly heard tales of the Lord Qedrim, who has the power to command stones. You have no doubt thought them to be mere tales, but now you see that they are altogether true. The Lord Qedrim is out of patience! He gives you one more opportunity to surrender, lest he take your walls and bury your city under them!"

A voice called from the city, a somewhat fearful voice, this time. "What conditions does the Kharmista of Higfrod offer?"

The herald answered, "The Lady declares that all the garrison may march out, and once they have stacked their arms, they may go where they will. There will be no sacking nor plundering of the city, nor its inhabitants.

"The city shall pay an indemnity of one thousand gold coins, or the equivalent value in silver.

"No man, noble or common, who served the Kharmost shall suffer. Save that certain nobles, to be named, shall pay a sum of one hundred silver coins. All nobles within the city shall make themselves known to the commander of the Lady's garrison. Who may, at his discretion, set them free on their spoken word to pay the agreed fee.

"These are the Lady's terms."

"And Morrkerr-eaten easy ones too," muttered Kw'bel.

Qedrim had to agree with that. He'd heard of instances where cities were given over to plunder for some time. Every adult male required to ransom himself and his family, or be sold into slavery. With nobles requiring huge sums in ransom, again with slavery the penalty for default.

He was also sure that, terms of surrender notwithstanding, for the first few weeks no citizen would have much recourse if some soldier decided he wanted some particular thing. Be it valuable or trivial.

Of course, there would always be a soldier or three who misjudged this 'free' period, and ended up suddenly surprised to find themselves accused and guilty of theft.

After a short silence, the answering voice from the wall said, "We will require another condition. That a limited number of troops be allowed within the city at one time."

The commander grimaced. The Lady had given him wide latitude as to terms he might accept. This was near enough to being beyond what he should allow. Then he shrugged, "Let them save some pride by dictating that one item to us. We agree."

So the herald shouted out to the spokesman on the walls to say that the commander accepted the stipulation.

There was another long wait. Then the city's gate opened, and the soldiers of the garrison began to march out and stack their arms.

THE STATE OF AFFAIRS in Daura settled into what might be described as a long holding of breath.

Surrender had been negotiated on certain terms, some of which could not be met until the Lady arrived. It was not totally unknown for a surrendered city to suddenly find the victors had nullified some or all of the conditions under which it had surrendered. And had required many things which the negotiators had forsworn. Such as plundering, and selling prominent citizens into slavery.

Qedrim did not believe this would be the case with the Lady. She would go by her word, even if her word had been spoken by a subordinate's mouth in her name. Of course the people of the city did not have that sort of assurance.

On Kw'bel's advice, Qedrim did not go around the city alone. "There's likely to be one or two dozen out there don't like the thought of being ruled by foreigners. Some them might be brave enough, with or without a skinful of wine, to try to take it out on one of the foreigners who happened to wander alone into their sight.

"I know I'm not letting my men go out except in groups of three at the least."

"I'll take your word for it."

THIS MEANT, GIVEN THE attitudes of the men to himself, Qedrim did not go out much at all. This in turn meant Qedrim's mood had not improved greatly by the time the rest of the army came in.

One of the first things he did was go out, in Malsan'to's company, to sample the wineshops. Genilabas was back in the Healer's tents on the battlefield.

"It was a bad poke he took but it didn't get his gut, so he'll likely be all right," Malsan'to gave Qedrim a look of concern. "Should you be drinking like that?"

"I don't know. D'you know any way I can drink faster?" Qedrim smirked as he lifted his rhyton to his lips.

Malsan'to frowned. "You know, I believe the preferred manner is to drink slowly enough to enjoy the sensation of the whole world beginning to fall into proper alignment. Rather than simply swallowing wine until one passes out."

"A very pretty speech, indeed. I've just spent the last year, or so it seems, either in the company of soldiers who're afraid I'll bring down the wrath of the Kharmista on them, or drop boulders on their empty noggins, or in the company of people who hate me because I'm a foreigner who's invaded their city," shot back Qedrim.

"And that makes the situation even more puzzling, then. Because now that matters are changed, your good friends—one of them at least—is here, and now you want to drink yourself into a stupor," replied Malsan'to grimly.

"And my most noble friend is trying to make me talk instead of drinking. I find this at least a little upsetting, to say the least." Despite this, Qedrim moderated his drinking.

"I don't suppose you'd favour me with the true story of how you brought the city to surrender. The tale I've been hearing is you dropped most of the city walls on the citizens' heads. This is obviously untrue, because the walls are still standing. Mostly. And there doesn't seem to be any great lack of citizens around," queried Malsan'to.

"Huh! The whole thing was because of my backside," answered Qedrim sheepishly.

Malsan'to frowned at him in puzzlement. "How does that work out?"

"Well, you know we force-marched all the way here, didn't you? So by the time we arrived, my backside was sore from the long ride, so sore I'm not sure it'll ever be right. So when the herald called them to surrender, and they refused, I was very close to pulling down their walls and dropping the rocks on them.

"What I did, though, was pull a whole lot of stones from the front wall, overlooking the gate. Pulled them down and stacked them carefully in plain sight of the wall."

Qedrim smiled slightly at the memory. "I think that must have convinced them we weren't going to fool around with any sieging or storming. And that their walls weren't going to do them much good. So the herald called them to surrender, and they asked the terms. Then they put in one little condition about limiting the number of soldiers who were in the city at one time, and Kw'bel agreed. On behalf of the Lady.

"And that was it."

Malsan'to shook his head, "Qedrim, Qedrim, you may have all the stones in the world, but you certainly can't tell a story. You should brag a bit. Gods know you have the right."

Qedrim shook his head. "Just isn't me, Malsa. Bragging just makes people look at you, think about you like a target." Even as he said it, Qedrim remembered a good deal of his life had been like that. Bragging, making himself a target, before having to dig like mad to get out from under.

'Wonder if that blond fellow is still back there in Higfrod? Wonder if he'd even recognize me anymore, being high-class like I am?'

"So, now what are you thinking about, Qedrim, with that faraway look on your face?"

Qedrim shook his head. "Just remembering myself back in the days when I wasn't a Lord and all. You wouldn't have liked me back then, Malsa."

Chapter 12

The boy was likely eight summers old, and very scruffy-looking. His clothing had once been fine cloth, well-tailored, the sort someone of high quality would wear. By now, though, it was stained and showing some wear at the knees and elbows. He stared up at the Lady with a truculent look.

The man who had brought him in was a servant, an upper servant from his well-fed look and his own good clothing.

"This is the son of the late B'tlas, Lady. I felt you would wish to have the disposal of him for yourself."

The Lady looked at the servant. "Whatever else I may be, I do not make war on small boys, nor carry over my anger from father to son. I appreciate your bringing him here. Someone give this man ten silver pieces for his trouble, and get him out of my sight."

The servant, who had surely been hoping for something more. Perhaps a place in the Lady's service. He opened his mouth to protest, then shut it. He may have misjudged the Lady's attitude toward her late enemy's son. But he understood all too well protesting could only worsen his situation.

The Lady barely waited until he was out of the room before she turned to the boy. "What is your name?"

"I am B'tlas, son of B'tlas!" he said defiantly. "Did you kill my father?"

"Not with my own hands, but he died in battle against me, so I suppose I could be said to have killed him."

"He told me if you ever got hold of me, you'd feed me to the dogs. I don't care; you can kill me, but you can never make me serve you!"

Such defiance, from such a boy, in in face of armed enemies, affected everyone.

Qedrim knew the boy had no idea what sort of danger he might be in, but saw as well that he was determined to be brave. He also knew the best course for the Lady would be to have someone quietly do away with B'tlas son. Despite that, he doubted the Lady would do so.

"No, B'tlas, I won't throw you to the dogs, or anything such. I shall take you home as a foster-son in my household. When you grow old enough, if you are equal to the task, I will give you your father's lands to rule."

Qedrim realized this went over the boy's head, save perhaps the knowledge that no one would throw him to the dogs. Having steeled himself against this worst fate, he was not sure how to take this news.

The Kharmista looked up at those around. "Find me someone who knows how to care for boys. And make sure they know the difference between boys who are prisoners and boys who are guests. B'tlas son of B'tlas is a guest.

"Now, what of the boy's mother?"

"She hasn't been found as yet, Lady," answered Kw'bel. "We've been tracking rumours. There's one story that some group of servants are holding her prisoner. Hoping to get a better reward from you than they would from me.

"There're also stories about her hiding from your vengeance in this or that noble's household, disguised as a servant.

"None of those stories have proven to be more than great imagination, but we can't ignore them. There's even a tale she's set out in disguise to go to the King of Dai'vlash to plead for aid."

"She hasn't gone back to her father's household?"

"Her father died five years back, Lady. And I've heard that the younger brother, who inherited, has little use for her. Just to be safe, we've sent people off to her brother's estate, to inquire into matters."

"Well done. I'm sure we'll all feel better once the loose ends are tied up. See to it that more reward can be expected for living people than for dead bodies.

"Now, how has the fine-collection been proceeding?"

"Tolerably well, Lady. Only a half-dozen Lords have tried to evade payment. We caught three almost at once, and the other three, well, we're on their track, Lady."

"You've done very well, Kw'bel."

KASSIBANIO OVERSAW the destruction of the buildings in which B'tlas had worked his magic, along with all the notes and writings which the Kharmost had done regarding his work.

"There's going to be an uneasy quality to the land and air hereabouts for some time," he told Qedrim as they watched soldiers gathering papers to add to a bonfire, "I've done cleansing spells, and fire will complete the cleansing. Inasmuch as anything but time can cleanse it from what has gone on here."

He sighed. "There were a few worthwhile things in there. Some spells to help crops grow, to encourage desirable qualities in in crops grown from certain seed, in the offspring of certain animals. But the whole was just too tinged with baneful influences to be worth the risk."

"What risk would that be?" asked Qedrim.

"Possibly none at all. But there is too much chance anyone who uses works from that workshop will fall into less savoury practices, and always for the best of reasons. 'I will harm some in doing this, but I will help numerous others.' You see?"

"I believe so," replied Qedrim.

They continued to watch as the buildings crumbled as Qedrim helped to demolish the buildings using his ability to move stones.

Once the last brick was torn out and the bonfires grew dim,
Kassibanio cast a final cleansing spell over the ruins.

THEY LEFT A SMALL GARRISON under Kw'bel, to whom
Annavristi had given the title of Vice-Kharmost. Then they marched
for Higfrod.

A letter from King Faldisen of Dai'vlash waited for the Lady. She
had it read at a council meeting.

"He says, 'Let there be peace between Kharmosat and
Kharmosat, for this constant bickering between brothers offends my
soul.'"

Gwothernan looked up. "It's almost as if he hadn't been made
aware of the summer's campaign or its results."

The letter went on, "I greatly desire that the pottery soldiers
of B'tlas, along with all writings regarding their making and
employment, be sent to me. Such things are too dangerous to be left
in the hands of a subordinate."

"Now I understand," Gwothernan said. "Here is a King pressing
for an excuse to make war!

"He surely knew our intent was to destroy the pottery men and
all B'tlas' magical work. So, after the fact, he demands that they all be
sent to him. When we respond with the truth, we've destroyed the
whole filthy lot, he will claim we are hiding it from him, and declare
war."

"War again!" The Lady clenched a fist on the table. "We've
already had too much war! And we're too small to fight against the
King, especially not in light of the losses we've taken in the last
years."

"We can draw on Daura's resources; they haven't lost as heavily as
we."

"Yes," she said, "If it comes to a fight, we will do that. But we'll have to try to put off that day for as long as possible."

"Exactly," said Gwothernan. We'll send him placating letters and gifts for as long as we can. But I'm afraid, Lady, it will ultimately come to war."

"Which we won't win. The Kharmosat of Higfrod, even with help from Daura, against all the might the King can put forth. We're outnumbered."

"We'll have to play our own game. How many Kharmosts are there who would join us, if only for fear they might be next once the King has dealt with us?"

She smiled, just barely, then seemed to take heart. She looked at Qedrim. "Qedrim, I think we may be keeping you busy the next year or more. Going from place to place to juggle stones for the edification of our friends. Are you willing?"

Qedrim, who had found himself thinking that he'd like to kiss away those cares and worries from her face, sat up suddenly. "I'm yours to command, Lady."

"DID YOU KNOW THIS PLACE was at the utter ends of the earth, and over horrible roads besides, when you agreed to come here, Qedrim?"

"I knew fall was not a good season for travelling, Geni, but it has to be done."

"So tell me again, how is it that being your friends has us out here getting cold and wet and uncomfortable?"

"I agreed to take the job so long as I could pick at least two of the people who'll be travelling with me. So I picked you and Malsa, so I'd have someone to talk to."

"I wish you'd picked us to stay warm at home and think good thoughts towards you."

Qedrim grinned. "I couldn't show up at these people's cities all alone, like some travelling entertainer. You're along to add to my stature. And besides, you're now known as friends of the Close Friend of the Kharmista. By rising in my favour, you've risen in hers."

"By rising in your favour we've become cold and wet. Don't you think it's time to camp for the night?"

"Just over the next rise."

All the complaints were mostly good-natured. Though this good nature tended to become a bit strained after three straight days of fine, cold rain. The fire-starting talisman he'd bought from Shapak-ailesh continued to live up to its guarantee.

THE WORKMEN WERE TAKING advantage of a break in the weather to begin the wall for the New Garden—as much a title as a name—for the Kharmost. In trousers and short rain-capes, they began taking the stacked stones and setting them up within the boundaries marked by evenly spaced wooden pegs.

The garden itself had been tilled for several years previous and planted with rows of vegetables. It was only this year the Kharmost had decided to enclose it.

"You witness it here in the beginning stages, Lord Qedrim," said the Kharmost Yo'tapha, a stout and red-faced man. "Next year it will be something to behold!"

"Drystone, I see." Qedrim said it for something to say; he understood the basics of drystone work, but he was scarcely an expert.

"Oh, yes, drystone of course. It'll give when the soil subsides, without having the whole lot fall over."

Qedrim watched the workmen as they lay the stones. They were carefully choosing the right size and shape for a particular spot. The wall's base was broad, and would slope upwards from both inside and out. This would cause the stones to lock together, holding them place.

He began to pull stones from the stacks and set them on the walls. With shouts and curses. the workmen jumped back as the stones drifted over to settle in position. The Kharmost himself let go with an oath, "Destroyer's Teeth!"

Then, "Is this your doing, Lord Qedrim?"

"Yes. Have I not got it right?" he asked, as though the business of moving stones through the air were something very common.

Most buildings in the Arndals had been drystone work, mortar being stigmatized as a lowland affectation. Qedrim knew the basic techniques, though he hadn't put them into practice in years.

"Well, yes, but...." The Kharmost looked at him closely. "One hears stories, you know. And if one doesn't believe them all, that's just because.... But you are moving the stones, aren't you? You actually have power over stones, like they say?"

"Yes, I have an ability to move stones. I'm not sure just what tales you've heard, but there is at least some truth in them. I can move stones, lift them, stack them. And throw them, of course."

The Kharmost eyed the growing wall. "Is it safe?"

"Safe? Oh, I think it's as safe as any wall. I haven't done a great deal of drystone work recently, of course, but I think I can manage a simple garden wall."

"No, but, one hears about stones moved thus, that they're, um, unhealthy?"

"Unhealthy? You mean cursed? No, there's no curse involved. I suspect the tale of the "curse" comes from the fact that I've been using this power in battles. And that I can hit any target I can see.

"You will recall the Lady Annavristi spent a winter in refuge in the hills. During that winter, I did a lot of hunting with my sling, and my power over stones. And no one took any harm from eating the game I brought in."

Like many of his decisions, this business of helping to build the wall had been a sudden notion which, when he thought on it, seemed to be a very good idea. An even better idea, in fact, than juggling and balancing stones, with the implied threat of being able to throw them at anyone he considered an enemy.

Building something up showed the same ability to use stones, although there'd be an inference that he could also tear things down. It might leave a better taste in the mouth of the people he showed it to. Not quite so directly stating 'Think what I could do with these stones I'm juggling.'

"Yes," he thought as he put the wall together, "building things with stones might be altogether a lot better than throwing them at targets. But if the impression doesn't come through properly, I can always do the juggling."

MALSAN'TO CONFIRMED his new view of things as they went off to the next domain to visit with another Kharmost. "Brilliant notion, Qedrim, building that piece of wall for him. It's a subtle suggestion, on the lines of 'I can build this wall up. Think what I could do if I wanted to pull down a wall.'"

"That had occurred to me, Malsa, after I'd started building the wall. I just thought building something. Making something useful, would leave a better feeling than juggling stones. People would view the juggling as a threat, which would be useful in its way, but might just get people's backs up."

They were greeted by the Kharmost and shortly thereafter Qedrim went to work helping them rebuild their walls and dilapidated buildings.

"I COULDN'T ALWAYS BUILD someone's wall for them," he reported to the council when he and his companions returned to Higfrod. "But I always did something. I demonstrated that I could build a wall, put a bed of stone into a ford, or even merely haul all the stones out of a field and stack them neatly beside it.

"I think most of them were impressed. How much that means to our cause, I don't know."

"You did all that could be expected of you, Qedrim. Thank you again."

ANOTHER LETTER ARRIVED from the King. He declared himself grieved he had not received the information on the pottery men.

"We've already told him the pottery men have been destroyed, along with all information pertaining to them." Gwothernan said. "He's pressing on us. I think he may be more ready to go to war than we'd thought."

"Or perhaps he knows how unready we are," the Lady said. "But it gets worse. Listen to this: 'It has been made known to me that one among your folk has power over stones. I would see this person for myself. Only send him to me, and many other faults may be dismissed.'"

"For certain!" Gwothernan said. "If he has not already made the connection. As soon as he sees Qedrim he will know him for the one who faced him down with the 'stones of the Palace wishing to be rid of the Lady.' I doubt Qedrim would survive long."

"Yes. I think we had best claim Qedrim is ill. Not seriously ill, but unable to travel as yet."

Chapter 13

It was difficult, but not altogether impossible for a person to speak to Qedrim alone. Gwothernan assigned a pair of guards to be with him at all times, despite the annoyance it caused Qedrim. The commander only stated, "You are too important to the Lady to be risked to some fool with a knife in the marketplace. And in case you're thinking about evading the guards, understand you will not be punished, but they will be. Staying with you is part of their duty. If they fail, they can expect to be punished. Just as they could expect to be punished for coming on parade with a rust-spot on their spear-blade."

It would have been easier if the guards had irritated him, but they were always polite, though not servile. Qedrim could have evaded them from time to time. But to condemn a pair of decent fellows to punishment just because he, Qedrim disliked having Gwothernan rule his life? No, that was not something he could do.

If he were drinking in a wineshop, though, and had to go out to the alley to relieve himself, one guard would come to be nearby. But the fellow would not have the effrontery to stand at Qedrim's elbow all the while.

So if a person who had been drinking in the same wineshop went out into the same alley at the same time. He might stand within whispering distance of Qedrim, and mutter a message only Qedrim was able to hear. The guard would not interfere, unless the fellow moved too quickly, or appeared like he was about to draw a weapon.

In this case the man said, "There will be a message of some interest delivered to your table."

He didn't bother waiting for an answer, but finished what he had been doing and went back into the wineshop.

Shortly after Qedrim went back in, a man, not quite a beggar. But by his dress not far away from being a beggar, came to his table. "I have a talisman for sale here, a talisman to prevent the bad head which comes of drinking wine." He reached into his clothing, but one of the guards had a short sword pointing at his middle.

"Best not be any metal in that hand when it comes out, fellow," the guard growled.

The man stared at the sword. "Oh, no, no metal, Lord! Only a talisman, if the Lord is interested." He pulled his hand out, slowly, shaking with nervousness. Which caused him to fumble around, dropping several bits of paper and the talisman itself. It was nothing more than two feathers bound together with a thin leather cord.

"I think not, fellow. I know a bit about talismans. And despite what many people wish, there is no such thing as a talisman to prevent a wine headache. Best take it and try to sell it to someone more gullible."

The man bent over the table and extended his hands in entreaty, about to make a further plea. However, he moved a bit too fast, and one of the guards appeared, wrapping his arms around the man, hauling him away to the door and ejecting him.

Among the bits and pieces which had fallen when the man had brought his hand out of his clothing was a leather scrap, with a few words on it in the Common Language.

'If you are at your chamber door at the third hour after midnight, you may hear a proposition which may interest you.'

"Very interesting" Qedrim thought. "So someone can get agents into the Kharmista's palace. Or rather, they have them there already."

He had no concern about either guard being able to read the message. Few people could read, and soldiers were less likely than most to be able to read.

It seemed like a reasonable notion to listen to the offer before he turned the matter over to the guards.

'If I get myself killed, Gwothernan will hate me.'

THE MAN WHO MET HIM was in servant's dress. Though Qedrim realized he may have gotten the clothing elsewhere. The better to be able to walk the palace halls unchallenged. He was little and brown, and his face held no expression.

"Lord, King Faldisen has authorized me to present you with a purse of twenty gold pieces, if you will agree to enter his employ."

Qedrim shook his head only sightly. "I think not. I am in the Lady's service, and happy here."

He realized he could be in serious danger here; the King might well want to have him dead if he couldn't be bought. If the man tried to move to close, or too quickly—-.

"You're sure of this? The King can reward you amply."

"Yes, I'm quite sure."

The little man shrugged. "So be it." He turned to go.

A moment later he had whipped around, brought out a dagger, and lunged at Qedrim.

Qedrim, ready for just such a move, dodged right, slapped the knife inward, and kicked at the knee. He didn't connect squarely, but near enough to keep the fellow from attacking again. He flipped the knife toward Qedrim's face, turned, and ran.

Qedrim ducked under the knife and heard it go clattering against the wall. By the time he was ready to go in pursuit, the assassin had turned a corner of the hallway. By the time he got to that corner, the man was no longer in sight.

"Now," he thought, "if I go along opening all the doors, I'll cause a lot of excitement barging in on people. But I won't likely catch him, since he'd have worked out his escape in advance."

He went back to report the adventure to his guards, and to Gwothernan at least.

"YOU TOOK TOO BIG A chance." Gwothernan was angry, but not to the point of shouting. "You ought to have reported the first approach, then let us handle the matter."

"And how would you have done it, then? Have guards on all the hallways, so the fellow got scared off, leaving us with nothing?"

"Nothing, Qedrim, is what we're left with now. Only your report of the incident, and a description of a person, which may not be the person's true appearance at all."

"We know the King is worried enough to want to try to buy me."

"I think we could have guessed that without all this folderol. And I know you're about to say you did what you thought best. Next time let someone know. It's just possible someone might know better than you do."

DESPITE ALL EFFORTS at sending placating gifts along with reasons why the King's requests could not be complied with. the King lost patience at last and declared war as soon as the campaigning season was opened.

It was a bleak council which met that evening. "Well, there is one hopeful element in this," the Lady said. "several Kharmosts are unwilling to march against us."

"Huh!" grunted Gwothernan. "Only the ones we wouldn't have had to worry much about anyway, the ones whose armies are hardly worthy of the name."

"You could at least have left me something to feel better about, Old Wolf." She smiled at him.

He smiled back, a slightly forced smile. "Military facts are military facts, Anniki. We'll be invaded, likely from two directions, perhaps more. Which means on the one hand, we fight two battles, at least. But on the other hand, we will be not quite so badly outnumbered in any one battle. Unless we allow the forces to join before we fight them.

"And if we decide to fight them before they join. We'll be forced to use some long and hard marching, with all the wear on our forces *that* entails."

He turned to Qedrim. "What can you do for us here?"

Qedrim frowned. "On the one hand, we won't have to deal with invulnerable enemies. On the other hand, we'll have to deal with a large number of ordinary ones. I have some thoughts, though. Not being a military man, I must ask, how do you choose your battlefields? It's always seemed almost as if both sides march until they meet each other, then fight on the field in between."

Gwothernan barked out a laugh. "It's all a part of the business of generalship. To make sure you meet up with the enemy on a field that's at least somewhat acceptable to your force. Preferably with something to anchor your flanks, a river, or a good hill, a wood, or the like.

"Of course, you want to find this spot soon enough the enemy has to come at you from the front, and yet not so soon he has the chance to work round one of your flanks.

"Most times, a few contingents of light infantry or light cavalry take care of this flanking business. In the case of the numbers the King can bring against us, we can't be certain of that. So we have to arrange to meet him on a ground of our choosing. Or, at least near enough he doesn't have the opportunity to work round our flanks.

"Does that help you at all?"

"I wish I could say exactly yes or no. Suppose I lay out what I'm thinking of, and you say whether there's some way we could make it work."

Gwothernan bobbed his head shortly, "Go ahead."

TWO WEEKS LATER FOUND them marching toward Daura. A large contingent of Dauri would meet them on the march. From there, they would continue to where an army from two other Kharmosats was invading "in the name of the King."

Two Kharmosts led this invasion. Though one of them, Sosindas, had, or presumed, a trifle more seniority.

The Gafrodi leaders hoped they would be able to deal with these troops. Then march back along their track to meet the King, who would be invading from the other direction. With sufficient luck, they could meet the King before he had time to do more than invest Higfrod.

"Catching him with his forces spread out around the city might even be the best," Gwothernan had said "but we can't count on that much good luck."

"COME ON, QEDRIM, GIVE us a little hint," Genilabas' voice was almost querulous. "We know. The whole army knows. That you and Lord Gwothernan have worked out a plot between you to defeat Old Sosindas without the rest of the army having to draw a sword. Why can't you tell your closest friends?"

"Because if it ever gets out. And I'm not saying you nor Malsa are blabbermouths. But if it ever gets out, Gwothernan will have my hide. And I like my hide just the way it is. Attached to me."

"You say you know we're not blabbermouths. You say you trust us. But you won't trust us enough to give us anything to be trusted with. Some fine trust that is."

"Come on, Geni, look at this way. This is the Lady's secret, hers, mine, and Gwothernan's. You wouldn't want me babbling out the Lady's secrets, would you?"

The discontented nod was as much agreement as Qedrim had expected.

QEDRIM RODE BACK TO the main force. Two-score horse-archers accompanied him, just in case. Though it was a known fact the enemy were still a day's march away. "It's those 'known facts' which always turn around and bite you in the butt," Gwothernan had said.

It was another 'known fact' that Sosindas didn't have enough troops to waste any by making moves toward the Higfrod rear. Yet another 'known fact', this one being one of the more reliable facts, was that Sosindas was nowhere near to being an inspired tactician. Sosindas could probably be counted on to get a superior force to the field of battle, and array it in a reasonably sensible fashion. But after that it would be up to the troops to grind their way to victory. There weren't likely to be any clever tactical maneuvers.

He'd made a survey of the land where the enemy would likely be camping just before the battle. That kind of thing couldn't always be predicted with absolute accuracy. But being near to the mark would be enough.

Qedrim rode back through the Gafrodi lines, conscious of all the eyes on him. Any soldier who didn't recognize him was most likely standing next to someone who knew about him. The word would be passed that he'd been out looking things over. And there'd be four or five different stories as to what he planned for the day of the fight.

"Hope I can live up to your expectations," he thought.

THE MORNING OF THE battle came, altogether too quickly. "You're ready, Qedrim?"

Gwothernan had his helmet pushed back on his head, for better visibility. When the time came to fight, he'd pull the helmet down and depend on what he was able to see through the eye-slits.

"I am. You realize this is likely to stretch me a little? You have someone ready to take care of me if I fall over?"

"Of course." There was annoyance in Gwothernan's response, as if this ought to go without saying.

Well, that was too bad. It wasn't going to be Gwothernan passed out there on the field, vulnerable to anyone and everyone.

"Well, our lot are falling in, and the enemy are doing the same. Time to get to work."

Gwothernan turned and rode off before Qedrim had a chance to feel annoyed at the man for ordering him around. By the time he did, he realized Gwothernan might well have been talking to himself anyway.

It was time for Qedrim to get to work, though.

Qedrim's ability at moving stones seemed to be limited to stones within sight. Though he had been working at that, practicing picking up stones behind him. It was still a fact that he had to have seen the stone, wherever it might be, but he was able to manage it.

So now, he commanded all those stones he had seen in their places over in the area of the enemy camp to rise up. He'd never tried lifting so many, nor in such vaguely-defined places. But the effort it took indicated, from past experience, that he was moving a large number of stones.

He brought them over and stacked them in a long pile. Just in front of the lines of Gafrodi light infantry on the left flank. It hadn't been necessary to take the stones from where the enemy were. This had been a small ploy to shake the morale of the enemy before they came to battle. Which drove home to them the fact there was a man over here who could command stones.

In fact, it was necessary to augment the line of stones with more which had been gathered in oxcarts for him. Even the Gafrodi troops appeared a little rattled at the stones suddenly flying up to take their places in front. "And their commanders were supposed to have warned them last night, too," Qedrim thought.

"So now," he said to himself, and raised the stones. This was not a drystone wall, not by any means. It was a wall, of sorts, about three feet high, one stone wide, and at least fifty feet in length. Qedrim's will alone held the stones balancing on each other. He then moved the stone wall forward toward the enemy.

The enemy infantry who faced this wall looked a little uncertain. They lost their dressing badly as the stone wall advanced on them. As the stone wall collided with their ranks, most of them broke and fled. Those in that fifty-foot stretch who didn't flee were pushed back by the inexorable advance of the stone wall, which moved as one unit.

Abruptly, a whole section of the enemy line was fleeing. Those who had been on the flanks of the hole were shaken. Some officers tried to extend the line to cover the hole. But this only caused their dressing to become worse.

Then Qedrim brought the stone wall back. He had thought first to make it wheel, like a finely-drilled infantry force, but there wasn't time. Instead, he marched it rapidly to his left, then brought it back.

When the next fifty-foot section of enemy infantry found themselves trapped between a moving stone wall behind, and armed troops in front, their morale collapsed.

In a rushing panic they sought to escape on the flanks. On their right were their own troops. On the left was a small gap, which an evolution of Gafrodi troops was rapidly closing.

Qedrim wheeled his stone wall this time, in a broad circle leftward, to catch more enemy troops. And, to allow the remnants who had been caught in the first trap to flee.

Which they did, with no one attempting to rally when the wall was gone.

By now the Gafrodi troops had wheeled sharply to hit the enemy troops in the flanks of the now-larger hole.

Qedrim let his stone wall fall. The dust which had been a problem on other battlefields was a problem here as well. So he couldn't see how far down the rank the enemy's disorder had gone. Not that this mattered much. With the Gafrodi troops through a gap of over a hundred feet and rolling the enemy up. The battle was practically won.

Nevertheless, he urged his horse down further leftward on the Gafrodi line. It wouldn't take long for him to bring his stones from where he'd dropped them, if he needed them again.

As it happened, it wasn't necessary. Nor was he even so worn out that he collapsed. He did, however, fall asleep when it was clear he wouldn't be needed any longer. Not waking up until late the next morning.

"AND NOW WE MARCH AGAINST the King?" Qedrim, the success of his plan against Sosindas making him bold, found himself willing to speak up on matters of strategy.

Gwothernan shook his head. "We march on Higfrod. That's where the King will have been making for. Let's hope he won't have managed to trick the city into a surrender before we arrive."

"Surely they won't surrender the city as long as they are aware we're loose?"

"They shouldn't. But that sort of thing is like those 'known facts.' Suppose the King somehow convinces them he's already met and defeated us? What good would it do the city to hold out? All they'd get would be worse terms when the King eventually wins."

"So we'll go up on the assumption the city hasn't been taken, but we consider what we'll do if the worst happens."

"Or maybe I would be able to convince the King to bet his Kingdom against my ability to hit a target three times in five."

Gwothernan frowned slightly. But Qedrim's performance in the battle had been enough to gain him a little leeway. "The King has just finished some tricky work to gain the throne against bad odds. He'd need a good mind to be able to manage the ins and outs of that, good enough that he wouldn't be easily fooled."

Annavristi spoke up. "We know they tried to bribe Qedrim. I wonder how many bribes we didn't find out about?"

Gwothernan shrugged. "No way to know, except to take close precautions."

He turned to face Qedrim. "You too, Qedrim. All it needs is for someone to put a knife between your ribs, and we've lost a big advantage."

"Not to mention I'd be dead," Qedrim said, stung at being referred to less as a person than as an important weapon. "I don't think I'd care for that at all."

"I wouldn't like that either, Qedrim," said Annavristi. "Make sure you stay safe."

Sobeldanser, whose strong dislike of Qedrim appeared to have moderated to a general distaste for him, glowered slightly. "There are others who have served the Lady well, wielding more ordinary weapons in her service."

The Lady turned to him. "And so there have been, Lord Sobeldanser. And we appreciate your work as well. Without you, and warriors like you, Qedrim could only be effective up to the point when slingers or archers came within range of him. And without Qedrim, we might well have won this battle, but at the cost of being unable to fight the next battle, which will come all too soon.

"All those who risk their lives in my service are appreciated. No matter how they serve."

"Thank you, Lady." Annavristi's words appeared to sooth the old Lord. Though Qedrim wondered just how much.

"SOMETIMES IT SEEMS the Lady's service is one long forced march," groused Malsan'to. "Seems we're never satisfied with getting somewhere, we always have to get there fast."

"This isn't really a forced march, Malsa. Now the march to Daura, *that* was a forced march. *This* is just a bit of a hurry."

"Ah, Lord Qedrim of the Big Stones, having marched with the Lady's forces a few times, is now a veteran campaigner! And I suppose next thing we know you'll be lecturing us on the tactics Lord Gwothernan used, and telling us how they might be improved!"

Qedrim grinned. "No, I won't go quite *that* far. I will say my backside isn't as sore as it was on that march to Daura. My judgment about this march is based on that."

"Oh? And didn't it occur to you that perhaps your backside has gotten more used to riding? So that this time, though we're riding just as hard, it doesn't feel so bad?"

Qedrim laughed. "Don't worry. We're just making good time for a few days then we'll drop back to a more sedate pace. That way, we've gained a couple of days on the King, without ending up worn to a stub when we finally meet him."

"THE KING AND HIS ARMY are camped around the walls of Higfrod, Lord!" The dusty horse-archer brought the news to Gwothernan at the head of the marching column.

"Ah, good, good! Their strength?"

"My commander didn't take time for a careful count before he sent me off, Lord. But I'd say there's a third to a quarter again our force."

Gwothernan nodded. "That seems to be about what we estimated. As long as they don't have any other forces hidden away in the neighbourhood. Qedrim!"

"Yes, Lord." When Gwothernan spoke in that commander's voice of his, it took strong will-power to avoid answering like the merest of soldiers.

"You have an idea for this one? I don't think his Highness will allow you to scout out his campground, not even if you ask politely."

"I have an idea or so. It might not have the same morale effect, but I think I can give them something to think about. I'd still end up with the wall formation; it worked well enough last time, there's no sense changing a good thing."

"Unless you know your enemy will expect it. But I think you're probably right this time, they won't likely have heard what we did to Sosindas."

Chapter 14

The King had formed his army in front of them. "It would have been nice to catch them spread out around the town. With all the resultant confusion that would come from having to haul that sort of scatter into a battle line. Ah, well, we can't have everything, I suppose. Qedrim, you're ready?"

"Oh, yes, ready indeed. You did make sure the troops were warned there'd be stones going overhead today?"

"I passed the warning. You think it's going to be needed? They know you're with us, and at least the party that had to gather the stones for you are altogether sure of it."

"It might be needed. I'll go off to my place, now, unless you have any final instructions for me."

Gwothernan merely shook his head.

QEDRIM'S PLACE WAS a smallish beehive-shaped hut which he'd built the night before. It had just been a matter of stacking stones one on another, with a bit of care to balance, and though he wouldn't have liked to live in the thing for any time, it would do the trick.

Qedrim looked at the stone hut. "Up in the air now," he told it.

Up in the air the hut went. He sent it floating out, over the heads of the Gafrodi troops. He had supported these same soldiers in the previous battle. Gwothernan had thought they would be more used to the notion, and "not be too skittish about stones floating around and about their heads," as he put it.

Other than a few ducked heads, they did not react much as the stone hut floated over them.

One of the four men assigned to guard Qedrim muttered "Dark Destroyer's Teeth!" as the hut went flying away.

Qedrim knew he could have moved the stone house much faster. But he thought the slower approach would be better, giving the enemy a good look at what was coming toward them.

He set the stone hut down, slowly again, right in the middle of their ranks. It only killed a few, because most were able to get out of the way, but it did disorder their formation.

He let the house sit there for a bit. The enemy were loth to get close to it, fearing whatever magic or curse this might be would rub off on them.

Qedrim picked the house up again and brought it back toward the Gafrodi lines. he was moving the house rapidly this time, taking it apart as the house moved towards the line. This was the maneuver he especially asked that their commanders warn them about. Seeing the stones coming their way might well give the Gafrodi troops pause.

The lines did indeed shiver a bit. And Qedrim heard, vaguely through his concentration, the ten-commanders and hundred-commanders bawling out orders to stand their Morrkerr-eaten ground because the Morrkerr-eaten stone-handler was on their side.

At any rate, he dropped the mass of stones a fair distance out from their lines, and began to reform the stones into the wall. The moving house had just been a bit of a ploy to shake their morale. The Gafrodi army needed all the advantages it could get.

Insofar as fighting the battle was concerned, the wall would do the actual work.

Shortly, the command to advance went up, and the troops began to advance toward each other. The wall, now complete, advanced as well. The King's troops were even less willing to come into contact with the wall than had been Sosindas. At first a fifty-foot section of the front rank halted. Then the front backed into the ranks following it. Disorder erupted that no amount of shouting from ten-commanders or fifty-commanders could put to rights.

Then a section of the line, somewhat more than fifty feet in length, was taking to its heels. In most cases shedding spears and shields to run the faster.

In the manner that had served so well in the previous battle, Qedrim marched the wall to his left and brought it back against the rear of the King's troops.

Just as the wall was beginning to squeeze the enemy, Qedrim heard the sound of hoofbeats. Most of his mind was still engaged with the stones, but he looked back. Five horsemen, Sobeldanser and some men of his household, approached them.

"Now, what're that lot doing here?" he wondered to himself, abstractedly, as he concentrated most of his attention on the wall that was beginning to push against the rear rank of the King's men.

"So you're doing it again."

'Stating the obvious, if anyone ever did.'

"Sorry, Lord Sobeldanser, can't talk right this moment. I've got my hands full."

"Oh, indeed? Now, men!"

Qedrim was too involved in his own work to even be properly suspicious. His guards, however, had been chosen for their suspicious natures, and had, in an almost casual fashion, arrayed themselves between Lord Sobeldanser and their charge. The attack did not take them by surprise, for they were moving even as the Lord shouted his command. The Lord's four men each engaged one guard. Sobeldanser then rushed forward to attack Qedrim.

Distracted as he was with moving the stones, Qedrim was caught almost completely unawares. But Sobeldanser was slowed as he tried to get his horse through the fighting guardsmen. There was no straight path from the Lord to Qedrim, either. The guards had seen to that.

Still, Qedrim was just loosing his hold on the stones when Sobeldanser was beside him, sword swinging down.

As the blade bore down on Qedrim, there was no time to do anything but evade the blow. Which he attempted by flinging himself off his horse in the opposite direction to the Lord's attack.

The attempt was only partly successful, for he felt a blow against his hip as he went off.

Qedrim fell hard, though he'd been able to curl an arm round his head. Hooves moved closer. He heard the Lord's muttered imprecations as he maneuvered for the killing stroke.

There was a pebble beside Qedrim's head, a small white thing the size of his first thumb-joint. Still half-dazed, he sent the pebble up towards the Lord's unseen face above him. He heard the yell, and rolled himself laboriously over on his side. The Lord was riding away, one hand clapped to his left eye. Qedrim was trying to pick up another pebble to hit the Lord's horse. Perhaps he could make the beast go wild and throw Sobeldanser. Suddenly everything faded away.

FROM THE SOUNDS OF men in pain, or men trying to swallow their pain with varying degrees of success, Qedrim assumed was in the Healer's tent once more.

A tired-looking young man in the Healer's costume, dusty-grey tunic and trousers with a powder-blue sash, approached him. "Ah, you're awake. How do you feel?"

"Like I've been trampled on by a Morrkerr-eaten horse. What happened?"

"You took a rather bad wound in the side, just above the hip. We've done what we were able to for the wound, but you've been sleeping nearly a day and a half."

"I assume we won? Otherwise I wouldn't be being treated so well."

The young face went blank. "'Won' and 'lost' are not things that Healers concern themselves with. The Lady Annavristi and the Lord Gwothernan both asked to be informed when you wake. One or both will be able to answer your questions."

Qedrim didn't bother to respond. He had no desire to enter into an argument about the battle, and whether or not it had been necessary. In fact, all he was able to remember was landing his house on the enemy. No, he had a picture in his mind of a sword rising and falling. Who had been holding the sword? No, his mind refused to recall that.

GWOTHERNAN SUPPLIED some missing bits of information. "That Morrkerr-eaten Sobeldanser! He was trying to win a place with the King, so he went after you! Left it a bit late, though. You'd already done messing up the King's right flank. Though not so badly as you did with Sosindas. The light infantry were able to exploit the gap, small though it was, and eventually the King's army started to fade away.

"It was another hard battle. Another Morrkerr-eaten hard fight. And a few more losses than I'm comfortable with. But we won."

Annavristi spoke up then. "Yes, we won. And much as I hate to be the one to say it, I think our next move has to be to march on Ga'tuitos, as soon as Qedrim can travel."

Gwothernan gave her an inquisitive look. "Not your usual attitude, Anniki. You're that angry because Sobeldanser tried to kill Qedrim?"

"I'm angry about that, Gwothernan, but that's a whole different matter. I'm going to have to defeat the King, and do it conclusively before he can recover and get an army together."

Gwothernan nodded. "I thought I'd have to tell you you're like the man riding the panther. The trouble is not so much in the riding, as in the attempting to dismount."

"And the rest of my life is going to be spent looking over my shoulder. Trying to see just who might be wanting their turn on the panther's back. I hope you don't want me to be happy about that."

Qedrim still couldn't remember anything about the fight besides dropping his house on the enemy, and that picture of the sword, evidently in Sobeldanser's hand, rising and falling.

He pulled his mind away from trying to force it to fill in the empty spots and said, "You'd best wait until I can at least be hauled along in a litter."

AFTER A WEEK, WHICH Gwothernan begrudged though he knew moving Qedrim too soon could be a mistake, they set out. The method adopted for carrying Qedrim was a hammock slung in an ox-cart. The ropes of the hammock and sling took up much of the jolting, but despite that it was not a comfortable ride.

It was Qedrim's turn to complain in the evenings lying, or later on in the journey, sitting up beside the fire. "Old Woman's Apron! I think the oxen are managing to hit every rock and rut and lump in the road. I wonder if this is their secret revenge for their castration."

"Ah, how he complains," said Malsa, grinning. "And this isn't even a forced march. For certain old Wolf Gwothernan isn't wasting any time, but a forced march, no, not like some I've been on."

"Oh, be quiet or I'll drop a stone on your head!"

"You wouldn't do that. So far you've only got two friends, Geni and me. Start dropping stones on heads, you won't have any friends at all. Except perhaps that you're a Close Friend of the Kharmista, and she won't come and keep you company while you gripe."

IN THE JOURNEY'S LATER stages, he could make his way around in the evenings leaning on a stick. As he did so, he noticed that the Lady's army was growing larger with strange contingents he'd never seen before. He was even present one evening as one such contingent joined them.

Aides ushered a tallish bearded man into the the Lady's presence. A Lord by the cut and ornamentation of his dress. He stood blinking a moment in the firelight. Then finally recognized the Kharmista herself. He dropped to his knees.

"O mighty Lady of Higfrod! I am Yoltsan, Kharmost of Djedjen. I have come to promise my aid and support in your present endeavour."

Qedrim watched all this with some distaste. He was quite sure Yoltsan would have cheered while King Faldisen's executioner removed Lady Annavristi's head. Now, because she appeared to have the upper hand—probably in no small part because she had the man who could command stones—he was in a rush to support her.

She surely knew all this as well Qedrim he did, perhaps better.

Her expression showed no sign of anything except welcome to this man who was suddenly switching alliances. "Welcome,

Kharmost Yoltsan, rise and be welcome among us. You will ride with me, of course?"

Part of Qedrim's cynical mind suggested Lord Yoltsan would have preferred to be safe at home. But another part said no. Lord Yoltsan would have had to have known that he would be brought along. He'd deserted one master. What might he do if someone else came to whisper in his ear? Someone with Royal aspirations and what seemed to be a foolproof plot?

Qedrim happened to be standing near Gwothernan while all this was going on. He worked himself a little closer to the Lord. "The Lady's picking up more troops, it seems."

Gwothernan's expression didn't change. Yoltsan might have noticed a sneer and cherished it in his heart as an insult to be avenged by selling his loyalty to someone else at a time inopportune for the Lady.

"Yes. So Long as I don't trust any of them in a real fight. We've been picking up bits and pieces of this sort, deserting the King's cause when he seems to be in trouble."

Qedrim nodded, understanding all that hadn't been said. Such desertions were a help to the Lady, making her seem stronger, while weakening the King by that little bit. How much reliance could be put on them if her fortunes seemed to change? Even a battlefield where the King seemed to have the more force might be too much for some.

It bore out altogether too well the statement he used to make. That everyone was out for themselves, and in a way, it was true. Everyone was out for themselves. What they wanted was not always the same thing, though. In Gwothernan's case for instance, everything seemed to revolve around preventing trouble for the Lady.

Chapter 15

At last the King halted his retreat to fight them. Several Lords had deserted the King, joining the Lady's cause. However, there were many others who had tied their positions too closely and too long to the King's, who could expect to fall with him.

That fall would be a long one for men and families used to having the King's ear and the King's favour.

So the army which the King was able to gather was altogether very near in size to the one that had served him at Higfrod.

"It's likely," Gwothernan said, looking at Qedrim, "that he's heard about the state of Qedrim's health, and wants to fight this battle before Qedrim recovers."

"I've been doing what I can to rebuild my powers. There's a fine line between practicing to a limit and wearing myself out so I never get better. I'm afraid all I can promise for tomorrow's battle is a small demonstration."

Gwothernan scowled, not in anger at Qedrim but in annoyance at the entire situation. "We can hope the King's men have heard all the extended horrors of your power. At least sufficient to make them nervous when they see some stones floating around."

Qedrim would have apologized for his inability, but he knew no one blamed him for anything. Nor did it help that no one blamed him.

THE NEXT MORNING THEIR army fell into formation, ready for battle. Qedrim, with an oxcart full of stones, stood behind one section of the line.

"I hope they've been told I'm not likely to be winning their battle for them," he thought. The next thought which came to Qedrim was the difficulty of trying to tell the army that. Without telling them they were in real trouble now. They'd won several fights with the help of Qedrim and his stones. How could they win without him?

Well, no help for it any longer. The armies were advancing. He picked out some stones, about the limit of what he could handle at one time in his condition. Then sent them out in a line in front of the Gafrodi. It was not at all like his wall, but it would have some effect.

He kept them right in front of the Gafrodi line until the two forces were closing. At that moment, he sent the stones hurtling into the enemy line.

No, it was not like the wall, but it caused severe disruption in the line for its whole fifty-foot length. However, Qedrim could not push them on very far. Suddenly, he had to let them go, slumping in the ox-cart, puffing and wheezing like an old man.

He pulled himself back up to look at what was happening. The Royal Forces were bending at the point where he'd sent in the stones. It was likely, if the Gafrodi maintained their pressure, they would break through.

Up behind the infantry a force of cavalry were coming. He wondered where they had come from. Of course, on horses, they'd be able to make a quick shift from one part of the field to another.

He wondered for a second if this had been some kind of stratagem designed to deal with whatever effect he might have on the infantry. That wasn't going to help the main problem, which was they might just negate what effect he'd had.

He couldn't heft enough stones to stop them, even to slow them. There was a fellow leading those cavalry, a fellow in fancy armour. Maybe....

He dropped a special stone into his sling, whirled it, and let go, steering the stone directly at that leader. Then his vision began to close in. He put a hand on the side of the ox-cart to support himself, and suddenly he dropped into blackness.

HE CAME UP OUT OF DARKNESS into a room, dimly lit by oil lamps. There was no one in the room, not even any other wounded people. He wondered how the battle had gone. It was likely they'd won, though it wasn't impossible the King had given orders to take him alive.

He was considering the possibility of calling out. Then it was day, and grey light filtered in from outside. He realized he must have dropped back to sleep.

He opened his mouth to call out, but all he managed was a whispery croak.

It surely wasn't enough to be heard anywhere, but suddenly there was an old Healer in the room. "Ah, you're awake! Good news. Don't try to speak just yet, let me give you something to drink first."

The Healer gently raised Qedrim's head and allowed him to take a few careful sips or water. From its taste, the water contained some herbs, but he drank it down thirstily.

He wasn't about to stir up the Healer's ire by asking if they'd won this time. Though this was a different Healer, he might possibly have moderated views. Still, he didn't need that kind of aggravation. Someone would have gotten word by now that he was awake, and then he'd find out what was happening.

Sure enough, shortly after the Healer left him, Gwothernan came in. "We won, then?"

"We won. Bloody awful battle, but we won. The King's dead. Killed by a sling-stone which smashed in his helmet. We know it was a sling-stone because there were stone-fragments still embedded in the wound.

"The way I understand it, he was moving with some horsemen to support his right flank when he went down. Some fools are even talking about a lightning bolt from a clear sky.

"When they saw him go down, most lost heart and pulled out, headed for their homes or whatever. A few charged home, but not quite enough to change the situation.

"But that was merely the cavalry force. We had hard fighting on our right flank, until their right started to go. A hard fight."

"Sorry I wasn't able to do more on my wing."

"You did what you could. Killing the King, that was a feat in itself. Not to mention you near killed yourself doing it."

"Near killed myself? Put my lights out for a bit, that's all."

"Put your lights our for four days. The Healers weren't sure you'd ever wake."

"Four days?" It wasn't like Gwothernan to joke about things like that, but still....

"Four days. We brought you into Ga'tuitos, installed you in the palace, with people to watch for any sign you were waking. There were a couple of false starts when someone misread a muscle twitch, but still, here we are."

"The Lady survived, of course." He was quite sure Gwothernan would have told him first if that were not the case, but just to make certain....

"She did. Left word that she was to be informed, day or night, when you woke. 'When' was her word, too. No matter how doubtful the Healers were, she knew you'd wake."

"I hope they didn't disturb her rest just for me," Qedrim muttered.

Gwothernan looked at him unsmiling. "She's got even less time to herself now she's Royal Lady of Dai'vlash. She's at present listening to a pair of canny fellows telling her how wonderful she is and how ardently they support her. Since they do both command powerful influence, she can't simply tell them to go Chaos Away. But believe me, she'll be here as soon as she can courteously disentangle herself."

"Oh."

Gwothernan gave him a stern look. "Listen, I thought I knew you well, once, when I looked into your past. At the time, I found that you seemed to be out for anything you could get, no matter how you got it. Didn't trust you. Didn't trust you for a long time. Even when you seemed to have thrown your lot in with us, despite our being a raggle-taggle bunch of starvelings in the hills.

"I'm still not sure how much I like you, Qedrim. But the Lady likes you, likes you a lot. I've been around long enough to know that people can change. But I've also been around long enough to know how some people can pretend to change to get something they want badly enough.

"I'm not sure how to judge you. You've served us well, but you have that past of yours. The Lady likes you, so I'll try to like you too. But I've been an 'uncle' to that girl since she was a small one in her father's house, and I won't see her made unhappy."

He stood and left them, before Qedrim was able to respond.

Qedrim spent some futile minutes preparing responses to Gwothernan, trimming and turning and polishing his phrases. Did the grim old soldier suspect Qedrim of some underhanded purpose? Was he threatening Qedrim with something if he made the Lady unhappy? Just how was he supposed to make the Lady unhappy? Or happy, either, if it came to that?

Of course Gwothernan was not around for Qedrim to use these words on. When Gwothernan did return some while later, Annavristi was with him. Her presence kept Qedrim from using any of those words he'd thought were so clever.

"I told them you'd wake! I came as soon as I could. How are you feeling?"

"Better." Qedrim saw Gwothernan's face over her shoulder, glowering at him, as if trying to tell him something without words.

"Good," Annavristi said. "Do you feel well enough for me to talk to you for a bit?"

"Certainly."

She turned to Gwothernan. "Would you leave us alone for a little, Gwothernan? I know you don't trust anyone when I'm around. But I'm sure you can admit Qedrim has demonstrated amply that he means me no harm."

Qedrim expected Gwothernan to make a token protest, or at least give him a parting glower. But the old warrior's face held no expression as he turned and left the room.

"Lady," Qedrim began, but she stopped him.

"At least when we're alone, Qedrim, I'd prefer you to call me Anniki."

"Anniki." He forced a smile. "Well, I'm afraid most nicknames people have called me from time to time are not the sort I'd like to repeat."

"Oh, I imagine we'll come up with something, in a while. 'Qedrim' will do for now. I'm glad you survived."

"So am I," he muttered. "The alternative does not appeal to me."

"We'll have to see to it you're properly rewarded. That small plot we've given you is not nearly enough for what you've done."

"Lad—-Anniki, I didn't do this for any reward. And any reward you give me is going to upset someone else. Sobeldanser wasn't the only one who dislikes me."

"Oh, I know that entirely too well. There are so many who think me just a girl who can be swayed by clever words. And when they find out otherwise, they get upset.

"I have to maintain a service of people who gather information for me, who this Lord or that Lord is talking to, what they do and say.

"So I seldom make promises. Save to consider their words before I make my decision. And I've managed to arrange a situation where most of the Lords respect me.

"Beneath it all, of course, two thirds of them think they could do my job, and do it better.

"I take a risk if I declare someone my heir. Because if that person doesn't get the notion on his own, several of his friends will try to convince him to replace me without waiting for my death.

"If I take a consort, there is the same problem. I have to have a man who has some ambitions, but not a man who has so much ambition that he decides to replace me.

"So now I'm Royal Lady of Dai'vlash, and the situation remains the same, though the stadium is larger. And still I dance my dance of keeping them happy enough so they don't rebel, but not letting anyone come close to me."

"It's not a cheerful prospect for a life, Qedrim. I need someone to be able to share things with. Someone who won't be looking to rule in my place."

Then Qedrim realized where all this was leading. He then realized, in fact, why it had taken Annavristi so long to come to the point.

"You don't want me, Anniki. You'll set all the Lords to hating you, that's for sure."

"This is the right time to do it. After so many years of war, everyone's ready for peace. They won't be willing to start anything as active as a rebellion just yet. And I have that much more time to cement alliances with some of them, at least enough so the alliance against me won't be so large."

"But I'm just a wandering gambler, Anniki. I—-"

"You think I don't know all about your past? Remember the people who give me reports? If that disturbs you, I'm sorry, but I've already told you how I can't afford to take anyone on their first appearances. But I also know you've done a lot for us. That you stayed with me in the Wooded Budaba, when there was no certainty I would regain my Kharmosat. Let alone come so far as I have.

"So I ask you to agree to be my consort. You're one of a very small few I could choose without the fear that you'd try to unseat me."

She held up a hand to forestall his response. "Don't answer just yet. Think on it for a while, answer me when you're back on your feet again."

HE'D THOUGHT THIS CONVERSATION would keep him awake. But he found himself coming awake again, lying on his side, and realized he'd slept for a while.

The next thing he realized was that he was not alone. He turned over, laboriously—his wound was troubling him again—to see Shapak-ailesh looking at him.

"I suppose I needn't be surprised you were able to find your way in here."

"Ah, the hero is out of humour today. And in such circumstances, too!"

"You! Did you steer the Lady toward me somehow?"

"Not at all, O greatly suspicious hero! Not at all. I brought you here, and what happened has happened. Without my having to resort to love-potions or any such stuff."

"You keep jumping into and out of my life. I can hardly believe it's all happenstance."

The little man's face took on such an exaggerated appearance of shame that Qedrim didn't bother trying to convince himself of its authenticity. "Ah, the most perspicacious hero! I must sorrowfully admit that not all of it has been happenstance. Indeed, the very first meeting, I took my place in that spot. Knowing that I would meet you and knowing that, if you were approached properly, you would be the man for the job that had to be done.

"You see, the Lady of Praises, for whom I have the honour to carry out various commissions from time to time, had become most grievously aware of the bent of the magic of the late B'tlas. It was therefore entrusted to me to see to it that he was done away with. I chose you to carry out the mission.

"I brought you to Higfrod, confident that matters would work themselves out as they did, and so it happened. No, there is no saying that I might not have put in some sort of nudge, now and again, if such had been needed. But none was needed.

"And now here you are, about to marry your princess."

"You steered me into that as well?"

"No, no, a thousand times no! You moved yourself quite well, without any assistance from me!

"And if the old tales fright you, and you fear that I will come when your first child is born and demand him or her as payment. Rest easy, that is not my sort of bargain. When you dealt with B'tlas, you did all I needed of you.

"I only came here to explain to you how and why I had come into your life."

"So, are you telling me that if I wed Anniki, I will live happily ever after?"

"Ah, yes, the third part of the payment. 'Ever after' is a long time. And happiness is something which cannot really be known without occasional unhappiness to compare it with.

"I can tell you, though, that you and Lady Annavristi will most likely live as happily as two people can, in the circumstances."

"'In the circumstances.' You're leaving yourself a room for an excuse if everything goes Chaos Away."

"Unfortunately, O dissatisfied young hero, I cannot tell the future. If I were able to, I would not. All I can say is that one ought to seize the day, make the most of what one has."

"Indeed? And had you not best leave, before the guards hear us and look in?"

"O young hero of such little faith! Do you think I would come in here without having made sure that nothing which was said in here would be overheard?

"Farewell, hero, until we meet again."

Before Qedrim could respond, Shapak-ailesh faded before him and was gone.

THE WEDDING OF THE Annavristi, Royal Lady of Dai'vlash, to Lord Qedrim of Arndal was a fine spectacle. The Royal Lady had declared that, given the demands of the recent years of strife, no outrageous sums should be spent on it. Even that permitted sufficient ostentation to satisfy the people that this was a true Royal Wedding.

A great platform was built, on which the Royal couple, along with sundry attendants, were seated. A crowd of common people milled about below, shouting good wishes to them. In order to allow as many people as possible to take part, the citizens were urged to keep moving. Which most of them took well.

Around the platform's base a double rank of light infantry were stationed, to watch the crowd. Thaldo now a Fifty-commander, muttered out of the side of his mouth to the Fifty-commander next to him, "I knew him when he first came to Higfrod. He was a bit rough, but even then I knew he was going places."

Up on the stage Gwothernan smiled grimly at everyone. Everyone knew he wasn't entirely happy about the Lady's choice of consort. The more snide suggesting he wanted to fill that role himself.

Somewhere closer to Qedrim stood Malsan'to and Genilabas, finely dressed, and wearing smiles.

And off in the crowd, seemingly immune to the urging of the soldiers to keep moving, was a little broad-faced man in a leather cap leading a mule.

Don't miss out!

Visit the website below and you can sign up to receive emails whenever J P Wagner publishes a new book. There's no charge and no obligation.

https://books2read.com/r/B-A-EKQG-OUORB

BOOKS 2 READ

Connecting independent readers to independent writers.

Also by J P Wagner

Avantir
The Guardian of the Sword

Talisman Series
Stonecaller
Talisman of the Winds

Standalone
The Search for the Unicorns
Railroad Rising: The Black Powder Rebellion
Maid of the Westermoor

Watch for more at www.revjpwagner.com.

About the Author

J. P. Wagner was both a sci-fi/fantasy writer and a journalist. While his editorials and informative articles could be found in publications such as the Western Producer and the Saskatoon Star Phoenix, Railroad Rising: The Black Powder Rebellion is his first published novel.

A self-proclaimed curmudgeon, but known to his family as a merry jokester, his words have brightened many lives. Sadly, J. P. Wagner passed away in 2015 before the publication of Railroad Rising: The Black Powder Rebellion.

While this may be the last book he finished before he died, it doesn't mean that this was his only book. In addition to his career in journalism, he wrote many novels throughout his lifetime. All of these works have been passed down to me, his daughter and now I will share them with you.

Read more at www.revjpwagner.com.

www.ingramcontent.com/pod-product-compliance
Lightning Source LLC
Chambersburg PA
CBHW030531030726
47495CB00004B/943